CAGED LIGHTNING

MARINA FINLAYSON

FINESSE SOLUTIONS

Cover design by Karri Klawiter
Model stock image from Taria Reed/The Reed Files
Editing by Larks & Katydids
Formatting by Polgarus Studio

Published by Finesse Solutions Pty Ltd
2018/02
ISBN 9781925607017

Author's note: This book was written and produced in Australia and
uses British/Australian spelling conventions, such as "colour" instead
of "color", and "-ise" endings instead of "-ize" on words like "realise".

A catalogue record for this
book is available from the
National Library of Australia

For all the wonderful readers who have followed Lexi's journey. Thanks for coming along on the ride!

1

It's a strange thing to meet your brother for the first time as a grown woman.

Well, I'd met him before, but that was before I knew he was my brother. That one little fact changed everything between us—and made me feel more than a little guilty about some of my past judgements of him. I mean, if Apollo really was a douche, then finding out he was my brother didn't make him any less of one. But when I was Artemis, and actually knew he was my brother, I'd been prepared to give up my godhood, at least temporarily, to save him. Which kind of suggested that I hadn't considered him a douche at all, and that maybe I—human, amnesiac, Lexi-I, not the forgotten moon goddess-I—had misjudged him.

And I did so hate to be wrong.

I scowled as I threw another rock over the cliff. The wind whipped my dark hair, which had come loose from its ponytail, around my face and brought the salt smell of the waves to my nostrils. The sea spread out below me, a vast blue mystery reaching all the way to the distant horizon. If I'd turned my head to the left, I would have seen the little town of Berkley's Bay, my home for the last few months, huddled around the curve of the shoreline. But I didn't look—I'd come up here to escape my problems while I tried to get my shit together. Most of those problems were down there, and I didn't need any reminders.

Jake was—possibly—down there, though for all I knew he'd headed back to the city already. He had a house on the cliff not far from here. A mansion, really. Nothing but the best for the Master of the South-East, and one of the strongest fireshapers on the Ruby Council. Or, at least, he had been. Who knew who was on the council anymore, now that Apollo had started weeding out the traitors?

I'd just broken up with Jake, though our relationship had barely begun, and my heart was still smarting at the wound. The stupid man had developed a sudden case of cold feet when he'd discovered I was really a goddess. Hey, how did he think *I* felt? I'd been happy being plain old Lexi. No one had asked *me* if I wanted to be a goddess. Hades had been sure I'd be thrilled to take back my old life as Artemis, goddess of the hunt and his niece. Shame his little trick of disguising me as a human had worked so well that I had no memories, now, of that former life.

He was down there, too, my manipulative uncle, along with most of the people I cared about in the world. Like Holly and Joe, friends and neighbours. Like Syl, my best friend. How was I going to tell her I was a goddess? She knew something weird was going on with me, but not the depth of the shit I'd landed myself in this time. I'd headed out of town after my final confrontation with Jake, not ready to face anyone else yet, and had ended up here, on this familiar stretch of coast. I'd walked along this clifftop path many times, admiring the view. It was from here that I'd hurled the mayor's stolen altarpiece into the sea below, right before all my adventures with gods and monsters had begun, and my life had started to unravel.

The blue sea was darkening as the approach of night leached the colour from the world. I'd been up here for hours. Syl and her new boyfriend, Lucas, would be back from the underworld by now, probably wondering where the hell I was. I should head back, before they all started panicking that I'd been snatched by the shadow shapers—which was a possibility now that I'd lost my human disguise. I mean, I still looked the same, but my powers were back in full force. Other gods would be able to sense them. Shadow shapers, too—and, unfortunately, it didn't work the other way. Shadow shapers had too little divine power in them for me to be able to sense them, so I had no early warning system. But I was too chicken to move. I was scared stiff of meeting my brother.

I remembered a brother, with golden hair just like Apollo's, but he'd been human, like me. Turned out that he was a false memory, implanted by Hades in his attempt to disguise me as a human. Even though my main memory of this fake brother was of watching a group of men carry his body away, his golden hair matted with blood, I was still reluctant to let go of him completely. I'd searched my mind for any memories of Apollo in that role but had come up empty-handed. Apollo was just a rather annoying guy I'd saved from death a couple of weeks ago. Except now he was my brother. If he expected me to be his sister again, he was going to be sadly disappointed. And I hated letting people down almost as much as I hated being wrong.

Finally, the sea, and the edge of the cliff in front of me, disappeared into the blackness of night. I couldn't put it off any longer. Reluctantly, I stood, stretching out legs cramped from sitting so long in one spot. I brushed dirt and grass off the back of my jeans and cast my mind out, searching for animals to bond with—I needed to boost my night vision before I went arse over turkey off the cliff edge in the dark.

The bright spark of a fox trotting through the bush caught my attention. I linked to him and the blackness around me suddenly became individual trees, bushes on the cliff edge, rocks and pebbles. I tied my hair in an impatient knot to stop it whipping into my eyes and turned my back on the vast, whispering darkness of the sea.

I trudged down the dirt track that led back towards town, the night around me alive with the bright sparks of animal life. Lines of light connected them to each other and to me, forming a web of life, with us all interconnected and dependent on each other. The natural world was a beautiful thing, softly glowing with energy. Now I knew why I could see these life sparks, how I could link with them—I was a goddess, and power over animals was my thing. But I was the goddess of the hunt, which made me wonder—did I use my power to track them, or, worse still, control them so I could kill them? Because that would be cheating. There was no point boasting about your hunting prowess if the animals literally couldn't get away from you.

I had so many questions about the person I used to be. I hoped I would like her, but if she had pulled stunts like that, we weren't going to be friends. I wasn't even sure I wanted the memories of a person like that.

Still, I shouldn't judge her on the limited information I had. That was what I'd done with Apollo.

The lights of Berkley's Bay winked through the trees as I came to the edge of the bush. The track ended at a gravel car park, and I crunched across it to the road. Berkley's Bay wasn't a big place, just a handful of streets arranged to make the most of the view across the bay, with a couple of wharves stretching out into deeper water for the fishing and tourist boats. Down here, we were sheltered by the headland, and the breeze was only light. I soon arrived at the end of the main street.

My footsteps slowed as I got closer to home. I lived above the town's tiny bookshop, right across the street from its only pub. The blinds were drawn in the windows facing the street, and a large figure's silhouette moved behind the kitchen blind. Probably Lucas, which meant Syl was home.

I stopped on the pavement outside the café. I should go up there and fill her in on what had happened. Or I could stand here and beat my head repeatedly against the front windows of the café. That might be more fun.

Dammit, I needed a drink.

I escaped into Alberto's pub, opening the first of the doors with relief. I wasn't being a wimp, just ... fortifying myself. There was nothing wrong with that. Making sure the outer door was shut, I opened the inner door, and the noise and light of the pub hit me, the swell of sound a welcome distraction. The two doors were part of Hades' role-playing. He'd lived here for years as Alberto, the famous vampire publican, and the two doors were never supposed to be open at the same time, to protect him from any light that might get in. He'd put a lot of effort into his cover story.

I took a seat at the long wooden bar with its front carved with wattle flowers and eucalyptus leaves. It was old, but beautifully maintained, Alberto's pride and joy. I wondered how someone who was thousands of years old could care so much about a hunk of wood. Was it part of the act, or did hundreds of little things to care about add up to a reason for an immortal to still find pleasure in life? What were *my* little things that kept me grounded? Somewhere, there must be a whole life that I'd left behind, full of people and interests and maybe wooden bars to keep polished to a perpetual shine.

Winston sat alone at a table in the corner, and I waved to him. He nodded back. He was wearing his civvies tonight, a pair of grey trousers and blue shirt. Only if you saw the gold ring on his right hand might you guess that he was actually a priest of Apollo.

Apollo's uncle—and mine, as it turned out, and that was going to take some getting used to—now in his familiar vampire guise, came to serve me. Dark hair slicked back from a pale, high forehead, lips blood-red against his white skin, Alberto looked every inch the classic vampire. I marvelled anew at how convincing the con was. No one would ever suspect, looking at him, that he was actually a Greek god.

"Everything all right?" he asked, smiling in a way that didn't reveal his fangs. "You don't look happy."

I restrained an urge to punch him right in his aquiline nose. Why would I be happy? I'd just received the unwelcome news that I was a goddess—and it was his fault that I hadn't known—and had lost my new boyfriend over it. Also his fault, come to think of it—he was the one who'd blabbed to Jake. I really *should* deck him. He'd completely screwed up my life.

"No," I said brusquely. "I need a drink."

"Beer?" he asked, reaching for my usual poison.

Beer wasn't going to cut it tonight. "Something stronger."

He asked no further questions and soon deposited a shot glass full of some clear liquid in front of me. Vodka, maybe. I tipped my head back and swallowed it in one go. Whatever it was, it burned all the way down in a most satisfying way.

I slammed the glass back down on the bar, enjoying his slight wince at this mistreatment of his precious bar top. "Another."

Pointedly, he put the glass back on the coaster before refilling it. I sculled this one as quickly as the first, then sighed. A pleasant warmth spread from my stomach into my limbs. At least becoming a goddess hadn't destroyed my ability to get drunk. A few more of these and I could forget about my problems for a while.

"Another."

Alberto raised an eyebrow. "It might be time to switch to beer. I'm not carrying you home."

"Seriously? You're cutting me off after two shots? What kind of a lightweight do you think I am?"

He began filling a glass with beer. "We have work to do.

The time for drinking will be when every last shadow shaper has taken up residence in my kingdom. Then we'll have something to celebrate."

"This is not the celebratory kind of drinking."

"Jake didn't come around, then?"

"No." I stared morosely at the foaming head on the beer. "It's ironic, really. I became a goddess because it was the only way to save him—and you—but becoming a goddess means that I lost him."

"Well, I'm grateful, at least. And he'll come round eventually. Just give him time."

I wished I shared his confidence. Time seemed to be something we were running out of. Hestia, at least, was convinced that if we didn't get Zeus back soon, it would be too late for him. And if I was about to go haring off on another adventure to try to save the father of the gods, I wanted Jake by my side, dammit. He was a handy guy to have around in a fight.

And speaking of fights …

"I'm surprised you're still here. Isn't it dangerous for you to hang around, now that the shadow shapers know where to find you? Why aren't you back in the underworld?"

Out of habit, he glanced around to make sure no one had overheard that. He'd been protecting his real identity for years now. Sneakiness was a way of life. "I'm not staying. I've just been setting things up with Harry—I told him I'm going on a long business trip."

"Does that mean you're coming with me?"

"Where are you going?"

Good question. "Hestia said we needed to reunite the parts of Zeus's lightning bolt so we could get him back out of the wires, but how are you and she and everyone else so certain that's where he is? Couldn't he be held prisoner somewhere by the shadow shapers?"

"If he was, he'd have one of their infernal collars on, so he wouldn't be able to access his power at all to send us these little hints."

"So maybe he's injured somewhere?"

He frowned. "Gods don't stay injured this long. And if he was still in this world, he could call the lightning bolts back to himself anyway. No, this is the only theory that makes sense. He used the wires all the time to travel—it used to drive Hera crazy, because she never knew where he was. He wasn't limited to jumping between his temples—he could go anywhere they had electricity." The frown deepened. "Naturally, he boasted all the time that only someone as powerful as he was could manage the trick. Thor, for instance, couldn't do it, a fact which pleased my brother greatly."

"And now he's lost his power, he's not strong enough to … become corporeal again?"

Hades rubbed at a non-existent spot on the bar, still frowning. "I'm surprised he's lasted this long, to be honest.

It must be draining whatever power he has left to hold himself together." He sighed. "I think Hestia's right. If we don't find him soon, he'll dissipate and be unable to reform."

That sounded nasty. And kind of an ignominious end for the father of the gods, to dissolve as if he were no more than sugar in a cup of tea.

"So, the clock's ticking, and we don't know where to start."

"That pretty much sums it up. We are Zeus's only hope at this point, and I fear he may also be ours. The shadow shapers are proving depressingly resilient."

"Like cockroaches."

"But, unfortunately, much more dangerous. We need a power like Zeus's to exterminate the vermin properly."

A customer called to him from the other end of the bar. The place was starting to fill up now, and the noise of conversation threatened to rise from a background hum to a dull roar.

"We'll talk more about this later," he said, moving off to greet the customer with an easy smile.

I sat back and looked around. Winston was still sitting by himself, a large glass of water in front of him, so I took my beer over to his table. "Hi. How are you?"

"Drowning my sorrows," he said.

I took a closer look at the glass on the table in front of

him, but it still looked like water. Either that or it was the world's biggest vodka shot. "In water?"

He smiled, but there was a distracted air to his smile. He looked miserable. "I have no head for alcohol."

"That would make the sorrow-drowning easier," I pointed out. "Cheaper, too. You'd get drunk faster. What's wrong?"

"I crashed Holly and Joe's new car. I feel terrible."

Was that all? I'd been expecting some new disaster among the fireshapers, or the disappearance of another god, or something equally dire. "Nobody got hurt. It's only money." And Apollo had plenty. I would make sure he parted with some of it to make this right.

Of course, that meant I would have to talk to him. To my brother. I shifted uneasily on the hard wooden seat. The thought still petrified me.

"Only money," he repeated, shaking his head as if he couldn't believe I could dismiss it so easily. For that matter, Artemis probably had bucketloads of cash stashed away, too. Maybe I could skip talking to Apollo altogether and fix it myself. The thought had a certain appeal.

I took a long sip of beer, cold and satisfyingly sharp on my tongue. Of course, I'd have to face him sooner or later. I had questions that needed answering. But no need to rush. Maybe Winston and I could drown our sorrows together. Tomorrow would be soon enough to face my brother. Perhaps even the day after.

"I took Councillor Steele back to Crosston this afternoon," Winston said, after a long period of frowning at his glass of water. Of course, to achieve the proper effect, I'd have to persuade Winston to try something a little stronger than his current tipple.

I determinedly contemplated various spirits, trying not to notice how my heart leapt at the mere sound of Jake's name. And how it sank again as the meaning of Winston's words sank in. He was gone, then. We'd definitely need something stronger than our current drinks. Maybe Winston would like rum?

"He burst into the temple in a tearing hurry," Winston went on, "demanding to be taken to the Ruby Palace. He quite scared my acolyte."

"So you took him." Apollo had given Winston a ring that allowed him to teleport between the god's temples, just as Apollo himself could. I'd told Jake about it last night. Last night, when the future had seemed so full of promise—before Jake had recoiled in horror at the sacrilege of bonking a goddess.

"Of course."

"Are you always so obliging to random fireshapers?"

"Councillor Steele is not a random fireshaper. We may not have been formally introduced, but I know who he is. I've seen him at the temple on feast days." That would be the Great Temple of Apollo in Crosston, not the hastily rented house that served as a makeshift temple here in Berkley's Bay. "He seemed … not himself."

My turn to stare moodily at my drink. "He got some bad news."

Winston didn't ask, and I didn't elaborate. Seemed like there was nothing but bad news lately. A traitor among the gods; Zeus falling apart, perhaps dissipating into the electrical system; shadow shapers everywhere, spying on us. Killing us.

I was sitting facing the door. Old habits. At least I didn't have my back against the wall—that was progress, surely. So I was the first to see when the inner door thudded open and a shining figure appeared in the doorway. Not literally shining, though I knew from experience he could do that, too—just shining in that extremely blond, exceptionally gorgeous way of his. The eyes of every woman in the room—and possibly some of the men—were drawn to his magnificence like a magnet. I was probably the only one there who didn't want to jump his bones. Because, you know, eww. He was my brother.

I sighed as his gaze fell on me. "And speaking of bad news …"

2

I stood, legs trembling, as Apollo approached. He wore tailored pants and a slim-fitting shirt that clung to the hard contours of his chest, both black, as usual. Maybe I should take him clothes shopping, give him the sisterly hint that there was a whole rainbow of other colours he could try.

He stopped in front of me, blue eyes intent, and I swallowed nervously. What did one say in a situation like this? *Hi, I hear you're my brother, nice to meet you?* Or maybe, *Sorry for thinking you were a dick all this time, how about we start again?* He said nothing for a long moment, while his gaze bored into me. Was he disappointed in me? Did he even know yet?

Then a smile of such delight and relief spread over his face that he looked like a different person. I'd never seen him so happy.

"Arti," he breathed. "It *is* you!"

He hugged me so hard I thought my eyeballs would pop. Maybe that's why they started to leak a little. No one had ever sounded so happy to see me before. I had vague memories—most of them sad—of my imaginary brother, but this was different. I could really get used to being this popular.

"I couldn't believe it when Jake told me." He pressed a kiss into my hair and his arms tightened around me, though a moment before I would have said it was impossible for his grip to be any tighter. "I thought they had you, too."

"Apparently not."

"Why didn't you tell me?" he asked, stepping back and giving me a little shake by the shoulders. "I was looking for you everywhere, and all the time you were right here, wearing this form. It's not *that* different, but you felt human, so I never even thought …" His brow furrowed in a frown of confusion. "Why can I sense you now, when I couldn't before? What have you done?"

Music still blasted over the pub's speaker system, but most of the conversations in the room had died. I took a step back, uncomfortably aware that more than half the people in the room were staring at us, including Winston, who looked between us with raised eyebrows. Tomorrow, the rumours would be swirling around the town.

Apollo still stared at me, tears in his eyes, as if afraid I would disappear again if he looked away.

"Maybe we should discuss this somewhere more private," I said, dashing the moisture away from my own eyes. "Let's go back to my place. You, too, Winston."

Apollo nodded, as if dazed, and let me drag him out into the night. Winston trailed obediently behind us, looking mystified. Mentally, I steeled myself to break the news to him, and to Syl, too. Might as well get it all over with at once. At least she wouldn't do a Jake on me. She had no great reverence for the shapers' gods. Maybe Lucas had even told her already. He'd found out before I had.

She was watching TV, as it turned out. Lucas was sprawled on the couch beside her, his long legs stretched out in front of him, one arm draped loosely around her shoulders. They looked so ridiculously normal, Syl slumped against his side, their dark heads close together. Just a regular Thursday night at home. I wanted to plunk myself down on that couch with them and pretend that that was my life.

But it wasn't even Syl's. She looked up as we came in, alert for danger. If she'd been in cat form, her ears would have been pricked. She was no more used to "normal" than I was.

Her lips curved into a welcoming smile as Apollo and Winston came in behind me. "Hi, guys. Want to watch the latest home renovation show? With all your money, you ought to be able to afford a decent reno, Apollo."

I snagged the remote control from the arm of the couch and switched off the TV. Obviously, Lucas hadn't said anything to her. Damn. "We need to talk."

Her feet hit the floor as she sat up straighter. "What's wrong?"

Lucas also straightened, mentally preparing to meet a threat.

"Nothing's wrong," Apollo said, as I opened my mouth to reply. "I have my sister back."

Syl glanced at the closed door, as if expecting this sister to walk in.

I sank down on the nearest armchair. Apollo perched on its arm, as close as he could get without actually sitting in my lap. Having lost me once, he clearly wasn't risking it again.

"It's me," I said. "I'm his sister."

Winston gasped and fell to his knees on our stained old carpet.

Syl took a little longer to figure it out. Her eyes were huge and, unconsciously, her hand sought Lucas's. "You're ... a demi-god?"

"I'm ..." I looked down at the floor. The sight of their joined hands pained me. If only Jake were here.

"She's Artemis," Apollo said, smiling fondly at me. "I've been looking for her everywhere, and she was hiding under my nose all the time."

"Mine, too," Syl said faintly, giving me a wounded look. "Why didn't you tell me?"

"I didn't *know*. Oh, for God's sake, Winston, get off the floor."

He teetered a little as he attempted to rise, so I jumped up to give him a hand. He was older than dirt and shouldn't be kneeling for anyone. The stupid man shied away from my hand, so I hauled him bodily to his feet.

"My lady, you shouldn't—"

"Don't you 'my lady' me," I snapped at him. "My name's Lexi, and don't you forget it."

Shocked into silence, he nodded and hurriedly sat down in the other armchair. Possibly before his knees gave out on him.

Apollo frowned. "What's wrong, Arti?"

"Oh, nothing. Except I'm now a goddess and I *still* have no memories. I have no idea what's going on."

His eyes widened. "You don't remember being Artemis?"

"Nope."

"What … not *any* of it?"

"Not a thing. As far as I'm concerned, you're just some guy I met a couple of weeks ago."

He said nothing, though hurt shadowed his eyes. Maybe I could have put that more diplomatically, considering how happy he'd been to see me.

"And that's why you were all shiny at the end, there, in

Brenvale?" Syl asked. "Because you … found your godhood, or whatever?"

I nodded.

Apollo sighed and ran a hand distractedly through his golden curls. "You'd better tell us exactly what happened in Brenvale."

I sat back down, leaning forward in my seat, and did just that. Lucas added a couple of details, since he'd been the one passing messages between me and Hades as I discovered the truth, locked in my cell with Cerberus, and he could explain more fully what Hades had said. But the story still didn't take long—there wasn't much to tell beyond the fact that Artemis had decided to hunt shadow shapers and Hades had helped by hiding her divinity, but it had worked too well. Artemis had forgotten herself and had ended up believing her cover story—that she was a human called Lexi. Me.

Syl rounded on Lucas, pulling her hand from his. "You knew this and didn't tell me?"

"I …" Lucas looked decidedly uncomfortable as he glanced from Syl to me and back again. "Lexi said she'd tell you herself. It wasn't my place to go blabbing."

Not his *place*? That was an odd thing to say. I wouldn't have blamed him for telling Syl—she was his girlfriend and my best friend, not some random person on the street.

"Telling me would not be *blabbing*," she muttered

darkly, but she left it that. Lucas was good people. Not everyone would be able to resist telling a story like that. Whatever his reason for keeping mum, I was lucky it wasn't all over Berkley's Bay by now. Imagine if Tegan had heard! She dealt in gossip as much as she did in haircuts. "But this is good news, right? You're the goddess of the hunt, so hunting for Zeus should be easy for you."

"Not if he's lost in the wires. I can hardly hunt him there. We'll have to search for the pieces of the lightning bolt instead."

Her face dropped. "And now your avatar's out in the open, the shadow shapers will be after you to steal your power."

Apollo spoke for the first time since I'd finished my story. "Jake said you didn't remember, but I must admit, I didn't quite believe him. I didn't think it was possible for one of us to forget our own identity. But if Hades was involved, that explains a few things."

"Didn't Jake tell you that he was?"

The sun god looked a little sheepish. "I didn't really wait for the whole story. Once he told me you were Artemis, that was it—I came straight here to see for myself."

I bristled a little on Jake's behalf. "Did you think he'd make something like that up?"

"I hardly dared to hope it was true—it seemed impossible that I wouldn't have been able to tell. It doesn't matter what outward appearance we wear, gods know when they're in the presence of another god—we can feel each other's divinity. And everyone's feels slightly different, so we always know who we're dealing with. Since I couldn't feel yours …" He shrugged. "But now I can. Impressive of Hades to manage to hide that. Do you think you could do it again?"

"No."

"That's a shame."

I rolled my eyes. He thought it was that easy? "The price for not broadcasting your divinity to other gods is apparently losing your memory. That might be too high a price to pay for the ability, no?"

He frowned. "You really don't remember *anything*?" He couldn't seem to wrap his head around it, as if being a goddess somehow made me bulletproof. "Like, what's the name of the Sapphire Adept?"

"Melissa Durante," I said, without thinking.

"That doesn't prove anything," Syl objected. "She remembers how to speak, and read and write. She probably still knows her times tables, how plants synthesise light, and the history of the Human-Shaper Wars, too. Those kind of factual memories are different to our own personal memories. The brain stores them differently."

Apollo sighed. "I don't suppose knowing how to contact Poseidon would be a factual memory, by any chance?"

Nothing sprang to mind. "Nope."

"Damn. You were always his favourite—something about the closeness of the moon and the tides. You had some special way to find him. I've been trying, but so far none of my usual sources have come up with anything. I think he's the logical place to start. We know for sure he has one of the pieces of the lightning bolt, and he may know who has the last one. Unfortunately, he's hard to track down when he doesn't want to be found."

My turn to sigh. Nothing was ever easy. Hades had confirmed that Poseidon had a piece of Zeus's lightning bolt, so I guess it made sense to start our search with him. If we wanted to reunite the three pieces and give Zeus the strength to return from his strange exile, we would have to locate the god of the sea eventually.

"Will your memory come back?" Syl asked, cutting right to the heart of the matter.

"Hades said he didn't actually take it, so he thinks it's still in there somewhere, buried deep. He's hopeful it will return." Not half as bloody hopeful as I was. This was such a frustrating way to live, with people expecting me to know things I didn't. Who knew what bombshells my memories had in store for me, and when they would choose to drop them? Hades had told me he and I had actually been there when the lightning bolt had come screaming out of the sky to land at Poseidon's feet. But, like so many other things, I could only take his word for it, since I couldn't remember it for myself.

Apollo clenched his fists. "Time. It always comes back to that. Zeus is running out of it, and we don't have enough of it to sit around waiting for your memories to return."

"Maybe if you went somewhere familiar—familiar to your old self, I mean," Syl said, "it might jog your brain into remembering."

Syl was in problem-solving mode, but I still wasn't one hundred per cent sure I wanted that old self back. "Doesn't it bother you that I might become someone else if I recover those memories?"

It sure seemed to bother her boyfriend. Lucas sat on the couch beside her with his arms folded across his chest in a defensive pose, looking quite unlike his usual laidback self. He wasn't saying much, either, which was also unusual.

She shrugged. "I've never been friends with a goddess before. Should be fun. There's got to be a few perks, right? Just don't turn me into anything freaky and we'll be cool."

"I'm a goddess, Syl, not a magician."

"That never stopped Zeus," she muttered darkly. "He's always turning people into weird shit in the old stories."

I turned to Apollo, who was frowning at us. Hades had said we'd been close, and that if anyone could tell me about my lost past, it would be my brother. "What do you know about my old life? Could you take me somewhere familiar?"

"You were living in Albany, in one of the southern shaper territories, before I was captured," he said. "You had a sort of combined gym and martial arts school there, for women only."

Martial arts? Not an archery range? I was handy with a knife, but I'd never found myself busting out any karate moves in a fight. I tried to picture myself throwing fancy kicks and punches, but no memories came bubbling to the surface. And who had I been teaching? "Did I have friends?"

He blinked in surprise, as if wondering what kind of weirdo loner wouldn't. "Of course. You talked a lot about Ophelia, your partner—"

My stomach dropped in horror, and I almost forgot to breathe until he completed the sentence.

"—in the gym." Only a business partner. Not competition for Jake. "A couple of other women, Brianna and Claire. You used to go on hunting trips with them into the mountains." He smiled fondly. "You were always boasting about the size of the wild boars you would bring down on those trips, with nothing but your bow and arrow."

"Show-off," Syl said. "Sounds like you."

In other circumstances, I might have stuck my tongue out at her, but my brain was fully focused on the partner thing. If he was about to tell me I had a boyfriend—or a girlfriend, for that matter—that I couldn't remember, things were going to get mighty awkward. "What about a … a non-business partner? Did I have anyone … special?"

I held my breath until he shook his head. "I don't think so. Not recently, anyway."

Well, that was a relief. Jake was my one and only.

Apollo eyed me shrewdly. He knew why I was asking. "Jake seemed upset when I spoke to him earlier."

What did I say to that? "He is."

"If it's any consolation, he's not too happy with me, either. I told him I've decided to make him Ruby Adept. He was so horrified he almost argued with me."

He smiled, but I gritted my teeth. Jake's ridiculous obedience to the will of the gods didn't extend to satisfying their romantic wishes, unfortunately. And dammit, he would be so busy as Ruby Adept that he wouldn't have any trouble avoiding me. Why couldn't Apollo have picked someone else?

"The investiture will be in a couple of days. You should come."

Jake wouldn't have changed his mind about us in a couple of days, but my stupid heart lifted at the thought of seeing him again anyway. "I'd like that."

"Good. Once the ceremony's over, I can leave Jake to handle the Ruby Council and we can focus fully on the search for Poseidon. I'll send you something suitable to wear."

"Why? Is there something wrong with my clothes?" I asked, preparing to take offence. No one whose wardrobe consisted of black, black, and more black was going to get away with criticising my fashion choices.

"Your clothes are fine." He ran a dismissive eye over my current outfit of jeans and a sky-blue T-shirt. My wardrobe didn't vary much from that: jeans and T-shirt, jeans and singlet top—these were my regular uniform. "But I doubt you have anything suited to such a formal occasion. We need to make a statement." He put one arm around my shoulder and flung the other out in an expansive gesture. "Sun and Moon are together again. We will send a warning to these shadow shapers that we are not to be trifled with."

He seemed a lot braver now that he had his sister back.

"Yay, us," I said drily. What exactly did he mean by "formal occasion"? I didn't like getting dressed up, and I hated having a whole bunch of strangers staring at me. If it wasn't for the lure of seeing Jake, I'd be running the other way as fast as possible instead of attending this ceremony.

"You'll need to look the part," he said. "At the moment, you don't even look like a huntress, much less the moon goddess." Then he frowned and looked around the small room. "Where is your bow?"

"In my bedroom."

He drew in a sharp breath. "You didn't have it with you in the pub—did you leave it here on its own?" He marched

27

into the bedroom, returning with my bow and quiver, a scowl as black as the pits of Tartarus on his face. "Do you want to end up dead? You can't just leave your avatar lying around like a discarded T-shirt. Have you forgotten what the shadow shapers can do with a god's avatar? You keep it somewhere secure, or you carry it with you. Always."

"Okay, okay, keep your shirt on. Syl and Lucas were here, anyway."

His expression clearly indicated that he didn't find a cat shifter and a werewolf sufficient security for my new fashion accessory.

I took them from him with a sigh and his face softened.

"I don't want to lose you again, Arti."

My irritation vanished at the concern in his eyes. I had a brother, and he loved me. That made up for a lot.

3

I cradled the hot mug in my hands, inhaling the delicious aroma of coffee as I gazed out at the blue waters beyond our little town. The sparkling sea stretched all the way to the horizon. Somewhere out there was Poseidon—all we had to do was find him. No pressure.

Still, that was a problem for another day. Today was Jake's investiture as Ruby Adept, and that was a big enough deal for one day. I closed my eyes and took another sip of coffee, digging my bare toes underneath the couch cushions to keep them warm. The apartment was unusually quiet, since Syl and Lucas had spent the night at his parents' place after some big werewolf thing, and I was enjoying the early morning peace. Later, my day would be full of pomp and ceremony, new people and the strain—or was that the thrill?—of seeing Jake again. For now, I was content to stretch out on the couch, admire the view of the ocean, and do my best to think of nothing at all.

Not that I'd ever been much good at that. If I had a book to read, I could sit still, but apart from that, I preferred to be up and doing. Maybe I should go for a long walk on the beach instead.

But then I'd have to take my bow and quiver. Apollo had been so ticked at me leaving them behind last time, and Syl and Lucas had been there then. He'd go apeshit if I left them now. Not that I blamed him. I had no desire to become a victim of the shadow shapers. I just wished my avatar wasn't quite so cumbersome. Apollo had the right idea with his small, go-anywhere ring. What had Artemis been thinking when she chose a bow and arrow for an avatar?

My gaze fell on the shimmering silver dress Winston had delivered a short time ago, draped over the back of one of the armchairs in a waterfall of shining fabric. It was long, with a figure-hugging bodice that plunged low at the neckline, and a flowing skirt. It looked like something an actress would wear to a movie premiere, something hideously expensive and exclusive. Something that really didn't belong in the wardrobe of Lexi Jardine.

Was this the kind of dress Artemis was used to? She must be a very different person to me if this was a normal part of her wardrobe. On the bright side, it would look good on me, and the idea of Jake, who was used to seeing me covered in dirt and sweat, seeing me in something like this instead was pretty enticing. His eyes would light with that hungry look I loved, as if he couldn't wait to peel me out of it.

At least, they would have, once. Maybe now he'd only feel a hint of regret. Or, worse, seeing me in such a dress would confirm his belief that I was too far above him, that we could never be together.

I set my empty coffee mug down with a sigh. Regardless of what I wore, I was still the same person. A silver gown didn't make me a goddess.

A gentle knock sounded at the door, but it opened before I could get up, and Holly peeped around it.

"I thought I heard you earlier," she said, coming in. For once, she didn't have Mireille with her. "You're up early today."

"I couldn't sleep. It's Jake's investiture today."

Holly knew how those sentences were connected. She'd been there when Jake had walked away from me, despite my pleas that she had politely pretended not to hear. "How do you feel about that?"

"I'm not sure. Part of me is excited to see him again. The other part is dreading it."

"That's understandable," she said. "Maybe he'll have changed his mind, now he's going to be the Ruby Adept."

"Maybe." But I didn't think so. The Ruby Adept might be the head of the fireshapers, but that was a long way short of godhood. And Jake was stubborn. It was going to take more than a promotion to change his mind. "Let's not talk about it or I'm going to chicken out of going. How was your pack thing last night?"

She sat on the arm of the armchair across from me, looking unusually awkward. "Actually, that's what I wanted to talk to you about."

"Oh?" I didn't like the way she said that, not meeting my eyes. What did pack business have to do with me? Was I going to need another cup of coffee for this conversation?

She wiped her hands along her jeans, as if her palms were sweating, though it wasn't particularly hot in here. In fact, my bare feet were still cold. I tucked them closer against my body. "Lucas told the pack last night about you. About who you really are."

"Oh?" I said again, mentally cursing Lucas. He hadn't even told Syl, and now he'd gone and told the whole pack? What was with that? He'd been acting strange since we got back.

"The alphas sent me as their representative, since I have the closest relationship with you of all the wolves."

Well, that was weird. Since when did Norma and Ray need a representative to talk to me? I sat up a little straighter, watching Holly's bowed head cautiously. "Is there a problem?"

She looked up at that. "No, not at all." Then she slipped from the armchair to kneel on the floor. "They wanted me to offer you our fealty."

"Get up," I said sharply, revolted by the sight of my friend on her knees. I sprang up myself, scattering couch cushions, ready to pull her to her feet if necessary. "What is this, the Middle Ages? Nobody pledges their fealty to anyone anymore."

She stood up, a look of distress on her face. "I told Norma I was the wrong person to do this. I knew I'd muck it up."

I took her hands and spoke in a gentler tone. "You haven't mucked anything up. I just don't understand. I didn't think you werewolves followed the shaper gods."

She stared at me in disbelief. "You can't be serious. We don't give a shit about the other gods—but you! You are the goddess of the moon, and we are its creatures. *Your* creatures. Who the hell else would werewolves worship?"

"But, I—" I stopped, at a loss for words. She'd caught me completely by surprise.

She stared down at our joined hands. "This is blowing my mind. I can't believe I'm here with you. Who ever expects to meet their goddess in person?"

Who, indeed? We'd just gone from weird to outright freaky on the crazy-o-meter. Werewolves worshipped Artemis? It made sense, in a way. No wonder Lucas had been acting so oddly.

My mind replayed one of my earliest conversations with Lucas. *What would you say if I told you the gods were real?* I'd asked, and he'd replied: *I'd probably wonder what you were trying to sell me.* He'd never struck me as particularly religious. How the hell were Holly and I having this conversation now?

"Lucas told me once that he only visited the shrine on feast days," I objected. "I got the distinct impression that he was only going through the motions and didn't actually believe in the gods. None of you have ever mentioned religion before." A slightly accusing tone had crept into my voice. This was just getting too ridiculous. What next? Statues of me in the town square? People feeding me grapes and carrying me around lest my delicate feet get dirtied?

Holly shrugged, still clinging determinedly to my hands. "We don't talk about it outside the pack. It's no one's business but ours." And now mine, apparently. "Our legends say you created our kind, in the quest for a perfect hunting companion—merging the loyalty and ferocity of your hunting hounds with the intelligence of a human."

"Really?" I said faintly. I was *not* going to ask exactly how I had combined humans with hounds. Some things were better kept as legends. I dragged my mind from the horrendous images it was contemplating and said, in a firmer voice: "Okay, but that's legends. This is the twenty-first century. There's not even a temple here. Surely you can't still …" I trailed off, unwilling to say "worship me". It was too weird.

Holly grinned at me, as if this was all so amazing, but I was not finding the same delight in the situation. "We have our own shrine, out in the bush where no one runs but the wolves. We visit it on full moons, and sometimes other times, too. I prayed there for a baby."

And I had delivered—literally. I'd delivered Holly and Joe's baby in the back of a stolen car as we careered down the freeway. The absurdity of it took my breath away.

"Don't look at me like that," I said sternly. Her eyes were shining. "You and Joe did all the baby-making on your own. It was nothing to do with me."

"You saved her," she said, with absolute certainty. "She wouldn't be here except for you. Neither would I."

"Of course I did!" Exasperated, I dropped her hands and stalked to the window. Outside, blue sky smiled down on blue sea. Two people were walking their dog on the beach, and out beyond the point, the dark shapes of surfers bobbed on the water, waiting for the perfect wave. "Because you were my *friend*, not because you prayed to someone." *Please don't make this any weirder than it already is.* "Seriously, Holly, that's all I want. Just friends. Not worshippers. I *need* friends."

Syl would be thrilled, and say she'd told me so, but after the events of the last couple of days, I was more than ready to admit it. Hell, I was happy to shout it from the rooftops: I was not an island. I needed my friends. Becoming some remote figure in a silver gown, an icon to be worshipped, was no part of my agenda.

She moved to my side and laid a gentle hand on my shoulder. "You know I'm your friend. It might just take me a little while to get used to this news."

"You and me both." We shared a smile and a knot of tension in my gut unwound.

"I just want you to know that the pack will be there for you if you need us," she added.

I sighed and turned my back on the view. Despite my churning feelings, I had to try to be gracious. The support of the pack was no small thing. "Thank you. That's good to know." And it was, even though I had no intention of endangering them by dragging them into this. "Actually," I added, as my gaze fell on the sparkle of silver draped over the back of the armchair, "there is something you could help me with. Just you, I mean, not the whole pack."

"What?"

"This dress. Apollo sent it for me to wear to the investiture today. And now that I see it, I realise I don't have any shoes to go with it." I had sneakers, combat-style boots, and a single pair of brown sandals. "And I don't know what to do with my hair. This is kind of a big deal, according to Apollo. I'm not sure I can pull it off."

"Is it safe for you to be out in public? If you're a goddess, you're in danger from the shadow shapers, too. Should you really be making public appearances?"

I'd asked Hades the same thing, forgetting it applied to me, too, now. He was planning on disappearing to the underworld; soon, I would be leaving, too.

I shrugged. "Apollo says we need to make a statement. I think he feels the need to stamp his authority on the remaining fireshapers in Crosston. Show that the new Ruby Adept has his full support."

"Well, I hope you're not going to make a habit of it," she said, frowning.

"I'm not sure that anywhere is truly safe anymore," I said. "At least not until we find out who is behind the shadow shapers and how they manage their attacks." As soon as we located Poseidon, I would be leaving Berkley's Bay, doing what I did best: hunting. Then we would see who was the better hunter: the shadow shapers or the goddess of the hunt.

She nodded, still frowning, and held the dress up against me. The slinky silver fabric caught the light from the window and threw sparkles all over the walls.

"I think strappy silver sandals," she said. "Norma has a pair that would fit you. I'll text her and get her to drop them over. And maybe a nice upswept style for your hair? Ask Tegan. She'd be more than happy to help. What? What's wrong?"

I grimaced. "I don't have time to stuff around in Tegan's salon." What I really meant was that I didn't want half the world staring at me while Tegan interrogated me on everything that had happened. My feelings were still too raw.

Holly nodded sagely. "Wait here."

She slipped out, but didn't leave me waiting long. A few moments later, she was back, with Tegan at her heels. Tegan was big and bold, an unstoppable force of nature. Today, she wore a leopard skin print skirt that on anyone else would have been scandalously short, but on Tegan just looked right. She had a thing about leopard print—said it satisfied the inner tiger to wear the skins of her rivals. Even though her rivals' skins were probably not made of stretchy synthetic. It was the thought that counted.

"I hear someone needs a formal do," she said, dumping a bag full of hairdressing tools on the dining table. "Come pull up a pew and let's see what we can do."

I sat obediently in the dining chair she indicated, mentally steeling myself for the flow of questions to begin. But they never came. She kept up a steady stream of harmless gossip about the doings of the town, but never asked a thing about what I'd been up to. I'd have to find out what Holly had said to her; I was in awe.

Gradually, I relaxed as I sat there, being beautified by the expert as Holly smiled encouragement. She was finished in remarkably quick time, and stood back, comb in hand,

and surveyed her work with pride. "That should do it," she said to Holly, "though you'll need to do something about her face."

"What's wrong with my face?" I asked, indignant.

"You look like you haven't slept in a week," Tegan said, brutally frank as ever. "People will be wondering who this hag is with the beautiful hair."

"Thanks."

"No problem." She swept her tools into her bag and gave me a wink. "Knock 'em dead, sunshine."

She left, and Holly glanced at her watch. "What time did you say this thing started?"

"Winston said he'd be back for me around mid-morning. The new Ruby Adept has to take office at midday, when the sun is at its height. That's why the ceremony always takes place on a Sunday, too—it's a sun god thing."

"You'd better get into that dress, then. Tegan took longer than I thought she would. Have you got any makeup?"

I hesitated. Makeup hadn't really been a priority for a while.

"At least some concealer?"

I shook my head.

"Fine. You get changed. I'll see what I've got that will work with your colouring—your skin is darker than mine." She headed for the door.

I took the dress into my bedroom and shimmied into it.

The silver fabric clung to my body like a second skin over my breasts and hips, then flared out into a full skirt that fell to the floor. I nearly tripped on it as I headed back to the lounge room. I couldn't get used to the feel of the silken fabric whispering around my legs as I walked.

The door opened and Syl came in, carrying a pair of silver sandals. "Norma asked me to bring these home with me. Wow, you look like a model. What have you done with your hair?"

I touched my hair self-consciously. The apartment still reeked of the three gallons of hairspray Tegan had sprayed on it to hold the style in place. "Tegan did it for me. Apollo sent the dress. He wants me to make an impression."

She considered me, her head tipped on one side. "Well, you'll certainly do that. You look … you don't look like yourself."

I didn't feel like myself either. Holly came back in before I could answer, hands full of makeup. I strapped on the borrowed shoes under her approving eye; they fit, more or less, though the heels were a lot higher than I was used to. Then I sat back down in the same chair as before.

"I can put my own makeup on, you know," I grumbled, as she swiped concealer over the dark circles under my eyes.

"I know," she said, "but let me do it anyway. I want to help."

She was very quick and, when she was finished and showed me the effect in the mirror, I had to admit she'd done a better job than I could have.

"Wow, thank you." What would Jake think when he saw me like this?

A thin wail rose from the apartment next door: Mireille, ready for another feed.

"I'd better go," Holly said. "You look stunning! Have a great time."

"Thanks," I said, forbearing to point out that I wasn't going to a ball, even if they'd dolled me up like Cinderella. Having a great time wasn't really part of the deal. The ceremony would be full of cowed fireshapers, and I'd have to make like a goddess and pretend I had a clue what I was doing. All while being close enough to Jake to touch him, with him doing his best to ignore me, no doubt. Yes, this was going to be a super fun event, for sure.

Syl had gone to get changed, since I'd decided I needed the moral support and had wangled an invitation for her, too. I strode down the hallway, practising walking in the heels, and nearly twisted my ankle. Too bad if the shadow shapers attacked while I was dressed like this; I'd never be able to run.

Limping into my bedroom, I surveyed the final effect in the full-length mirror on the inside of my wardrobe door. A stranger stared back at me, her green eyes luminous, widened and emphasised by expertly applied eyeliner and shadow. Dark hair was piled on her head, with curling strands falling in front of her ears in an elegant yet casual style. Deep red lips were parted uncertainly. And the dress! She was wearing liquid moonlight, sparkling as she moved. I could believe that this woman was a goddess.

In short, I looked beautiful, but I didn't look like me. Did I really want to become this person, who seemed so different? This whole goddess thing was scaring me. I liked myself and the friends I had just fine. What if being a goddess changed me into someone else? Would they still like me? Would I? The beautiful reflection frowned at me. This was all so weird.

I took refuge in the practical. Apollo's insistence on my carrying my bow and quiver everywhere was going to be a problem. They definitely weren't the right kind of accessory for this dress. I'd feel like an idiot, but I didn't dare leave them behind after how he'd gone off at me the other day.

Let's face it, I felt like an idiot anyway. This look wasn't me—I was awkward as a kid playing dress-ups in someone else's clothes. I teetered on one foot, removing the first strappy sandal. I certainly wasn't going to convince anyone of my divinity staggering around in these ridiculous heels. How did Norma even walk in them? I was more likely to provide the comic relief when I went arse over apex down the stairs.

The other shoe came off and I sighed in relief. Even after such a short time in them, the balls of my feet were stinging from trying to walk in the high heels. Then I considered the dress. It was beautiful, but too long without the strappy sandals. I'd be tripping over the hem every second step.

A few minutes later, Syl walked in and stopped with a gasp, hands flying to her mouth in horror. "What are you *doing*?" she squeaked.

"Fixing this dress," I said, without looking up.

"Fixing it? You've ruined it! Are you crazy?"

I concentrated on what I was doing; the snip of the scissors, the soft sigh of fabric falling to the floor. Nearly done. The dress now came to just above my knees. Okay, the hem was a little ragged, but the length was much more practical.

"Did I miss the part of the invitation that said 'come as a homeless person'?" she continued.

She looked lovely, in a red halter neck dress that clung to her curves and a pair of nude shoes. She wore no jewellery, but she didn't need it: her black hair cascaded alluringly over one shoulder. She was enough, just on her own.

"I couldn't do it, Syl." The last piece of the dress slithered to the floor and I did an experimental twirl in front of the mirror. The hem was only slightly uneven— good enough. "If I have to be a goddess, I'm going to do it on my own terms. I'm not a goddamn princess."

I strapped on a belt that held my favourite knife in a sheath, then sat down and pulled on my combat boots. Syl watched me lace them in silence.

At last, I was ready. "What do you think?"

"I think Apollo is going to be pissed." She shook her head, grinning. "But I like it. Homeless person chic looks good on you."

4

Winston smiled encouragingly, resplendent in what I thought of as his official uniform of long red robes and strange little hat. It was meant to be a stylised silken sun, but it looked to me more like an octopus perched on his thinning hair. "Ready?"

I nodded and took his outstretched hand. Syl took his other one. "Ready."

Together, we stepped forward. The world shivered around us and my foot landed, not on the worn carpet of his tiny temple, but on the smooth tiles of the Great Temple of Apollo in Crosston.

A blast of trumpets nearly scared the crap out of me. Two trumpeters, one on each side of the huge double doors to the street, currently closed, blew a fanfare which echoed in the vast space. I flinched and glared at the offending musicians, but they ignored me, their gazes fixed straight ahead, standing at attention.

There were fewer people in the large circular chamber than I had expected, but they were all looking at us. A little knot of priests in celebratory red, same as Winston, stood together in front of the great statue of Apollo that dominated the room. More red-robed priests formed a guard of honour, creating a sort of aisle from the closed temple doors, around the sacred fire to where the other priests waited at the base of a dais in front of the statue. Syl fit right in in her gorgeous red dress.

Where had she gotten that dress? Her wardrobe was even more limited than mine, owing to the fact that she'd spent most of the last few months in cat form. I leaned over to whisper to her as the priests bowed in sync like a red wave.

"Did Apollo send you that dress, too?"

"No. I borrowed it from Holly." That made sense. They were about the same height and build.

The great golden statue of Apollo loomed above the priests. It showed Apollo seated, playing a harp, his golden curls tumbling about his shoulders. In the centre of the circular chamber, the sacred fire leapt in its hearth, directly under the dome that soared overhead. A row of windows circled the base of the dome like a necklace, allowing natural light to fall on the tiled floor below and offering glimpses of blue sky above. That and the sacred fire were the main sources of light, though small torches were spaced at intervals around the walls. I knew from my previous visit that the temple had electric lighting. I looked up and saw that, today, they were all dark. We were going old-school for the ceremony, apparently.

In front of the statue of Apollo, raised above the waiting priests, two thrones sat on the dais. There were no other chairs. I hoped it wouldn't be a long ceremony, since the spectators were obviously expected to stand throughout.

Another trumpet blast made me jump. This time, the priests sank to the floor. Apollo stepped out of thin air in front of his statue, appearing on the dais. He wore the familiar black, but on his chest glowed the most enormous ruby I'd ever seen, suspended on a thick gold chain. Ignoring the priests, he took the steps down from the dais and strode across the floor toward me. The priests parted to let him through. My ears were still ringing from the trumpets, but I heard him clearly as he took my hand and leaned forward to brush his lips against my cheek.

"You look beautiful."

I cast a triumphant look at Syl, who shrugged. "You don't mind that I ... modified the dress?"

His lips twitched as he tucked my hand into the crook of his elbow and drew me toward the dual thrones. "Modified. Is that what they call it? No, I think it was a good call. It's time we put the fear of the gods back into the forefront of our enemies' minds. Appearing as the huntress is a good reminder of what will happen to those who defy us."

The priests rustled like a field of wheat in the wind as we passed among them. Apollo led me up onto the dais. Standing in front of the thrones, we turned to face the audience. Nearly everyone in the chamber was a fireshaper. With the return of my divine powers, I could tell that at a glance now, without having to see a demonstration of their ability. The ones who weren't priests mostly wore black, like their god, men and women alike. There were also a few shifters, like Syl, and a handful of ordinary humans.

Apollo took my hand and gave it a reassuring squeeze. "I am happy to welcome my sister to our ceremony today," he said to the waiting assembly. The rustling had subsided, and his voice rang proudly in the cavernous chamber. "Sun and Moon together will welcome the new Ruby Adept."

A buzz of whispers flew around the room, and all eyes turned to me with renewed interest. Miracle enough to have one god walking among them, but two! These were strange times indeed for the local fireshapers. Winston beamed proudly at me from where he stood with Syl, close to his fellow priests but slightly apart, perhaps indicative of his new status. Whatever that was. He was something more than a simple servant of the Great Temple now, though his new duties hadn't been clearly defined, as far as I knew. Was he a high priest of his own tiny temple?

Yes, strange times, when a lowly priest with only weak fireshaping could become so favoured of the god. Difficult times, too. If these were all the fireshapers left, numbers were way down. Not really surprising, considering how many Apollo had killed in his rage, and how many more had fled with the traitorous former Ruby Adept. The fireshapers were at a fraction of their former strength.

"I thought there'd be more people here," I whispered to Apollo. The small crowd was not enough to stop the temple from feeling empty and echo-y. "Isn't creating a new Ruby Adept a pretty big deal?"

"Usually," Apollo said. "Though I've never actually attended one of these things before. But, normally, it's a three-day festival with crowds and parades. The temple is packed, and they broadcast the ceremony live. Under the circumstances, I thought it was better to get it done quickly and quietly, with the minimum of fuss. Only the fireshapers and a handful of their higher-up human servants are here."

Apollo sat down, so I hurriedly sat, too, placing my bow across my knees. As if that was the signal, the great doors to the temple creaked open and one of the priests broke from the little knot in front of the dais. His octopus hat was bigger and more elaborate than the other priests', golden instead of red, so he must have been important. Probably the high priest.

"Let the candidate come forward," he boomed in a deep

voice that seemed to come out of nowhere, as he wasn't a particularly big man.

A figure stepped inside, silhouetted against the bright light from the street. Jake, of course. I leaned forward to get a better look, squinting against the glare. He was dressed in white pants and a long white tunic with red embroidery around the neck and hem. His feet were bare.

My heart did a little flip at the sight of him. He'd had a haircut since I'd seen him last, and the shorter length made him look younger. Still good enough to eat, though the shapeless tunic did nothing for him. The shadows under his eyes were nearly as blue as the eyes themselves. It looked like someone wasn't getting enough sleep. That seemed only fair; I wasn't sleeping that well, myself.

Longing welled up inside me. He looked oddly vulnerable in the oversized tunic, with his bare feet. I wanted to leap down off the dais and throw myself into his arms, kiss that tired, careworn look away. Instead, I smoothed the silken folds of my dress over my thighs and watched him pad into the temple, taking slow, measured steps.

The great doors boomed shut behind him, and one of the waiting fireshapers stepped up to meet him. He was only a little shorter than Jake and looked almost as tired. He wore black, like the other fireshapers. Though his clothing was no more elaborate than theirs, something proud in his carriage made him stand out from the others.

"Who's that?" I whispered to Apollo.

"That's Adani. Master of the West."

Ah. One of the masters on the inner council. Jake, who was Master of the South-East, was another. He probably knew this man well. Maybe they'd been burning the midnight oil together, trying to pull the tattered remnants of their organisation back together. Apollo had mentioned Adani's name before; he'd been overseeing the interrogation of the fireshapers, trying to root out the last of the traitors. Together, Jake and Adani paced between the rows of red-clad priests until they reached the central fire. Then Adani bowed deeply to Apollo, followed by a slightly shallower bow to me. "My lord, Lady Artemis—the Ruby Council offers its candidate, Jacob Harlan Steele, for your approval."

Jake stared rigidly at Apollo and I felt a childish urge to get up and wave my hand in front of his face, just to make him notice me. He hadn't looked at me once since he'd entered the temple. His tanned face was paler than usual; perhaps he was nervous. Or maybe he was still mad at Apollo for making him take on this role. Secretly, I hoped he was pining for me. He ought to be—he was making this way harder than it needed to be.

"I approve," Apollo said. "Proceed."

Adani bowed and resumed his place among the fireshapers. Alone, Jake paced around the sacred fire and stopped before the high priest at the foot of the dais.

"Jacob Harlan Steele," the high priest said in that sonorous voice. "Are you prepared to take on the duties and responsibilities of Ruby Adept, leader of the Ruby Council, protector and mentor of all fireshapers living in the lands within the council's purview?"

"I am."

"Kneel."

At a sign from the high priest, two priests brought forward a heavy red cape of some velvety material, richly embroidered with gold flames. Gently, they settled this cape about Jake's shoulders as he knelt on the hard tiles in front of the high priest.

Apollo sat, relaxed, in his chair, observing with interest, but I was tense. Jake's eyes were firmly on the floor. Was he seriously going to pretend I didn't exist? Staring at his bowed raven head, I wasn't sure whether I wanted to kiss him or shake him. Maybe a bit of both.

The high priest rested one hand on Jake's head. "Place your right fist over your heart and repeat after me: I, Jacob Harlan Steele, do solemnly swear ..."

In a clear voice, Jake echoed him. "I, Jacob Harlan Steele, do solemnly swear ..."

"To guide and protect the fireshapers of New Hollandia ..."

"To guide and protect the fireshapers of New Hollandia ..."

"To the best of my ability, always striving for the glorification of our Lord God Apollo, from whom our fire springs."

"To the best of my ability, always striving for the glorification of our Lord God Apollo, from whom our fire springs."

A priest stepped forward with a red velvet cushion bearing a golden circlet, too simple to be called a crown—and Jake was no king, anyway. Its main feature was a central ruby, large by most standards but dwarfed by the one around Apollo's neck. The high priest took this from the cushion reverently and lowered it onto Jake's dark head.

At once, all the gathered priests began to chant a long, monotonous prayer to Apollo, glorifying him and praising the new Ruby Adept who served him. I shifted uncomfortably in my seat as the prayer droned on, fingers curling impatiently around my bow. The quiver at my back made it impossible to lounge back against the throne as Apollo was doing. He appeared to be enjoying the priests' long listing of his many attributes. Jake remained patiently on his knees, an obedient statue—I bet he could have done with that velvet cushion by now—but I began to look around. How long would this go on?

Winston was absorbed in the prayer, chanting along with the rest of the red robes. Syl, next to him, looked as bored as I felt. She rolled her eyes when I caught her gaze, and I grinned back. Adani and the other black-clad fireshapers chanted, too, though Adani's eyes were roving around the temple as much as mine. Not religious, then. If only Jake were the same. I wondered what Adani thought of having his god actually in attendance, after centuries without any contact or any reason beyond faith to believe he actually existed. Most men would probably have found religion pretty damn fast. I liked the fact that he hadn't.

I leaned closer to Apollo. "How long are these guys going to be singing your praises?"

His blue eyes, so like Jake's, sparkled with amusement at my evident restlessness. "Sometimes they go on for hours."

"No wonder other gods don't normally come," I muttered. "No offence, but I don't need chapter and verse on your magnificence."

"Then you're in luck. I believe today they're reciting the shorter version of this prayer. They should be finished soon."

Zeus's balls. If this was the shorter version, I'd hate to hear the long one. I fiddled with my bow, my fingers stroking the smooth wood over and over. Why had I come? There was no point seeing Jake when Jake refused to see me. No one liked being ignored. And this ceremony only emphasised how hopeless my cause was. Jake was the Ruby Adept now, with a massive workload. He was tied to this city, probably even tied to the Ruby Palace. He was no longer free to run around the world with me, rescuing gods and killing shadow shapers. His life would be full of paperwork and council meetings. I certainly didn't envy him—I could hardly think of anything worse.

Finally, the interminable prayer ground to a close, and the priests fell silent. Jake rose. If his knees were screaming, he gave no sign. Accompanied by a priest on either side, he moved to face the sacred fire and bowed his head.

"What's he doing?" I whispered, when nothing else happened.

"He's praying to me," Apollo said.

"They're not going to start chanting again, are they?"

"Don't sound so horrified. No, this time, it's just Jake, asking for strength for the next part of the ceremony."

"Can you hear him when he prays to you?" I asked, suddenly diverted.

"Of course."

"Do you hear everyone that prays?" That would be horrifying. Millions of people, all begging for things inside your head. "Why can't I hear anyone praying to me?" Surely someone, somewhere, was praying for Artemis's help.

"You learn to tune them out. You probably don't even realise you're hearing them. Occasionally, something catches my attention, particularly if the supplicant makes a good sacrifice."

I shook my head. Sacrifices? The surprises just never stopped coming with this god thing. Prayers and supplicants would have to go in the *too hard* basket for now. "What's the next part of the ceremony?"

"You'll see. He's nearly finished."

I couldn't help wondering what Jake was saying, but it seemed rude to ask, so I watched his bowed head instead. He looked foreign in the magnificent red cloak and ruby diadem, not like the Jake I knew at all. Was that man gone, buried under the weight of his new responsibilities?

No, I wouldn't believe that. Cloaks and jewels didn't change a person, any more than shiny silver dresses did. We'd both taken on new roles but, fundamentally, we were the same people we'd always been. Just better dressed.

Jake finished his prayer and nodded to the two priests flanking him. They stepped forward and removed the heavy cloak with a ceremonial flourish. One draped it over his arm and stepped back. The other waited while Jake removed the ruby circlet and then, surprisingly, the long, shapeless tunic.

Not that I would complain about any opportunity to admire Jake's broad, muscled chest, but this seemed a little odd. What now? I caught Syl's eye, and she cocked a puzzled eyebrow at me. I lifted one shoulder in a shrug.

We weren't left wondering long. Now clad only in a loose pair of white pants, Jake took a deep breath and walked straight into the sacred fire. I sat bolt upright in surprise, fingers clenching on my bow. The fire burned in a vast bowl, sunken into the temple floor, several paces across. But Jake wasn't pacing anywhere, just standing there as the flames danced and flickered across his skin.

I glanced around, unnerved. Sure, he was a fireshaper, but this seemed a little excessive. "If he fries, do they decide he's not worthy or something?" I whispered to Apollo.

"It's a test of his power," Apollo murmured. "Throwing a few fireballs is much easier than withstanding the temple fire playing over your body. The sacred fire is no ordinary flame. The previous Ruby Adept only lasted a little over a minute, I'm told."

Therefore, Jake had to do better, to prove himself to the remaining fireshapers, who would be looking for a strong leader to help them rebuild. *Relax*, I told myself. *He's not going to get crisped*. But my fist stayed clenched around the bow.

His face was expressionless, eyes fixed on some point on the far wall. Strands of his dark hair lifted gently, wafted by the fire's heat, but otherwise he was still. Dazzled by the flames, I could only stare and count off the seconds.

In the darkness beyond the fire, something moved, and that was my only warning.

An enormous gust of wind sprang up from nowhere and ripped through the vast chamber, scattering the sacred fire and knocking the gathered people from their feet. It forced me against my chair, my quiver digging into my back. My heart pounded in shock as all the torches blew out in the same instant, plunging us into shadow. The only light came from the tiny windows circling the base of the dome far above.

Barely knowing what I was doing, I reacted on pure

instinct, my hand reaching over my shoulder for an arrow in a well-rehearsed movement. I nocked it to my bow and stood in one smooth motion. The great room was dim, but not too dim for my eyes. The bow string twanged; the arrow flew, and in the shadows, a man went down.

Apollo leapt up, his reactions slightly slower than mine, and flung his arm out. Flames roared back to life in the sacred bowl.

"Watch out!" I snapped, leaping down from the dais as his flames leapt hungrily at the lower reaches of the dome. He'd burn us all to cinders if he didn't get his inner sun god under control. The scattered fireshapers struggled to their feet, but kept well clear of the massive flame.

Jake sprawled on the tiles in front of it, knocked aside by the tornado. I dropped to one knee at his side, but before I could feel for a pulse, his eyes flickered open. Time stopped as we stared at one another.

"Lexi," he said, his eyes shining with love.

I smiled down at him. Zeus's balls, but he was handsome. I could drown in those blue, blue eyes of his.

His hand reached out to me, and then a shadow crossed his face and he sat up, drawing away. "I mean, Lady Artemis."

He held himself stiffly, as if the separation cost him an effort of will. Stupid, stubborn man. How many times did we have to save each other before he admitted that we were meant to be together?

Apollo appeared at my side. He reached down and took Jake's hand, helping the new Ruby Adept to his feet. "Are you all right?"

Jake ran a shaking hand through his hair, very careful not to look at me. As if it would hurt less that way. "I think so. What the hell was that?"

"Good question," Apollo said, moving around the roaring flames, which quieted as he passed. He stopped by a black-clad body that lay on its back in the shadows by the door.

"Who is it?" I asked, crossing to his side. The flames of the now-subdued sacred fire warmed my back as I stared down at the body.

Oh, damn. It was Adani.

Apollo waved his hand at the torches on the walls and they re-ignited, burning far brighter than they had before, raising the light levels in the great room considerably. Apollo's mouth set into a hard line as he contemplated the former Master of the West. The man had a surprised expression on his face and a golden arrow lodged in his throat.

"Oops," I said. "Maybe I should have left him alive for questioning."

"I already did question him," Apollo growled. "At length. And then let the bastard question half the other fireshapers. I thought he was clean. Now I'll have to start all over again."

Definitely not clean. And what was that length of pipe lying by his outflung hand? I knelt to examine it.

"Don't touch it," Jake said as I reached for it, his voice urgent. His instinct to protect me, at least, couldn't be suppressed. But I knew it couldn't harm me. Belatedly, the knowledge of what it was swam into my mind from somewhere deep in the murky layers of memory.

"A blowpipe." I picked it up, intrigued. I hadn't seen one of these in years. Decades, even. I'd used one myself, once, but that was long ago, racing barefoot through the jungle with—

What the hell? Where had that come from? The humid air, heavy on my skin, the calls of exotic birds and monkeys high overhead in the canopy, clouds of buzzing insects—it seemed as clear as if I stood on that spongy ground right now, and the temple around me faded. But when I pushed for more, the memory slipped away.

I drew a sharp breath and shook the blowpipe until two tiny darts dropped onto the tiles. The mysteries of my uncooperative memory would have to wait. That was a good sign, though, right? I'd remembered *something*, and I hadn't even been trying. Maybe that was the secret: to stop chasing it and let it come as it would.

The ends of the darts were smeared with some kind of dark paste that gleamed even in the low light of the temple, and I was very careful not to touch it as I picked one up and sniffed it. The scent told me nothing, but there was no prize for guessing it would be some kind of poison. But who was it meant for?

Carefully, I replaced the darts in the pipe. Unlike the one I remembered from that long-ago jungle, this pipe was made of metal, not wood. I held it out to Jake.

"Seal it. We don't want any accidents before we can get this analysed."

He nodded and pinched the ends together between his finger and thumb. I'd seen him work metal magic before, but it still astonished me. He made it look as easy as if the pipe had been made of clay.

Apollo took the now-sealed pipe from me and tapped it impatiently against his open palm, gazing down at the body with frustration in his face. "Who was his target? And why now? It makes no sense."

"Was his secondary air?" I asked, though I was pretty sure I already knew the answer. Still, it had to be asked. Shapers all had two powers, sometimes three. Whichever was stronger decided what kind of shaper they were—in this case, fireshaper. Their secondary power was usually much weaker than their primary.

"No," said Jake. "He was metal, like me."

"Which means that that wind he raised—"

"Must have been stolen from one of the gods," Apollo said, a touch of impatience in his voice. "Probably Zephyrus. Yes, obviously, he was a shadow shaper."

I'd been there when the shadow shapers had killed Zephyrus and stolen his power over the winds. I didn't remember Adani's face among the crowd, but some of the gathering had worn hoods—and besides, I'd been far more focused on surviving the experience myself and saving Jake than on identifying all the guilty parties.

"But what did he gain by revealing himself now?" Apollo asked, still worrying at the problem.

"If he didn't flee with the Ruby Adept—" I checked myself. The fireshapers had a new Ruby Adept now. "—with the *previous* Ruby Adept, he must have had a good reason for staying." Presumably, that reason had to do with capturing Apollo, or even myself, but this was an odd way to go about it. "There were two darts—were they meant for me and you?"

"In front of all these witnesses?" Apollo shook his head. "Maybe poison darts are how they are stealing the gods away, but a temple full of fireshapers would have had something to say about that. They can't *all* be damned shadow shapers."

I glanced around at the gathered shapers. The high priest was hovering uncertainly a few steps behind Apollo, with Syl and Winston right on his heels. The rest of them were keeping a respectful distance, though all eyes were glued to our little tableau. All except Syl's, that was. She was watching everyone else, alert for danger. A warm glow of pride bloomed in my heart.

"He's right," Jake said in a low voice, as a hundred ears strained to overhear our conversation. "That would have been a suicide mission."

"It turned out to be a suicide mission anyway," I pointed out. It didn't make sense. Why run the risk of exposure all this time, then throw it all away for nothing? How had he expected to get away with it?

"He probably wasn't counting on getting an arrow through the neck the instant the lights went out," Apollo said, giving me a look that was half approval, half frustration at being denied answers by my haste to loose that arrow. "I didn't tell anyone but Winston who the other throne was for. No doubt he intended to blame someone else, maybe even 'accidentally' kill the supposed villain in the confusion so we couldn't question them."

"So, if not us, who were the poison darts for?" Again, I looked around at the gathered shapers. The high priest? Killing him would mean some other priest would take his place. The shadow shapers could be trying to get one of their own into the top job, but for what purpose? He was powerful, but only in the temple structure. The members of the council had more power than the priests already, and more influence.

There was no one here who had more power than Adani himself, except one.

Jake met my eyes. "They must have been for me. If I

died, he would have been the logical choice for Ruby Adept."

If he had died, I would have torn Adani's heart out with my bare hands. I resisted the urge to kick the dead body, feeling a powerful satisfaction at the sight of my golden arrow embedded in the traitor's throat. I closed my hand on its smooth shaft and put my foot on Adani's shoulder. The arrow head scraped on a vertebra as I pulled the arrow out and wiped the gore off on the dead man's shirt. A murmur swept through the crowd. Did my actions seem callous to the onlookers? Too bloody bad. I wouldn't be shedding any tears for him.

Two darts didn't necessarily mean there were two intended victims. Even guided by the powers of the wind, a dart wasn't the most reliable of weapons. The second dart was insurance in case the first one missed.

I nodded. "You're right. With you out of the way, the shadow shapers would have had control of the fireshapers again. That was something worth staying here in the danger zone for."

Apollo was still frowning. "Now you'll have to start all over again," he said to Jake. "Question everyone he interrogated, see how many of these snakes are still hiding in the grass. Burn them out if necessary. I want them gone."

5

Syl came in the next morning and perched on the edge of my bed. "Are you going to lie there all day, or do you want some breakfast? Lucas is going to fry up some bacon and eggs."

"Lie here all day," I said, stretching lazily. I hadn't been asleep, just lying there watching the clouds move across the blue expanse of sky that was all I could see outside my window from this angle.

"I thought Apollo was taking you out today?"

"He is; I'm just kidding." I glanced at the time: just before ten. No wonder my stomach was complaining.

"Did you get a chance to talk to Jake yesterday?"

I threw the blankets back with a scowl and sat up. "Jake made very sure that he was never available for any private discussion. He seemed determined to demonstrate how very busy he's going to be as Ruby Adept." I shrugged.

"Whatever. A public ceremony and reception isn't really the ideal place for a tête-à-tête."

Not that I'd been left in any doubt of how he really felt underneath his very proper behaviour. That look on his face just after Adani had attacked, when he'd forgotten for a moment that I was a goddess, had given away his true feelings. He needed to work on his poker face if he truly wanted to convince me that he didn't care for me.

I peeled off the old T-shirt I'd slept in and lobbed it at Syl. She batted it away without comment, watching me rummage through my drawers for something clean to wear. "To be fair, he *is* going to be busy. The fireshapers are a mess; they've got traitors hiding under every rock and all those empty jobs to fill. Maybe your brother shouldn't have been quite so enthusiastic with the smiting."

Trying to ignore the oddness of her saying "your brother" so casually, I shrugged on a dark shirt that only had a small stain on one sleeve. All this adventuring certainly made keeping up with the laundry difficult. "To be *fair*," I said, gently mocking her, "most of the ones he killed were attacking him at the time, so keeping them alive probably wouldn't have been the best idea."

"Most," she said, and left it at that.

Okay, so maybe Apollo had lost his head. But we *had* been under attack and trying to save Jake from certain death. They weren't exactly ideal circumstances for clear thinking.

She wandered to the window and stood, contemplating the view. I peeked out, too, as I zipped my jeans: it was another glorious spring day outside. My window had the same mesmerising view of the ocean as the lounge room, and there was nothing but blue all the way to the horizon today. The sea was flat, with no white caps to disturb it. The surfers would be unhappy, but the scene looked like something off a postcard, with the green headland off to the right and the long sweep of white sand along the foreshore.

"I'm going to miss this," Syl said softly.

I paused with one shoe only half-tied, struck by the wistful note in her voice. "Since when are you going anywhere?" Surely it was too soon for her and Lucas to decide they wanted to move in together?

"Since you became a target for every psycho god-killer out there," she said, with some asperity. "We can't stay here, numb-nuts. The shadow shapers know where you live."

"*Numb-nuts.*" I finished tying my laces. "If only they all regarded me with as much reverence as you do, eh? Then we'd have no problem."

Lucas was clattering around in the kitchen, humming something so off-key I couldn't tell what it was supposed to be. The delicious smell of bacon cooking drifted down the short hallway and my stomach rumbled in anticipation.

Syl wasn't so easily distracted, however. "You can laugh all you want, but the one thing you can't do is stick your head in the sand and hope this all goes away. You don't see Hades hanging around to be slaughtered, do you? We were in the pub last night and there was no sign of him. Harry said he'd gone off on a long holiday. Holiday, my arse. That man has a better sense of self-preservation than you do. You're sitting here with a target on your back, practically begging the shadow shapers to come and get you."

I paused in the doorway. Syl was standing with her back to the window, her face in shadow, but I could still see the worry in her eyes. "As soon as we get a lead on Poseidon's whereabouts, we'll be out of here."

I didn't want to think any further than that. I loved this town; it truly felt like a home. I'd go if I had to, but I wasn't letting the shadow shapers drive me away if there was any hope of staying. Maybe Poseidon would know who had the other lightning bolt. Hell, maybe he had them both, and this could all be over in a couple of days.

"And how long will that take? Apollo's been searching for days already. It's not safe for you here, Lexi."

"Considering they know where I live, these shadow shapers are taking an awfully long time to get here," I said. For the first time, it struck me how odd that was. I mean, Becky had barely shaken the dust of this place off her feet and Hades had disappeared. Now they knew not only

Hades, but I, and sometimes Apollo, could be found here for the taking—and, instead of attacking, they were sitting on their hands.

It gave me a nasty feeling. They must be brewing some truly evil surprise.

"I don't care," she said. "We need to get out *now*. I'm sick of looking over my shoulder all the time."

"What about Lucas?" My stomach gurgled again. I could hear the bacon sizzling in the pan. Couldn't we continue this argument *after* breakfast?

"What about him?"

"Well, you said 'we' need to get out, as if you're planning on coming, too." Not long ago, she'd said Lucas was just a fling, but I wasn't so sure. They'd been inseparable since they'd met—but Lucas had another life back in Crosston, a life he could only delay returning to for so long. "Do you really want to go on the run and leave him behind?"

She shrugged, but her gaze slid away from mine. "Do you really think I'm going to let you go on your own? Lucas is a big boy; he can make his own decisions."

"Lucas can also hear every word you two are saying," he called. Damn werewolves. Keeping secrets around them and their exceptional hearing was bloody impossible. There was a clatter as he got plates out of the cupboard. "If you don't want this breakfast to get cold, you'd better get your arses out here."

Well, that was a plan I could get behind. I marched down the short corridor into the lounge room. "Smells good."

Lucas stood in the kitchen, bare-chested, on the other side of the bench that divided the tiny kitchen from the lounge room. It was a pretty nice view, if a very hairy one. Werewolves had almost as much body hair in human form as they did as a wolf. The male ones, at least—I'd seen rather a lot of Holly's body when she was giving birth, and she hadn't had anything like the same carpet effect going on.

Lucas thrust a plate at me, loaded with bacon and eggs swimming in butter, but his eyes were on Syl. "No one's leaving anybody. If you guys are leaving town, I'm coming, too."

"You don't have to do that," I said, when Syl didn't answer. "This isn't your fight."

"I think the pack might have something to say to that," he said.

I rolled my eyes. I didn't want to hear any more about the pack and their moon goddess fixation.

"And besides, someone's got to make sure you remember to eat." He grinned at me. Well, there was one werewolf, at least, who'd lost his awe at the moon goddess.

"I assure you, I never forget to eat—just sometimes there's no time." I shovelled bacon into my mouth and almost moaned at the explosion of salty, greasy goodness.

"That's settled, then." Syl sat down beside me. "We'll pack everything up while you're off with Apollo, ready to go when you get back."

"Go where?" I mumbled around a mouthful of bacon.

"I don't care," she said. "Somewhere that's not here. It's time to get out while we still can."

⁘

By the time Apollo arrived half an hour later, the bacon was just a beautiful memory, and Lucas had his shirt on, more's the pity. I mean, I wasn't about to poach on Syl's territory, but I had eyes, didn't I? I could certainly appreciate a well-built man, even if the man whose chest I would most like to see was being stupidly uncooperative.

Apollo wore a black T-shirt and tight black jeans, as usual, which reminded me of my plans for his wardrobe.

"One day, when this is all over, I'll have to take you shopping," I said, brushing my lips lightly against his cheek in greeting. I felt weird even doing that much, but his hug was much more certain. Guilt pricked at me, that he was so obviously happy to see me when I couldn't even remember him.

He raised an eyebrow. "Oh? Why's that?"

"So you can go into a shop a grim, black caterpillar and emerge a beautiful butterfly."

He frowned in confusion.

"There are more colours in the world than black, you know."

"But you were the one who told me I should wear black more often. Make up your mind, woman."

Syl laughed. Dammit. I knew someone must have told him to wear a lot of black. Hadn't counted on it being me, though.

"It looks good on you," I admitted grudgingly. "But don't you get bored of wearing the same thing all the time?"

He shrugged. "It's just clothes. This way, everything goes with everything else and I don't have to think about it."

Syl rolled her eyes. "Only a man could say that."

"It sounds perfectly logical to me," Lucas protested.

"My point exactly."

"Are you ready to go?" Apollo asked, ignoring her.

"Sure. Ready when you are." I was nervous as hell, but I wasn't going to tell him that. He was taking me to the martial arts school in Albany he'd told me about, where Artemis had lived, and I was tense with excitement mingled with dread. Would it bring memories rushing back? Would I meet people who had been important in my life? He'd mentioned a business partner—would she be there?

"Where's your bow?"

Crap, I'd nearly forgotten it again. I ducked back into the bedroom and emerged with bow in hand and quiver slung over my shoulder. "Lugging this thing everywhere is going to be a pain in the arse," I muttered. "And I'll probably get arrested."

Apollo eyed the golden bow thoughtfully. "You know, you never would tell me what your avatar was before. For the longest time, I thought it must have been your hunting horn, because you always seemed to have that slung on your belt. But then you went through a phase—I don't know, horns must have been out of fashion, or something—and you never had it with you anymore, so I was stumped. I figured it couldn't have been your bow, since I often saw you without it, but I've just had a thought ..."

"What? Don't keep me in suspense."

"You sometimes wore a silver charm of a bow and arrow on a chain around your neck. I would have assumed that was your avatar, except you didn't wear that all the time either. Now I'm trying to remember if the times you didn't wear it were also the times you carried your bow."

I was still waiting for further explanations when Syl snapped her fingers. "You mean the bow's her avatar, but sometimes she transformed the bow into a silver charm?"

Oh, right. Now I saw what he was getting at. "That would certainly be much easier to carry around."

"Easier to hide, too. You could just tuck it under your shirt."

"Your ring gave me the idea," I said absently, staring at

my bow. For centuries, it had been fine to walk around with a bow and quiver in plain view, but it had been a couple of hundred years since that kind of behaviour would get you arrested in most places, so I'd had to adapt.

"You remember that?" His voice was eager.

"Ah … yeah." But that was all I remembered. "No idea how I did it, unfortunately."

"It shouldn't be difficult. Your avatar is simply a physical manifestation of your power, after all. It's really a part of you. Just focus on what you want and direct some of that power into achieving your vision."

That *sounded* easy. Doubtfully, I shrugged off the quiver, then glared at it and the bow, trying to envisage a tiny silver charm on a chain. No one was more surprised than I was when they shimmered out of existence, leaving a charm swinging from the necklace in my hand. I nearly dropped the damn thing.

"Impressive," Syl said as I fastened it around my neck. "Now, don't forget what I said. We'll be waiting."

"Waiting for what?" Apollo asked as the two of us headed out the door. At the bottom of the stairs, we emerged into warm sunshine. Winston's "temple" was only two blocks over. Apollo strode off in its direction, and I lengthened my stride to match his.

"Syl wants to leave Berkley's Bay straight away. Go into hiding again."

My heart rebelled at the thought. I'd had enough of hiding, and especially of running. I liked Berkley's Bay and the friends I'd made there. I wanted to stay. But perhaps I'd felt that way about Albany once, too.

"She's right. I won't be making any more public appearances after this. Where will you go?"

He seemed to think it was settled. I wasn't stupid—I knew Syl was right, though it still struck me as odd that the shadow shapers hadn't already appeared. But I couldn't rely on them to leave me alone forever. We had to go, at least until we'd managed to defeat them. I just didn't want to. If only we could find Poseidon and get on with things. The waiting was killing me.

"I don't know. I think Syl expects us to go to Albany, but I'm not sure if that will work." I was hoping to find some information today to help me decide. Maybe Artemis had other properties. A little cabin in the woods somewhere would be nice.

"You know you're welcome to stay with me. Syl, too."

"Are you sure your places are secure? You told me once you'd gone to bed one night in your own bed and woken the next morning as a captive of the shadow shapers."

His face darkened at the memory. "That's true. The underworld may be the safest place for us both for the moment. Although I'm not sure I could stand it as a long-term option. At least we know that's one place the shadow shapers can't infiltrate."

And we knew we could trust Hades. "I just don't want to go to ground. We should be moving, going on the attack, not hiding away. Have you found Poseidon yet?"

"I would have mentioned it already if I had," he said, a little acid in his tone. Apollo was just as frustrated at our lack of progress as I was. He drew a deep breath and forced a smile. "But I'm hoping for a breakthrough today."

Ah, yes, the special secret method Artemis supposedly had to contact her Uncle Poseidon. He was pinning his hopes on a broken rod if he was expecting my memory to come through for us. "Are you sure Hades can't find him? He's his brother, after all, and I know they at least talk to each other." Unlike many of the Greek pantheon. There was always plenty of infighting to enliven things among the gods. But Hades and Artemis had been with Poseidon when the piece of Zeus's lightning bolt had come lancing down out of the sky, enjoying a fairly cordial visit, according to Hades' description of it, so I knew they got along all right.

Apollo shrugged. "He says not." He gave me a shrewd look. "Don't worry so much. I have a good feeling about today."

Well, that made one of us.

"Nobody there will know who I am, looking like this," I pointed out. "They'll probably just chuck us out."

"They may not know you, but Ophelia knows me. She

knows I'm your brother, and what we are. She'll believe me if I tell her who you are."

"*Will* you tell her?" What would be the reaction of this friend I didn't know when she learned I'd completely forgotten her? I felt the pressure of other people's expectations weighing on me. "I can't help thinking it would be easier if I could just break in and steal this thing, whatever it is."

Apollo grinned, a flash of real amusement. He looked a different person—a far more likeable one—when he smiled like that. "You picked up some terrible habits from your time as a human. You can't solve all your problems by stealing things."

"Do I look very different now?" Maybe she'd recognise me anyway. Although, if my own brother hadn't, that probably wasn't very likely.

He considered me, blue eyes thoughtful. "Not *very* different, but enough. The shape of your face has changed, and your hair is black, now, instead of dark brown. And there's something about your eyebrows that's not quite right."

"My eyebrows?"

We'd arrived at Winston's house, and he held the front gate open for me. "Maybe it's just because they always seem to be frowning at me."

Smart-arse. I pushed past him and strode up the concrete path to the front door.

"You're a little shorter, too," he added, "and not as well-muscled. But more tanned."

"Are you calling me flabby?"

"You asked," he reminded me.

I paused on the front porch. "How would I change my appearance back? Not that I want to. I'm just curious."

He gave me a disbelieving look, and I lifted my chin defiantly. I liked the way I looked, even if my muscle tone apparently wasn't up to goddess standards. I felt comfortable in this skin. But it was a fair question.

"You just …" He paused, an odd look on his face, as if he'd never thought about it before. "You have to *want* to. And then it happens. I don't know. It's like asking me how my muscles make my arm move. They just do. I don't have to do anything special. It just works. Like this."

In the blink of an eye, his face transformed. There was no melting or reshaping, no transitional phase. Just one moment, he looked like Apollo, and the next, he looked so like Lucas that I leapt back, startled, and banged my elbow against the door behind me.

"That is … that is *freaky*," I breathed, reaching out to poke doubtfully at his face. It felt exactly the way it looked, even down to the stubble that grazed my knuckles as I ran them along his jawline. This was no illusion—his face really had changed shape, colour, everything. A thought struck me. "Why don't you do this, then? This would be the best way to hide from the shadow shapers. Beats running and hiding. They can't find you if they don't know what you look like."

His face resumed its normal appearance, and he leaned past me and opened the front door, gesturing me inside. "Because if they get close enough, they will sense my divinity, whatever face I'm wearing. And besides, it takes effort to hold another form for an extended period of time."

I stepped into the small house, making room for him to shut the door behind us. "Even though you don't know how you're doing it?"

"Even though I don't know how I'm doing it," he agreed. "It gives me a filthy headache right here." He gestured at a point between his eyes. "And you can't keep it up when you're asleep. It's more of a party trick than anything—it doesn't fool other gods, only mortals. Zeus used to use it all the time to seduce women. Apart from that, there's not much advantage to it."

Not much advantage to it? There spoke a man who'd never wanted for anything a day in his life. What a boon such an ability would have been to me in my, ahem, previous line of work. No more clambering over rooftops and sneaking around. I could have changed my face, become someone with a right to be there, and walked boldly in wherever I wanted to go, secure in the ultimate disguise. Taken anything I wanted. There would have been no stopping me.

"How have I done it for so long, then?" I asked. "I don't have any headaches." And I was sure I didn't change appearance when I was asleep. Syl would definitely have mentioned *that*.

"I don't think it's you doing it," he said. "This is some work of Hades'. He's even better at such things than Zeus—look how often and how easily he slips into the likeness of Alberto." Admiration filled his voice. "He is a master."

"Maybe I should talk to him, then."

"Maybe you should. But I thought you said you didn't want to change?"

"I don't. Let's go." I held out my hand to him, eager to change the subject. It wasn't that I wanted to change back to my old appearance; it was more a natural urge to have every weapon possible in my arsenal. Though, I guess if shadow shapers could sense my divinity regardless, it might not be all that useful.

He took my hand. There was no sign of Winston or his acolyte, though the tiny sacred fire was burning in its bowl in the middle of the living room. Apollo nodded, and we took a step forward. The cramped living room of the little "temple" in Berkley's Bay disappeared, and I swayed as we transitioned to a place I hadn't seen before.

It was a temple, of course. Only a small one, but in good repair, unlike the little shack of a thing we'd travelled to when we had gone to see Hestia. Obviously, someone took the care of this one to heart. A bright flame flickered in the central pit, and fresh flowers stood in a vase at the foot of a life-sized statue of Apollo and Artemis holding hands and smiling at each other. Like the Great Temple in Crosston, this room was circular, but unlike that cavernous place, this one was flooded with light from the floor to ceiling windows around three-quarters of the circle. The rest of the room was taken up by large wooden doors of some glowing timber, carved with climbing roses.

Outside the windows was a sea of green. Dappled sunlight filtered through trees whose leaves swayed gently in a light breeze. A path leading away from the temple disappeared among tall trunks of silver and brown. The whole scene looked so idyllic that I half-expected to see rabbits and fauns come gambolling out of the forest.

"Where are we?" I asked. When he'd said we were going to a martial arts gym, this wasn't what I'd been expecting. Perhaps we still had a long way to go. He was limited to travel between temples, after all, and they weren't always situated very conveniently for his purposes.

He opened the carved door and led the way through a small antechamber. The outside door stood open, showing more greenery, and the breeze that ruffled the leaves brought a whole range of forest scents to my nostrils.

"On your estate," he said, setting off along the narrow path through the trees. It was dirt, crisscrossed by the roots of the trees that crowded in close on either side, and littered with small stones and leaves. A tension in my shoulders loosened as I stepped under the shelter of the overhanging branches. The place felt welcoming; the silence of the forest, broken only by bird calls and the sounds of our footsteps, was like music to my ears.

"Really? I own this?" Considering I'd been living from pay packet to pay packet in a rented apartment, the idea of owning a whole *forest* seemed absurd. Of course, I knew that the gods were rich, but this made that wealth more concrete in my mind.

"Yes, although no one but Ophelia knows that. Everyone else thinks that some big corporation in Crosston owns the gym and you are a kind of manager and live-in caretaker. Your cottage is that way." He waved a hand at a smaller path branching off to the right. I stopped to peer down it, but all I could see were trees.

"I live in a cottage?" I had enough money to buy a whole forest and I only lived in a cottage?

"Not all the time." He shot me an amused glance, as if he could read the confusion in my mind. "But it's a handy base for hunting, and you always used to laugh at my luxuries and tell me I was a sybarite. You said no one needed more than one toilet because they only had one arse."

I grinned. That sounded like me. "Clearly, I had never shared a house with Syl when I said that. When she's in human form, she hogs the bathroom like you wouldn't believe. I've never known anyone who takes such long showers."

"I don't think you've shared a home with anyone since we were children. You certainly like your alone time. Even your lovers rarely got asked to stay the night."

Now that *didn't* sound like me. What was the point of being in a relationship with someone if you didn't get to hang out with them? If I ever got—*when* I got—Jake straightened out, I would spend as much time with him as I possibly could. That was the whole point of relationships, wasn't it, to share your lives?

"You make me sound like some weird hermit," I said.

We emerged from the trees at the back of a large, flat-roofed building. It looked like a warehouse, plain and windowless, and seemed at odds with its setting. A bank of big air-conditioning units hummed away against the wall.

"No, I think you just preferred the company of women. You had a select group you hung with at the gym or out trekking and hunting in the wilds. When you weren't with them, you kept to yourself, mostly."

I followed him around the building, walking now on a concrete path. I liked to hang with my girlfriends and I didn't like romantic relationships. And, apparently, I loved the great outdoors. Did I read when I was being all antisocial? Because I couldn't imagine not being a reader, though I could see the appeal of nature. I glanced back at the forest behind us, so much more inviting than the bare concrete and ugly, industrial-looking building.

Some effort had been made at the front, at least, to beautify the area. Trees and small gardens broke up a large expanse of concrete parking lot. About a dozen cars were there, with room for three times that many. Facing onto the car park was a large glassed section, though the glass was tinted so I couldn't see in. Automatic doors slid open as we came up the front steps, emitting a blast of frigid air. A young woman in gym clothes, glistening with sweat, came out.

"Morning," she said as she passed us.

"Morning," Apollo said.

I turned to watch as she strode across the car park to her car. Did I know her? I could tell she was human, but nothing about her rang any bells. She could have been my best friend and I wouldn't have known.

I caught at Apollo's arm as we stepped inside, suddenly nervous. "Don't tell anyone who I am."

"What?" He glanced down at me, eyebrows raised. "Why not?"

"Because ..." I didn't really have a reason, just a sudden pit of nerves in my stomach. I wasn't ready to claim godhood here, when I'd hardly come to terms with it myself. I didn't want to deal with strangers' expectations, their disappointment when I didn't know them. How would that girl have felt if she *had* been my best friend and I'd had no idea who she was? "I just want to look around and get a feel for the place first."

"Are you sure? I thought you might want to move back here and take up your old life. People will need to know who you are." He was clearly disappointed. Perhaps he'd been hoping to get his real sister back by bringing me here.

"Please. Not yet. I need to ease myself into it."

He frowned, but didn't argue. Two long rows of treadmills were on our right, with another row of exercise bikes behind them. A large-screen TV was showing a morning talk show with the sound turned way down and music with a driving beat was pumping from the speakers on the wall.

A young girl with a big smile was behind the desk on our left.

"Hi, there!" she said cheerily as Apollo drew level with her. "Need some help?"

That sounded like a polite way of saying, *Hey, mate, this is a women-only gym. Where do you think you're going?*

Apollo returned her smile with a dazzling one of his own. "I'm looking for Ophelia. Is she in the training hall?"

"Um …" The girl's eyes flicked to a big clock on the wall. It was showing just after eleven o'clock. "She's probably just finished. She might be in her office. Shall I look for you?"

"No need," Apollo said. "I know where that is."

He treated her to another dazzling smile and strode on through, even though I was fairly certain that men weren't allowed in women-only gyms. But the girl was left blinking in his wake, as if she wasn't quite sure what had just happened. There might have been a little divine magic in that smile. I hurried after him before she decided to blame me.

A song that I thought I'd left behind in Crosston blasted over the speakers and I almost groaned aloud. *Ooooh, Lexi, you're so sexy. In my arms, babe, I feel your charms, babe.* What the hell? This hadn't been on the charts in nearly a year. It had been the bane of my life when I'd first met Syl—she used to sing it all the time to taunt me, fluttering her eyelashes at me and making what she fondly considered to be seductive faces. I shuddered and tried to ignore the insistent mewling of the chorus. I'd probably have the bloody thing stuck in my head for the rest of the day, now.

Apollo strode down a corridor past several smaller rooms for group classes and stopped at a door marked "Office". A strong smell of heated chlorine filled the corridor—there must be a pool in the complex. None of it was ringing any bells. They could have had a gladiatorial arena, too, for all I knew. Or a circus. Women's laughter sounded in the distance, and the banging of doors, as if a bunch of them had hit the change rooms at once.

"Ready?" he asked.

"No," I said, suddenly jittery. The woman in that office really *was* one of my best friends, apparently. What if I didn't recognise her? What if I *did*?

But it was too late. He'd already opened the door.

6

The office was small and drab. A bank of grey metal filing cabinets sat along the back wall, behind a black, industrial-looking desk, all sharp corners and reflective surfaces. There were no plants or spots of colour, no armchairs or other homey touches. The only thing it had going for it was that the wall to our right was glass from floor to ceiling, and it looked out over the floor of what must surely be the training hall, judging by the mats on the floor. We were up high, with a bird's eye view of two women in white uniforms sparring in one corner of the room, trading kicks and punches under the watchful eye of another whose white outfit was belted in black. Above them, a large neon sign on the wall proclaimed, "GIRL POWER!" in jagged green letters.

All this I took in at a glance—then my attention was claimed by the woman behind the desk. She looked up as we came in, and her dark eyes lit up at the sight of Apollo. When she stood and came around the desk with outstretched hand, I realised she was nearly as tall as him.

"Apollo!" she cried, and her voice was a deep boom. She had the chest of an opera singer and the longest hair I'd ever seen, scraped back into an impatient plait that snaked its way over one shoulder almost as far as her knees. Given her height, that was an impressively long way. Apollo flinched as she took his hand in a crushing grip and pumped it up and down in an enthusiastic handshake. "Have you found her?"

To his credit, he didn't even look at me as he lied. "Not yet, but I feel we're getting close. It's good to see you again. How are you?"

She shook her great head sadly. "Better for seeing you, but missing her still. This place is no fun without her."

Fun? Artemis was fun? That surprised me. She always seemed so serious in the legends. Cold and deadly, yes. Fun, no. But I guess even gods had to let their hair down now and then. I stared at the woman, trying to force a memory of her to the surface. If she and Artemis enjoyed each other's company so much, shouldn't I be able to remember her?

The woman gave me a curious look as Apollo drew me forward. Maybe the effort was showing on my face. I probably looked constipated.

"Ophelia, I'd like you to meet my friend, Lexi. Lexi, this is Ophelia Rasmussen."

"Pleasure," she said, thrusting her hand out.

I shook it, trying not to wince at the pressure. She was strong. It only took me a moment to realise why. I'd been so busy gawking at her hair and her height when I came in that I hadn't registered the most important thing about her.

She was a werewolf.

"Nice to meet you," I said, and she went rigid. If she'd been in wolf form, her ears would have pricked up at the sound of my voice. All her attention focused on me so tightly I felt like a bug under a microscope.

"Your voice sounds familiar," she said, glancing uncertainly at Apollo.

Werewolf hearing. You couldn't fool it. I said nothing—what could I say? She stepped closer, enclosing my hand in both of her large ones. I wasn't a small woman, but she made me feel tiny and delicate. Her nose twitched suspiciously. She was smelling me.

I mustn't have smelled enough like the goddess she remembered, because she finally dropped my hand, looking crestfallen. Guilt gnawed at me. Should I tell her? But surely that would only make her disappointment worse? I wasn't the friend she longed for.

Her skin was nearly as dark as her hair, like a night with no moon. I bet her wolf form was huge and black-furred.

A sudden image of such a wolf silhouetted in the moonlight came to me. Memory or imagination? I had no way of knowing.

Apollo was watching me keenly. If he was hoping for a breakthrough, he'd be sadly disappointed. My shoulders slumped. I was sick of this—sick of the not knowing, the pretence, the uncertainty. Sick of the pressure, too. I wanted to remember and I didn't, all at the same time. No, scratch that. What I really wanted was to go to bed and eat chocolate for a solid week.

"We were hoping to have a look around Arti's place," Apollo said. Of course, he didn't need the big werewolf's permission to do anything; he was a god. Nice of him to act as if she had a say in it. "I want to show Lexi a couple of things. I think we're close to finding Artemis."

Very smooth. He hadn't actually lied. We could be close to "finding" Artemis—or I could be doomed to spend another hundred years trapped in this limbo. No one could tell.

Ophelia shrugged. "Fine by me. Do whatever you need to do." She moved behind the desk and pulled open the top drawer, offering Apollo a bunch of keys. "You need the front door key?"

"No, thanks," he said. "It's good to see you again."

"You, too," she said as he shepherded me toward the door. "Let me know as soon as you hear anything."

"Will do."

Back down the corridor we went, past the smiling receptionist and out the automatic glass doors. Warm air laden with the scent of cool pine and hot asphalt hit us as we left the air-conditioned interior. I took a deep breath and felt my spirits lift. I wanted to dive into that forest and never come out again.

Apollo led me back around the building, past the dumpster and the air-conditioning units chugging away, and onto the path we'd followed before. This time, we didn't follow it all the way back to the little temple in the woods, but instead took the other branch that he'd pointed out previously. It led, as he had said, to a cottage, whose warm wooden walls and green steel roof blended into its surrounds. It sat among the eucalypts and pines as if it had always been there, part of the landscape.

I felt an immediate affection for the little cottage, though no rush of associated memories as we stepped up onto the planks of its wide veranda. The flyscreen door hung a little loose on its hinges and clearly wasn't locked. If the main door was locked, it wasn't obvious. Apollo may have been doing his god-thing, but he merely turned the handle and the door opened. It reminded me of Syl's comment about how he never knocked, just walked right in as if he owned the place, and I smiled as I followed his broad back into the narrow hallway.

The cottage was built on simple lines: a bedroom on our right, a lounge room on the left. We passed one more bedroom and a bathroom opposite before the hall ended in an eat-in kitchen. The place wasn't much bigger than our little apartment above the bookshop. The apartment smelled better, though—this place had that musty aroma that came from being locked up too long.

I ran my hand over the wooden surface of the dining table, big enough to seat eight. It looked like it often had, too—it was covered in scratches and odd gouges, as if it had seen a lot of company. It made me feel a lot better about Artemis. For some reason, I'd had an image of her as a bit of a stuck-up princess in my head, maybe because she'd looked so cool and unapproachable in the painting Hades had hanging in the foyer of his palace. But this table didn't belong to any princess. It was down-to-earth and practical.

"What do you think of the place?" Apollo asked, making an effort to sound casual.

But I knew what he meant. "You have to stop doing that. I promise you, if I have any flashes of recognition, you'll be the first to know."

His gaze slid away, toward the window over the sink with its cheerful gingham curtains. "I didn't mean to pressure you."

"Yes, you did. Trust me, I'm even more keen than you are to remember something—anything—about my old life.

But having you check in with me every three seconds is not helping." I took a deep breath, forcing my irritation down. "So, what are we looking for in here?"

"I don't know. There might not even be anything. Just wander around and check everything out. Don't rush yourself. Something might call to you."

Yeah, right. The only calls I was likely to get were on the phone tucked into my jeans pocket. I stifled a sigh and wandered off. Might as well start in the bedroom. Most people kept their most important stuff there, didn't they?

"And don't follow me around watching me as if I'm some performing monkey," I called over my shoulder. "Go for a walk or something."

His footsteps, which had started down the hall after me, abruptly halted and headed back the other way. I grinned as I went into the bedroom.

It wasn't a very girly room, which was another point in Artemis's favour as far as I was concerned. I really had to stop being surprised that we shared so many traits. We were the same person, in a way, though we had lived such different lives. Changing the outside didn't change who a person was on the inside. Maybe. Hopefully. I was still afraid that divinity might make more of a difference than I would like, but it was encouraging.

The bed was large, but not piled with pillows, and the quilt was a simple affair in a soft green colour. The curtains were also green—it didn't take a genius to guess what the goddess's favourite colour was. Despite the size of the bed, there was only one chest of drawers, on the right side of the bed, which suggested that it usually only had one occupant. On top of the chest of drawers was a photo of three smiling women.

The one on the right was Ophelia, her brown eyes crinkled into a grin of genuine amusement, her outrageously long hair sprouting free from her head as if she were Medusa. I didn't know the woman on the left, but she was laughing. Perhaps the woman in the middle had said something funny—there was a self-satisfied air to her smile. Clearly, she was Artemis. Even though she was smiling, there was something of that haughty look that I'd seen in Hades' painting. But there was a smudge of dirt on her cheek, and her long, dark hair was wild.

The three of them were outside, against a background of trees, and a familiar quiver stuck up over Artemis's shoulder. Perhaps this was one of those hunting trips that Apollo had mentioned that she liked to take with her friends. Artemis had her arms slung around the shoulders of the other two women in a casual display of affection. The little seed of hope that we might not be so different after all put forth a couple of tiny shoots.

I stared into the goddess's eyes, envying her free and easy smile. How long ago had this been taken? Before the troubles with the shadow shapers started, most likely, or she might not have looked so relaxed. Her cheekbones were sharp, and her skin was as pale as the moon. The differences between her face and mine were subtle, but enough that she looked like a goddess and I didn't, despite the fact that our hair and eye colour were much the same. She was only a little taller, judging by her height relative to Ophelia's, yet no one would have taken us for the same person. Hades had done a good job of "humanising" the goddess. My skin had never been that flawless, nor my nose so fine.

I replaced the photo gently and turned, catching a brief glimpse of myself in a mirror on another wall. For a second, I could have sworn I saw Artemis's face looking out at me, and my heart lurched in surprise. But when I looked closer, it was only my own familiar face reflected back at me.

Holy shit. I touched my cheek, heart still thundering. Surely I hadn't imagined that? The person from the photo had been staring out at me from the mirror. I focused on my own familiar eyes and tried to get that person back again. But, though my face went red with effort and the blood roared in my ears, nothing changed.

Taking a deep breath, I pulled open the top drawer. I was here to search for a way to contact Poseidon. I could try to reshape my face some other time, when I was less hurried and stressed. Whenever that might be. The twin deadlines of Zeus's possible demise and my own forced departure from my home were certainly making it hard to focus on anything at the moment.

The drawer contained socks and underpants, and I felt like a weirdo as I rifled through them. Hurriedly, I shut the drawer and opened the next one. That one was full of bras and fancier sets of matching underwear, little scraps of silk and lace that I bet she never wore on hunting trips. I slammed that drawer shut, too, before my mind travelled too far down the path of wondering for which occasions she brought out the things from the second drawer. They were all in my size. That red set in particular … I could imagine the hungry look in Jake's eyes only too well if he saw me in that. Not that that was likely to happen.

Her wardrobe, which took up most of one wall, was surprisingly practical. Most of it was the kind of thing I had in my own wardrobe—jeans, T-shirts, workout gear. There were only a few dressier outfits. I guess there wasn't much call for cocktail dresses out here in the woods. She could have had whole rooms full of fancier clothes somewhere else. She was bound to have more than one residence.

After I'd checked the shelves along the top of the wardrobe and found nothing more exciting than out-of-season clothes and blankets, I moved across the hallway into the lounge room. So far, this was a bust, and this room didn't look much more promising. There were a couple more photos on the mantelpiece, a small bookcase on either side of the fireplace, and not much else apart from a comfortable-looking lounge suite upholstered in a deep, rich brown leather. The most striking feature of the room was a stag's head mounted above the fireplace. Its liquid dark eyes sent a shiver down my spine. I had a hard time reconciling my own deep connection with animals with Artemis's role as the goddess of the hunt. Maybe I would have to find her memories before I could understand.

I moved over to the bookcase. It felt as though the stag's eyes followed me all the way. Zeus's balls. How could she stand to be in this room with that thing watching her all the time? Poor creature. He was a beauty, with such big antlers it was a wonder the weight of them didn't tear the whole head down from the wall.

Deliberately, I turned my back on him and began examining the books on the shelves. There were a lot of romances of the shaper-human kind, a few histories, and quite a lot of biographies. Who would have thought a goddess would be so interested in other people's lives? Was people-watching the thing that kept Artemis going over the centuries, the way Hades seemed so invested in role-playing as a vampire publican?

But there was nothing there to help me. I picked up the pottery vase that sat on top of the bookcase and tipped it upside down, but nothing fell out. The coffee table was empty but for an abstract sculpture that looked like a cross between a tree and something out of a nightmare. I gave that a good shake, too, and held it in my hands, trying to focus on it, to see if it "spoke" to me as Apollo had suggested. So far, nothing in this house was saying anything at all, and I had a bad feeling that we had wasted our time with this trip. We would have to rely on Apollo's sources to locate Poseidon eventually.

Which could take ages, dammit. We didn't have time to wait around. Hestia had infected Apollo with her urgency over Zeus's predicament, and Apollo, like the kind and generous soul he was, had passed the infection on to the rest of us. There was no way I could sit around for months, waiting, while the damn shadow shapers took pot-shots at us.

Frustrated, I banged the sculpture back down on the table rather harder than I'd intended, and then jumped guiltily at the noise. Fortunately, it didn't break. I gazed around the room in desperation. Was there even anything here to find? For all we knew, Artemis had some bloody mental connection with the sea god, and that was locked up tight with everything else inside my stupid head.

I caught the deer's sad gaze and shook my head. "What do you call a deer with no eyes? No idea. Get it?" The deer stared impassively back. "No-eye deer? Yeah, I know, you've probably heard it before. But that's exactly what I've got. No bloody idea." I moved closer and laid my hand on his soft nose. "Don't suppose you could give me a hint, could you? I bet you've seen a lot from your perch up there."

I ran my hand down the deer's neck in a regretful caress. Now I was talking to stuffed animals. Excellent. And a stuffed animal that I'd undoubtedly killed myself. He'd probably rather gore me than help me.

My fingers felt a slight unevenness at the base of the stag's neck, and I paused. Leaning closer, I could make out a fine line. I traced it with my finger and found it joined another, and then another. Together, they made three sides of a square the size of my hand, in fact.

Ooh, interesting. I dug a nail into the bottom line, then wormed my way under it. The flap of deerskin peeled back, revealing something that looked like a battery compartment, only bigger. It had a small indentation on one side, just the right size for a fingertip, so I levered it up, my heart beating faster with excitement. What was Artemis hiding in this funny little hiding place?

Knowing my luck, probably her sex toys, or a secret stash of chocolate. It was too much to hope that it might be the mysterious item I was looking for.

Or was it? Inside lay a shell, no bigger than the palm of my hand. Gently, I extracted it. Things were looking up. It had to be related to Poseidon, surely.

"Apollo?" I headed back to the kitchen, the shell cradled

in my hand. He would know what to do with it, wouldn't he? I sure as shit didn't. But he wasn't there. He must have taken my advice to go for a walk.

I stood uncertainly in the middle of the tiled floor, turning the shell this way and that in the sunlight streaming through the kitchen windows. It was just an ordinary shell—I'd seen plenty just like it washed up on the beach at Berkley's Bay. It even still smelled faintly salty. If it was a way to contact Poseidon, I had to say, an instruction manual would have been nice.

My initial excitement began to fade as I held it up to my ear. All I heard was the soft shushing of the blood pounding in my own head. No unearthly voices. No one picked up at the other end: *Hi, you've reached Poseidon—how may I help you?* I tried blowing into it, but that did nothing but give me a slightly salty taste on my lips and the sudden realisation that this shell had probably once been the home of a slimy sea creature, and maybe I didn't want to put it in my mouth.

Perhaps it was like summoning a genie and you had to rub it. Feeling like a complete idiot, I rubbed, gently at first, then more vigorously. Nothing happened, of course. Was it just a random shell? But I couldn't believe that. Surely no one in their right mind went to such lengths to hide something unless it was valuable. Of course, there was always the possibility that Artemis was cracked in the head.

I sure felt like it, standing in the kitchen and rubbing a stupid shell.

"Zeus's balls, Poseidon. Couldn't you have made it a little easier?"

"Couldn't you try asking nicely?" a deep voice boomed.

I whirled, but there was no one there. It had sounded as though a man were standing directly behind me. I peered suspiciously at the shell. It was buzzing against my hand, so faintly I might not have noticed it if I hadn't been so focused on it.

"Hello?" It was bad enough that I'd been rubbing the damn shell—now I was talking to it? "Who's there?"

"Have you gone senile since I last saw you, Arti?" the voice replied.

I glared suspiciously at the shell, but the voice didn't sound like it was coming from inside it. It reverberated in the air all around me.

"Surely you're too young to be losing your memory?"

"Yeah, that's a funny story, actually." Just as well my voice still sounded the same. "But one that I really need to tell you in person."

"Has something happened?"

"You could say that. Apollo and I need to see you. How do we find you?"

Apollo walked past the kitchen window, heading for the back door, the sun shining on his golden curls.

"Name the place and I'll be there."

Well, that was easier than I'd expected. "Berkley's Bay. When?"

"I can be there tonight."

Apollo opened the door, a quizzical look on his face.

"Great. We'll see you there."

Abruptly, the buzzing feeling in my hand stopped. Poseidon must have "hung up" or whatever you did with a shell phone.

"Tell me you got through to Poseidon," Apollo said, his face alight with hope.

"I got through to Poseidon," I said obligingly.

"And?"

"And we have a date. Berkley's Bay, tonight."

7

At eight o'clock that night, Apollo and I walked out onto the wharf at Berkley's Bay. The two big dolphin-watching cruisers were tied up, their decks dark. The fishing boats were already gone for the night. There was no one out here except the two of us.

I pulled my jacket closer around me, glad that I'd worn it. We were halfway through spring, but the sea breeze still had a bite to it once the sun went down and the warmth disappeared from the day. Behind us, the lights of the town glowed brightly as twilight faded into darkness. I could see our lounge room window from here. Syl and Lucas were there, watching TV.

True to her word, Syl had been all packed when we got back from Albany earlier, ready to move into hiding. Only the news that we were meeting Poseidon that very night had stopped her nagging me to leave town. It was a rather grumpy cat shifter that I'd left sprawled on the lounge with her werewolf boyfriend. She would rather have come with us, but Apollo said that Poseidon didn't like strangers, and she and Lucas had had to stay put. We were going to have enough trouble explaining my unfamiliar appearance to the sea god, without throwing in anyone else.

My boots clomped on the rough wooden planks of the wharf as we paced all the way to the end. The sea was calm tonight, with only a slight swoosh as the water coiled around the jetty posts beneath our feet. I turned my back on the town and looked out to sea, but only the lights of a distant fishing boat interrupted the darkness.

"Are you sure this is the right place?" I asked.

Apollo shrugged. "Once he gets close enough, he'll sense us. He'll find us."

I glanced back again at the town. What if Poseidon turned up in a chariot pulled by dolphins, or something equally outrageous? Even a yacht would excite comment. "Won't people notice there's another god in town?"

"Poseidon's no amateur. Stop fretting."

I fell silent, stamping my feet in their combat boots to stop my toes getting cold. A strand of hair had come loose from my ponytail and was attempting to beat me to death. The wind seemed to have picked up even since we'd come out here. Impatiently, I tucked it behind my ear. Then I shoved my hands in my pockets to keep them warm ... and found the pockets unusually empty.

"Damn."

"What?"

"I just realised I must have left my phone on charge."

"I'm sure you'll manage to survive a couple of hours without it."

All at once, the wind died, and only its sudden absence made me realise how loud it had been. I eyed Apollo, uneasy.

"He's coming," he said.

I strained to see anything in the blackness to seaward, but even with my night vision boosted, it was a hopeless task. The salt smell of the sea rose up all around me, very strong.

"How can you tell?"

"Just wait."

Steam started to rise from the dark water beneath us. No, wait—it wasn't steam. As it rose, it coalesced, until thick mist was swirling around my knees.

"I shouldn't be alarmed by this, right?"

"All perfectly normal," he assured me.

"Good." It never hurt to check these things. I'd seen some screwy things lately, and most of them had been trying to kill me. The mist thickened at an impossible speed, flowing down the jetty behind us until the whole town was hidden from sight. In fact, I could barely see Apollo, and he was standing close enough to touch. "Is it just me, or is it getting colder?"

Something loomed out of the mist, something that towered way over our heads, like a mountain made of mist itself. I gazed up at sheer white sides, at cracks and lines that streaked through the behemoth like flaws through marble, and my mind boggled at the sheer impossibility of it.

"Well, that's a new one," Apollo said, as cool as a cucumber. "Last time, it was a floating island. I've never seen an iceberg before."

It didn't make any sense. We were way, way too far from the southern pole for an iceberg to be floating up to the jetty at Berkley's Bay. How had it not melted? But then, how many of the things that had happened in the last few weeks had made any sense? After dragons made of fire, three-headed dogs, and statues come to life, how odd was an iceberg in these temperate climes, really? Poseidon wasn't even trying.

A door opened in the side of the iceberg, though before it opened there had been no sign that a door existed. A woman in a white fur coat with long hair the colour of seaweed stepped out onto a flat part that was almost level with the jetty and bowed.

"Please follow me. Lord Poseidon is expecting you."

Apollo gestured for me to go first, so I stepped up onto the surface of the iceberg. I expected it to be slippery, but it was so dry I could have been walking on wood or concrete. The iceberg was so big that it didn't rock or move in any way, as if my weight meant nothing compared to its own enormity. I couldn't quite get my head around it—icebergs were meant to have most of their bulk under the water, but that surely couldn't be the case here. The part I could see was gigantic, and I knew the water here was nowhere near deep enough for another ninety per cent to be lurking underneath the surface. More magic, I supposed.

Perhaps it wasn't even an iceberg, just an illusion cast on something else. It was sure cold enough to be one, though—the green-haired woman's breath was forming white clouds in the air in front of her face. That fur coat wasn't just for show.

"My lady," she said, bobbing into another little bow as she waved me through the door.

The temperature dropped at least twenty degrees as I passed inside, and I pulled my leather jacket a little tighter around myself, wishing I had a fur coat like hers instead. Everything was white, with the floor and walls forming one seamless whole. It looked like someone had carved tunnels out of the ice. Points of light marched along the ceiling at regular intervals, but they weren't light bulbs, just lights, and too bright to stare at long enough to make out what was causing the glow. More magic?

"I thought you guys had all updated into the twenty-first century?" I muttered to Apollo as we followed our fur-clad guide along the stark white corridor. A luxury yacht might have been nice. "I'm going to freeze to death before we even get to see Poseidon."

He took my hand, and his was as warm as if he were strolling along a sunny beach, not deep in the bowels of a bloody iceberg. "Poseidon is old-school. He enjoys his little extravagances. You *are* cold. Gods can adjust their own body temperature, you know."

"No, I did *not* know." Having the power didn't mean I knew how to use it. My teeth ached with cold, and it felt as though every outward breath was extracting more of my body heat, leaching it all out into the frigid air in clouds of steam. "No one ever tells me these things."

He grinned at the petulant tone in my voice and patted my hand in a deliberately patronising way. "There, there. Poor little Arti. Just think yourself warm. It's easy."

Easy for him, maybe. I would have sighed, but I was trying to limit my breathing to the bare minimum necessary. How could these people stand to live like this? I stared at the back of our guide's green head and tried to "think myself warm". I imagined a warm golden light spreading from the centre of my chest out through my body, filling my arms until the aching cold receded from my fingertips. I willed warmth and feeling back into my frigid toes and warmed my frozen face. A sensation like blushing spread over my cheeks as the warmth swelled up from my neck in a wave.

"Don't overdo it," Apollo said. "Your face looks like a tomato."

"Thanks," I said, dialling the golden light back a notch. I felt so much better. Now I could look around and enjoy the wonder of being inside this impossible iceberg, watching the frozen walls glitter like a fairyland, instead of fearing my extremities were about to drop off from frostbite. "That helps a lot."

"You *will* remember these things eventually," he said, though whether he was trying to persuade himself or me, I wasn't sure.

Our corridor crossed another. Music was playing somewhere down the other hall, a soft guitar piece with a mournful tone. A man came out of another one of those *now you see them, now you don't* doors. He stopped short at the sight of us, then dipped into a hasty bow. He was still bent over when I looked back, his green hair falling about his face.

Did everyone here have hair that looked like it was made of seaweed? I wanted to ask Apollo if our guide was a nymph or perhaps a Merrow, but it seemed rude to chat about her behind her back, so I contented myself with admiring the glittering white walls and listening to the echo of our footsteps in the long blank hallway.

I'd "met" a Merrow before, but I'd been underwater in the pitch-black canal at Brenvale at the time, too busy fighting for my life to catch a glimpse of whoever was trying to drown me. If it hadn't been for the arrival of the mysterious Mac, who had chased the Merrow away, I wouldn't have survived the encounter.

We seemed to have been walking down this corridor much longer than should have been possible, even inside something as big as the iceberg, when we arrived at a set of double doors. There was nothing hidden—or even tasteful—about these ones. They were gold, and covered in carvings of Merrow and fish. Some of the Merrow were twining around each other in ways that made me look away hastily, fixing my gaze on the ornate handles that were as long as my arm.

Our guide thrust the double doors open, revealing a large room that was remarkably comfortable despite being basically an ice cavern. Glittering icicles hung from the ceiling like stalactites, poised above our heads like clear daggers. Colourful rugs were scattered across the floor, and I wondered briefly what stopped them getting wet, before I reminded myself: magic. How long would it take me to get used to its constant presence in my life? Lounges grouped in a loose circle stood in front of a fireplace where bright flames crackled merrily.

A fireplace. Inside an iceberg. Right.

At our entrance, a man rose from a truly stupendous piece of furniture—sort of like a cross between an armchair and a clam shell—upholstered in a satin that matched his piercing green eyes. Apart from the eyes, his main feature was a white beard that foamed down his chest nearly to his waist. He wore a long robe, also green, and looked rather like he should be playing the role of wizard in a children's story book.

"Told you he was old-school," Apollo whispered.

"Lord Apollo and Lady Artemis, my lord," our green-haired guide announced, before withdrawing and pulling the great golden doors closed behind her.

Poseidon crossed the carpet with sure strides for someone who looked so old, his green robe swirling around his feet. He shook hands with Apollo. "Welcome, my boy. You haven't changed a bit." Then he turned to me with a frown. "You, on the other hand ... why are you wearing that face when your own is so lovely?"

Nice one, Poseidon. Way to tell your niece that you think she looks like a troll. "I don't actually have a choice at the moment."

The frown deepened. Those thick white eyebrows drew together, and he looked less like a kindly wizard than before. More threatening. It reminded me that Poseidon's temper was legendary. "Why not?"

"I told you it was a long story, remember?"

"Why don't we sit down?" Apollo asked. "This could take a while."

In the end, it didn't take as long as I had feared to bring Poseidon up to date, though his frown grew truly thunderous at a few points in the tangled story. When we'd finished, he sat back in the giant green shell and pondered the ceiling for a while.

"Trust that stupid brother of mine to stuff things up," he said, eventually. "Why did he have to go messing with your head?"

I stiffened a little at this criticism of Hades, who was still my favourite uncle despite everything. My initial anger with him over my situation had had a chance to cool, and I'd been forced to admit that he'd only done what I'd asked. Poseidon, on the other hand, switched too fast from smiles to frowns, as changeable as the sea.

"I'm not exactly thrilled at the results myself, but apparently it was my idea, and if he hadn't done it, Apollo would probably still be a captive—or worse."

"But that's not why we're here," Apollo cut in smoothly, giving me a warning look. Okay, I could take a hint. No upsetting the sea god. "Hestia thinks—and I agree—that it's time to do something about Zeus."

"We should have done something about Zeus a couple of thousand years ago," Poseidon grumbled. "Starting with neutering him."

I snorted, and the sea god turned twinkling green eyes my way. At least he had a sense of humour. "You know half of you—us—wouldn't exist if it wasn't for his wandering eye."

"True." He studied me with a smile. "We wouldn't have had you, which would have been a sad loss to Olympus, though I daresay we could have done without Athena or that drunkard, Dionysus."

"You don't like Athena?"

He lifted one green-robed shoulder in an indifferent shrug. "Nothing wrong with her, I suppose. Her insistence that she knows everything becomes wearisome very quickly." His gaze settled on my face again. "Are you sure you can't change your appearance back? Have you tried?"

"Of course I have." I ignored Apollo's sceptical glance. Okay, so maybe I hadn't really tried that hard, but I'd had other, more urgent tasks. "I'm sure it will come back to me eventually."

"I hope so."

Gods above, the guy had the tact of a charging rhinoceros. It clearly didn't occur to him that he was insulting me every second time he opened his mouth. But I wasn't supposed to upset the sea god, was I? So, I let it slide. It was kind of funny, in a way. Didn't everyone have one of those embarrassing old relatives who insisted on speaking their mind, no matter what? Poseidon was obviously mine.

Apollo did his best to steer the conversation back on topic. "Hestia thinks if we reunited the three parts of the lightning bolt, we could generate enough power to draw Zeus out of his hiding place."

Judging by the beetling of those thick white brows, that wasn't a popular suggestion. "She does, does she? That woman's almost as bad as Athena for thinking she knows everything." He folded his arms across his chest. "Has it not occurred to her that their separation may be the only thing that is keeping Zeus safe from the shadow shapers?"

"You do still have yours, right?" I asked.

"Yes, I've got it. Safe and sound, right here, where no shadow shaper could ever find it."

"I shouldn't think it needs protecting from shadow shapers," Apollo said. "The one I saw hurled me through the air when I touched it. I doubt a mere shadow shaper would survive the experience."

"Hurled you through the air?" Poseidon stared at my brother in frank disbelief. "You can't be serious."

Apollo raised a haughty eyebrow. He didn't like having his word questioned. "I assure you, I am. Artemis was there; she saw it."

"It's true," I said. "It was sizzling and spitting so bad that no one else even dared to try. Hestia had to build a shed around it to protect her people."

"Oh, well, *Hestia*," he said dismissively, as if that explained everything. "It probably just doesn't like *her*. Mine is as calm as a summer sea."

"Really?" Now it was Apollo's turn to sound disbelieving.

"Really." The sea god bristled slightly; clearly, Apollo

wasn't the only one who disliked people questioning his word. "I'll show you, if you like."

He got up and walked over to one of the walls, laying his hand almost lovingly on the frozen surface. We joined him as the ice beneath his palm began to flow and reform. Not *melt*—no water dripped. It just became fluid, and moved where Poseidon directed it, then solidified again. The palms of my hands tingled, as if they itched to try the pretty magic for themselves, but water was Poseidon's element, not mine. All that would happen if I laid my hand on that frozen wall would be that my skin would get stuck to it. Not going to happen.

Anyway, the wall rippled apart, forming a deep shelf the length of my outstretched arms, fingertip to fingertip. Light burst forth from the recesses of the shelf, startlingly bright. I squinted as Poseidon reached in and pulled out what had been hidden in the depths of the ice.

It was, of course, the lightning bolt that had come lancing out of the sky to embed itself into the deck of his yacht that day Hades and I had been visiting. I could still see it there, quivering, and smell the ozone in the air. I recalled the shock on the faces of my companions, which was no doubt mirrored on my own—

Holy shit, I was *remembering*.

I latched onto that scrap of memory, my heart hammering in excitement. There had been scorch marks on the deck all around the lightning bolt, which sizzled and hummed as if it were as shocked to find itself there as we were. Poseidon had thought we were under attack—he'd leapt up, his trident appearing from nowhere in his hand, his brows drawn together in fury, and he'd said … he'd said …

Zeus's *balls*, it was gone again. No matter how hard I strained after it, it slipped through my fingers like a handful of sand, until I was no longer sure of anything. Was I really remembering, or just imagining?

The lightning bolt was no longer sizzling or spitting energy the way the one in Hestia's care had done. It lay quiescent in Poseidon's grip as he held it out to us. I shook my head, trying to focus on the present moment.

"Touch it," he said. "It's perfectly safe."

Looking at the bolt too long still made my eyes water, but it wasn't as bright as that other one, either, and it was possible to make out more of its shape beneath the glare. About the length of my arm, its surface was smooth, with no joins or marks anywhere. Sundering it from its other two parts had left no trace on the gleaming surface. It had to be one of the side pieces, judging by its length. The piece Hestia had was the height of a man. I reached out and stroked it hesitantly but, as Poseidon had promised, nothing happened. It was warm to the touch, but not uncomfortably so.

Apollo paused in the act of reaching out to the bolt and looked up, like a hunting dog that had caught a scent. "Are you expecting someone?" he asked Poseidon.

The sea god nodded. "A friend of mine. Though I believe Arti has met him, too."

He looked at me expectantly, but I had no idea what they were talking about. What had Apollo sensed? Should I have sensed it, too? Trying not to be obvious about it, I sniffed the air, but the hint of ozone from the bolt was the only odd scent in the room. I sent my senses out, searching for animal life but, though there was a great deal of it in the seas outside the iceberg, there was nothing inside it to help me.

A few moments later, the great golden doors opened again, and the same seaweed-haired woman poked her head in, putting me out of my misery.

"Manannan mac Lir to see you, my lord."

"Send him in," Poseidon said, his bearded face breaking into a smile, and someone I did indeed recognise strolled in.

8

Poseidon strode forward, one beefy hand outstretched. "Manannan! Good to see you again. I believe you know my niece already?"

Manannan mac Lir. The Celtic god of the sea. Well, that would explain a few things. He was wearing shorts and a brightly coloured shirt every bit as loud and tasteless as the one he'd been wearing the night I'd met him on the canals of Brenvale. Syl, Lucas, and I had been checking out the shadow shapers' mansion where Hades had been held when the Merrow had capsized our little boat. If not for this guy appearing out of the night in his massive cruiser, we would have been toast. At the time, I'd thought him an extraordinarily powerful watershaper. Since Brenvale was the capital city of the watershapers, and dedicated to the worship of Poseidon, that had been a reasonable assumption. What reason would a sea god from a different pantheon have to be there?

Once he'd shaken hands with Poseidon, Manannan grinned at me. He had the appearance of a young, fit guy, with streaks of blond in his shoulder-length brown hair that suggested a life lived mainly outdoors, and a tan to match. Tattooed Celtic knots stretched up his left arm all the way from the back of his hand until they disappeared under his shirt sleeve.

"You told me your name was Mac," I said reproachfully.

"And so it is," he replied, flashing white teeth as his smile widened. "Partly, anyway."

"Why didn't you tell me who you really were?"

He shrugged. "Why didn't you? You said your name was Lexi. I sensed no godhood about you then, though there was certainly something odd there."

"Long story." I sighed. How many times would I have to tell it?

"Wonderful!" He threw himself onto the nearest lounge and put his feet up. They were bare, and a few grains of sand brushed off onto the cushions. "I love a good story."

"It's very simple," Poseidon said, sinking back into his shell lounge and laying the lightning bolt across his knees, where its soft glow lit his face from below. "Hades made her human so she could hunt shadow shapers without being targeted herself, but in the process, she's lost her memory and really believes she's a human. Called Lexi." He snorted. "What sort of a name is 'Lexi'? It sounds like a dog's name. Here, Lexi! Good dog, Lexi."

I shot him a glance even colder than his stupid iceberg. Screw him. Lexi was a great name. Apollo was smirking, too, though he wiped that off his face quick smart when I turned the glare on him.

"It's short for Alexia, and there's nothing wrong with it, thank you very much."

"Well, that's not a very entertaining story, Poseidon," Manannan said. "You've spoiled the ending and left out all the good bits."

"Allow me," Apollo said, and proceeded to provide enough embellishment to please even the fussiest of audiences. Even I, who'd lived through the whole thing, found myself leaning forward, enthralled, as Apollo wove the tale of the last few weeks of my life. I guess there was a reason he was the god of minstrels. He had a way with words, my brother. I even came out of it sounding all heroic, so I forgave him for smirking at Poseidon's dog comments.

When he'd finished, Manannan sighed like a man who's just finished a satisfying meal, and gave Poseidon a reproving glance. "Now *that's* how you tell a story."

"How about you tell one, now?" I asked. "I'd like to know how you managed to be there on the canal that night, at exactly the right time to rescue us from the Merrow."

He laughed, flashing those white teeth of his. "You were so suspicious, weren't you?"

"You must admit, it looked bad. I couldn't believe it was a coincidence. I thought you'd set them on us yourself."

"But now, of course, you realise that I was truly your knight in shining armour."

"Of course." His smile really was infectious. "But I still want to know how you did it."

He pouted a little. "You won't accept that it was my sheer magnificence and leave it at that?"

"Stop flirting with my niece," Poseidon said. "You're old enough to be her great-grandfather."

"But better preserved than you, my friend," Manannan pointed out.

Poseidon didn't move from his lounge, but a different person was sitting there. Young, dark-haired, impossibly handsome and dressed in a sharp suit and tie—only the green eyes were the same. In this form, he looked a lot like Jake, and I sighed and looked away.

Not to be outdone, Manannan had changed form, too—only now he looked just as Poseidon had before, complete with a long white beard and formal robe. I could just see the beginnings of his tattoo peeking out the bottom of the long sleeve. That was interesting. Everything but that had changed. Did he really like that tattoo, or was it an integral part of him?

"Gentlemen, could we stick to the point, please?"

Both of them flashed back to their normal appearance,

and Manannan continued as if nothing had happened. "To tell the story properly, I must go back before that. A couple of weeks ago, I received an unexpected visit from Hades. He was more agitated than I'd ever seen him. He told me of the trouble your pantheon has been having with these shadow shapers. I knew, of course, that Hephaistos had died, but I had never heard how it happened. I was shocked to learn of such a coordinated effort against a whole pantheon."

"So it's not happening to yours? Or any of the others?" I'd suspected that, but it was still a shock to have it confirmed. Someone had it in for us, specifically. Yay, us. The Greek gods: collecting enemies since prehistoric times.

"No. How could it? Yours is the only one I know of with this strange system of using avatars."

"We are?" I looked at Apollo, expecting a nod of confirmation, but he looked as surprised as I did. I was used to not having access to crucial information, but it seemed this particular tidbit was news to him, too. "So, you guys walk around with all your power in you, all the time? How do you manage to pass yourself off as human?"

"I can't speak for the other pantheons, but all of us have these tattoos." He held up his left arm, with its intricate inking. "You might have noticed mine. I'm not going to give away any trade secrets, so I'll say no more, but it was about this, and related matters, that Hades sought me out."

"Two weeks ago, you said?" That put it about the time Hades had disappeared. I'd thought he'd been chasing Becky, the local spy for the shadow shapers, but it seemed he'd had other things on his mind.

Manannan nodded. "He said he'd been visiting the gods of all the different underworlds, to see if any other gods had died, or whether the shadow shapers were only targeting your pantheon. You may know me only as the god of the sea, but I do have other duties, one of which is to escort our dead to the underworld. I couldn't give him the answer he hoped for, however. None of ours have died. He was very thoughtful when he left."

"Then that proves that this whole thing is an attack on us by another pantheon," Poseidon said. "Probably by that bastard Loki."

"No, it doesn't," I said, earning a scowl for disagreeing with him. "Whoever's leading the shadow shapers has got to be someone we all trust—how else are they getting to us so easily? Would Apollo have let Loki get near him without taking every precaution, if he even agreed to meet with him at all?"

"You and Manannan may be friends," Apollo said, "but most of us steer well clear of the other pantheons. No offence, Manannan."

"None taken. Call it professional jealousy or a keen instinct for self-preservation, but most of our lot keep to themselves, too."

"That's shark shit," Poseidon said. "Why would one of our own turn on us like that?"

"It's not as though it's never happened before," I reminded him. "The Olympians turned on the Titans."

"That's not the same thing!"

"Maybe not," Apollo said, "but I agree with Lexi. I think this is an inside job."

Poseidon folded his arms, his scowl growing blacker, as if he could see the logic but didn't want to admit that we might be right.

"Do you know where Hades went after that?" I asked Manannan, wanting to move on. Somewhere, the shadow shapers had caught up with Hades and dragged him off to Brenvale. That part was still unclear to me.

"He didn't say. But our conversation made me uneasy, so a few days later, I paid a visit to my old friend here." He indicated Poseidon with a wave of his hand.

"I'm surprised you two aren't rivals," I said. Particularly since Poseidon didn't seem the type to share his toys.

"We aren't competing in the same market, as the humans would say. We sea gods have the world pretty well divided among us all, and there is very little cross-over. The good thing about being a sea god is there can be clearly delineated territories. It's not like being a god of love, or wisdom, which is an airy concept. You won't find any temples to Poseidon on my turf, and I have no worshippers on his either."

"That seems very civilised." There were a few individuals who wanted to kick the status quo—I thought of the mayor of Berkley's Bay, and his altarpiece of Manannan that I'd stolen. It seemed so long ago, now, though it had only been a few weeks. He'd been a secret worshipper of Manannan's, despite the region's official adherence to Poseidon. Still, a few oddballs did no harm, I supposed.

"Even the most bloodthirsty god gets tired of war after a couple of centuries," Manannan said. "Unless you actually *are* a war god, of course—then it's your bread and butter. But I was sick of it, and I thought the other sea gods might be amenable to a different arrangement."

I glanced at Poseidon, who was nodding sagely, and wondered how long it had taken Manannan to talk Poseidon into this arrangement of his.

"It's been working for millennia now," Manannan said, with justifiable pride. Anyone who could talk gods into being reasonable was allowed a little self-congratulation. "Make love, not war, right?"

Poseidon rolled his eyes. "Now you sound like Zeus."

"No, he likes to do both," Apollo said. "Preferably at the same time."

I shuddered. "Let's not talk about Zeus's love life, if you don't mind." Turning back to Manannan, I asked, "So why did you visit Poseidon?"

"When Hades told me how bad things were getting over

here, I was worried about him. I suppose I wanted to see for myself that he was safe, and that he had appropriate security in place."

"Of course I did," Poseidon said. "This place is a fortress. Nobody gets in or out without my say-so. But, since he was here, I asked him to check out some rumours I'd been hearing from the Merrow. I would have gone myself, but protecting my brother's lightning bolt is my first priority. I won't leave the fortress even for a moment while it's here."

"What rumours?" Apollo asked.

"There was a lot of power swirling around the canals. Merrow are particularly sensitive creatures. They could taste it in the air. Some of them were worried another god had moved into my territory."

Sensitive creatures, huh? Not the ones I'd met. A chill ran through me as I recalled the feeling of a cold hand closing around my ankle, yanking me down to my death. Not a pleasant sensation at all. "But hang on—it was the Merrow who attacked us. They were working for the shadow shapers the whole time, so why would they go blabbing to you about it?"

"That was only a couple of renegades," Poseidon said. "It was the loyal ones who came to me."

"And the loyalists didn't know who their fellows were working for," Manannan added. "Or where. The shadow shapers had a cosy little nest in Brenvale, as you discovered, but it took me several days to locate it. Then I kept watch for a couple more, trying to understand what I was sensing. It seemed to me that there was more power there than could be explained by a few jumped-up power-stealers. Turned out that was Hades I could feel, since, by that time, they'd dumped him there. I had loyal Merrow watching the place. When they reported spies, I was intrigued. I was already on my way to see what you were up to when you were attacked."

"Fortunately for us."

"Yes." He grinned. "Fortunately for you."

"It couldn't have been Hades you sensed, though," I pointed out. "He had a collar on by then, which blocked his power."

Manannan and Poseidon turned identical frowns to me. Maybe it was a sea god thing. "Then who was it?" Manannan asked.

"Possibly our traitor," Apollo said, looking grim.

I nodded. "Maybe. Or maybe there were just so many shadow shapers there that it felt bigger to you. There were at least twenty of them the night we freed Hades, and some of them had taken power from more than one god."

"So what now?" Apollo asked.

The lightning bolt still lay across Poseidon's knees, quiet as a lamb. Quieter, actually. Lambs had a tendency to spring about at random, but the lightning bolt showed no desire to gambol. If anything, the intensity of its glow had lessened since Poseidon had first pulled it out of the wall. It was possible, now, to look at it without squinting.

Poseidon lay a big hand on it in a protective gesture. "If you've come to ask me to give this to Hestia, you can jump overboard and swim back to shore. Unless you can find the other one, and there's actually some possibility that we could get my stupid brother back, it's not leaving here. That woman couldn't protect a hen house from a fox. I'm not trusting her with this."

"She's kept the one she has safe enough," Apollo pointed out in such a deliberately patient tone that I could tell he was annoyed at the slur on Hestia. He was very fond of her.

"Only because no one can get near the damn thing. You said so yourself." He glared back at his nephew, and I sighed. What was the point of arguing about it? He'd obviously made up his mind.

"I'm all for finding the other one." I was also keen to keep them focused. "Do you have any idea where it is?"

"Are you sure Hades doesn't have it?" Poseidon still looked grumpy. "He seems the obvious choice."

"He says he doesn't, and he has no reason to lie about it. Who else would Zeus have trusted?"

"One of the other sky gods, perhaps, like Thor?" Manannan suggested.

Poseidon rolled his eyes, and I was tempted to do the same. Just because Manannan had brokered a peace between the sea gods didn't mean that any of the others could get along so well.

"Please," Poseidon said. "Zeus has a hard time even admitting that other sky gods exist. There's no way he'd send part of his power to one of them. He'd be afraid he'd never get it back."

"What about Hera, then?" I asked. "She's his wife."

Poseidon laughed. "Only because she hasn't got around to killing him yet."

"Okay, not Hera. Aries?"

Poseidon shook his head. "Haven't seen him in forever. He's made himself very scarce while this whole thing's been going on. Perhaps Demeter? She was always Zeus's favourite sister."

"Hades has already checked with Persephone and Demeter. They don't have it."

"Then who else is left?" Manannan asked. "Aphrodite?"

Poseidon guffawed, and even Apollo smiled as he shook his head.

"Athena, then?"

A long pause followed while they considered the idea.

"I suppose it's possible." Apollo sounded as though he didn't like the idea.

Poseidon nodded thoughtfully. "She came from his head. She knows his mind."

"And she's his favourite child," Apollo finished.

"Does that bother you?" I asked. Should it bother me? It all felt rather academic, since I had no memory of ever meeting Zeus. What did I care who his favourite child was?

"Of course not," he said, a little too quickly. "I don't need Daddy Dearest's approval for self-validation."

"Self-validation?" Poseidon echoed. "You've been spending too much time among the humans, boy."

It was odd to hear one thousands-of-years-old man call another "boy", but I supposed these things were relative. Poseidon had been around before there were even humans, when the Titans still walked the earth.

"Regardless, it probably is Athena—which is a pain in the arse."

"Why's that?" I asked.

"Because she hasn't spoken to the two of us in over a thousand years."

✦

Many hours later, the iceberg was floating at rest in the tiny cove of a remote tropical island, and the four of us were standing on the small, flat part of the iceberg, looking up at the mountain that towered above the centre of the island.

"Are you sure this is the place?" I asked.

Jungle stretched as far as the eye could see, from the thin

stretch of white sand at the water's edge up onto the knees of the black mountain. Bright birds flashed through the sky above the treetops, and monkeys—or something—called to each other from deep in the jungle. There was no sign that people had ever been here. It looked like virgin jungle, completely untouched by human habitation.

"Where does she live?"

"Up there," Poseidon said, waving a vague hand at the mountain. He was being deliberately uncooperative, still sulking about being dragged into the action. But he was the only one of us who knew where Athena lived.

"You'll have to talk to her," Apollo had told him last night. "She won't listen to me or Arti. I doubt she'd even let us in."

Ah, sibling rivalry—such a wonderful thing. Apparently, we'd had a falling out with our sister way back when, though Apollo hadn't told me why. It was probably something stupid, as such things often were.

"I told you," Poseidon had returned, the scowl returning to his face. "I'm not leaving this iceberg while the lightning bolt is under my care."

"The three of us can look after it," Apollo said.

"Artemis doesn't even know which way's up, and you've already been caught once by the shadow shapers, boy." Poseidon wielded his usual tact and diplomacy. I was almost used to it by now. "I wouldn't leave you in charge of an ice cream stand. And I'm not sure I want to get involved in this mess. I have the lightning bolt to think of."

"You're already involved." Apollo was rapidly losing patience. We'd been going round and round in circles for what seemed like hours. "Don't imagine you're safe just because you hide in this iceberg. You're a target, too, just like the rest of us. But if you're too scared, tell Manannan where this damn island is, and *he* can take us there."

"How dare you!" Poseidon had roared. "I'm not scared, but I have a duty to safeguard this bloody lightning bolt. And if you're right about there being a traitor among us, how do we know that they won't be lying in wait for us there?"

"No one's going to be lying in wait for anyone," I said. "How would they know we're coming when we've only just decided it ourselves?"

Before Poseidon could burst a blood vessel, Manannan stepped in. "Let me go ashore. I don't have an avatar, so I have nothing to fear from any shadow shapers. You can wait at a safe distance."

"Athena won't listen to you," Poseidon growled.

"If she doesn't, I can invite her to come out and hear it from you, Poseidon."

That had seemed to satisfy him, and so we found ourselves here, in the morning sunshine, contemplating the looming peak of Athena's island.

"I'll come with you," I said now to Manannan. "For company. I can wait outside while you talk to her."

Manannan glanced at Poseidon. "Do you think that will upset her?"

"Breathing upsets her. I've never known such a one for getting miffed over the smallest thing."

Pot, meet Kettle. I sighed. I was itching to get off this iceberg and look around the island. "Maybe I'd better not, then."

The shore was still a good way off, the water changing from deep blue where the iceberg floated to a beautiful, clear green next to the beach. Manannan stepped off the edge of the iceberg but didn't sink—the sea held him up as if it were as solid as the ice.

"Nice trick," I said.

He winked at me. "I know how to impress the ladies."

Walking on water would have been impressive enough, but he didn't have to exert himself so far. A wave rose up under his feet and bore him into shore, gently depositing him on the beach. It looked like he was riding an invisible surfboard.

"Can you do that?" I asked Poseidon.

"I wish." He stared after the Celtic god enviously. "I've been asking him for a thousand years to teach me that trick, but the bastard won't give it up. I've even tried getting him drunk, but those Celts can hold their liquor."

As Manannan trudged up the beach, small black cones like witches' hats popped up out of the sand just before the tree line. He paused and glanced back at us.

"Any idea what those are?" he shouted across the water.

"Keep going," Poseidon called. "It's the only way to find out."

"Easy to say when you're standing out here," Apollo said, earning himself a glare from our uncle.

The cones gleamed in the sun as if they were made of metal. I probed them, searching for a spark of animal life, but they were as dead as the metal they appeared to be. Manannan still hadn't moved, and neither had the cones. There must have been fifty of them, spaced at regular intervals all the way along the small beach.

"Is this the only access to the island?" I asked.

"No," Poseidon said, "but it's the easiest. This is the lowest point. The other side's all cliffs. If you had wings, you could fly right in. Where's Hermes when you need him?"

It was a rhetorical question, but Apollo answered anyway: "I haven't seen hide nor hair of him since Zeus disappeared. He's lying low somewhere."

"Some messenger," Poseidon grumbled.

Back on the beach, Manannan was on the move again. His first couple of steps were tentative as he watched the black cones for a reaction. When they didn't move, he strode more confidently towards the trees.

"See?" Poseidon said. "Nothing to worry about."

No sooner were the words out of his mouth than the whole beach erupted. Sand fountained into the air as the cones surged skyward. My mouth fell open as giant armoured warriors appeared. Like the iceberg, their bulk had been hidden beneath the surface. The cones turned out to be only the tips of their helmets.

"Shit," Apollo said as Manannan beat a hasty retreat back down the beach.

In unison, the warriors thumped the butts of their spears down into the sand. They carried shields as well, and the hilt of a sword protruded over each armoured shoulder. Each warrior was twice the height of a man, but they weren't men. They were statues, the faces beneath their helmets only featureless, metallic surfaces.

Water lapped around Manannan's ankles as he stopped in the shallows. The warriors stood motionless, barring the way into the jungle.

"What do you think?" he called. "I may be immortal but I'm not keen to spend the next few months regrowing my limbs."

"See what happens if you approach them," Poseidon suggested.

Obediently, Manannan moved back up the beach toward them. The statues responded by marching down to meet him, so the sea god turned tail and fled back to the safety of the sea. Once he was on his way back to the iceberg, the statues returned to their former position at the tree line. The message was clear: the way to the mountain was barred.

"This is your field," Poseidon said to Apollo. "Can't you do something with them?"

Apollo snorted. "I could melt them to slag, but that might not endear us to Athena. Hephaistos is the metalshaping expert. *Was* the metalshaping expert. My power over fire gives me only basic metalshaping abilities."

I contemplated the giant warriors. Hephaistos had been the god of metalshaping, and now that he was dead, metalshaping was becoming more and more difficult. What we needed was another metalshaping expert—someone, perhaps, who already had experience with moving giant metal statues and bending them to his will.

"What are you smirking about?" Poseidon asked.

"Just remembering the time that Jake woke the giant statue of Apollo in the Plaza of the Sun and set it on Erik Anders," I said. Good times. "You should have seen him run, with those huge horses and the chariot chasing him across the plaza. And when the statue threw its spear, I thought he was going to wet himself."

Apollo was quick on the uptake. "Are you suggesting that Jake might be able to help us here?"

"Who's Jake?" Poseidon gave us both a suspicious look.

"My new Ruby Adept," Apollo said.

"A fireshaper? Nonsense. How could a fireshaper succeed where a god cannot?"

"His secondary is metalshaping," I said, offended on Jake's behalf at the sea god's scorn. "And he's bloody good at it."

"Much as it pains me to admit it," Apollo said, "metalshaping is not really my thing. I had no need to bother learning the fine art of it with Hephaistos around. Jake is probably much more suited to the task."

Poseidon shrugged. "Fine. Let's get this Jake person, then."

Later, when the island was only a tiny speck on the horizon and Poseidon and Manannan were swapping raucous sea god stories over a flagon of wine, Apollo leaned closer and murmured: "Are you sure you only suggested Jake for his skills in metalshaping?"

"Of course." I batted my eyelids at him in mock innocence. "Why? What other reason could I possibly have?"

"As long as you're not trying to tempt away my Ruby Adept. I need him, Arti."

"Mm-hmm." I took another sip of my wine. *He* needed him? "I think Jake has already made it clear which twin has his loyalty."

He said no more, apparently satisfied. Naturally, my

first thought had been of Jake when we needed an expert metalshaper. But that didn't mean it had been my *only* thought. I had every intention of using any means at my disposal to steal Apollo's Ruby Adept away from him. But there was no point arguing about it now. He'd figure it out soon enough.

9

We left Poseidon's iceberg out at sea, and Manannan dropped us back at Berkley's Bay in the same luxury yacht that he'd picked us up in the night the Merrow decided to capsize our little rowing boat. The shadows were long, and the heat had gone from the day by the time we left him and headed straight for Winston's little temple.

"I'll come with you," I said to Apollo as we stood on the footpath outside the small brick house in the late afternoon sun. We'd been gone nearly twenty-four hours. Syl would be worried. I hadn't expected our visit to Poseidon to turn into an overnight jaunt to a distant island.

"No need." He frowned impatiently at me. "I'm perfectly capable of retrieving Jake without your assistance."

"I know, but ..." But I couldn't wait to see him again. And maybe I was just a little worried that Apollo might run into trouble. Syl's nerves had infected me. After all, as

Poseidon had pointed out just hours before, the shadow shapers had already captured him once. Every time he went out in public, especially in a big place like Crosston, he was basically walking around with a target on his back.

"But you're eager to get your hands on my Ruby Adept?"

"Jake is too proper for that." But I'd wear him down, somehow. What we had was too good to let go without a fight. "I guess I'm just a little worried. Syl's got me imagining shadow shapers around every corner."

"Then stay here and guard your back. Or, better yet, figure out a way to persuade Athena to give us her part of the lightning bolt."

"That's assuming she's even got it."

"Who else would have it? Poseidon's right; it makes sense that Zeus would send it to her. He makes no secret of the fact that she's his favourite child."

"Maybe that's exactly why he wouldn't. Too obvious. Perhaps the reason Hermes has disappeared is that he's guarding it."

He sighed. "If you're determined to be gloomy, go home and mope with your friends. If she doesn't have it, we'll keep looking. Let's just take one problem at a time, eh?"

He leaned forward and gave me a peck on the cheek, then headed up the path to the house. I watched him go, touching my cheek self-consciously. He'd kissed me. My brother had kissed me. That was going to take some getting used to. Conflicting feelings surged through me—pleasure at my rediscovered, if dysfunctional, family; frustration at my inability to remember them or anything much else; a fierce longing to be kissed in a completely different way by the man Apollo had gone to get.

Well. It wouldn't do to still be standing here on the footpath when the two of them returned, looking like a lovelorn teenager. I turned smartly on my heel and marched down the street, in the direction of my own home.

Syl whirled as I opened the door into our apartment. She'd been standing at the big window that looked out towards the sea. Her worried expression changed to one of sheer relief, then almost as quickly to fury.

"Where the hell have you been?" she demanded, stalking across the floor like a lioness about to spring on her prey.

"I told you, Apollo took me to meet with Poseidon."

"That was yesterday! Do you have any idea what time it is?"

I couldn't help it; my mouth twitched. "You sound just like a mother."

"Don't you laugh!" She jabbed me in the chest with her finger. "I've been worried sick. I thought the shadow shapers had taken you."

"I'm afraid you're still stuck with me. Ouch!" She'd just jabbed me again, even harder. "Syl, quit it! It took longer than I expected, and I left my phone behind and didn't have any way to get you a message. I'm sorry, all right?"

"Sorry? I'll make you sorry," she muttered.

"Oh, for goodness' sake." I pulled her into a hug, and she sagged against me like a puppet whose strings had been cut. She really had been wound up. "You're awfully violent for someone so small."

"I thought you were dead!" she wailed into my shoulder, and I hugged her harder, stroking her dark hair.

"Where's Lucas?" I would have expected him to be here, keeping her fears under control.

"He went out to look for you. I stayed here, in case you came back." She drew back, sniffing, then jabbed me one last time for good measure. Her finger felt as though it was made of steel. "Don't you *ever* do that to me again."

I rubbed at the sore spot on my chest. "I'd love to be able to promise you that I'll stay safe, Syl, but this is a war we're fighting. You can't wrap me in cotton wool."

"You need a bodyguard." She folded her arms, her expression grim. "Leave it with me."

"That sounds ominous."

"I'm not the only one who worries about you, so ..." Evidently pleased with whatever scheme she was plotting now, she threw herself down on the couch in a sudden change of mood and looked at me expectantly. "So, tell me everything. Where have you been all this time? What happened?"

And just like that, she stopped being angry at me. Talk about sunshine and storms. Good old feline curiosity to the rescue. I sank into one of the armchairs and began the story of our voyage in the good ship *Iceberg* to see Athena. She interrupted me with exclamations of surprise when I explained that the mysterious benefactor who had saved us from the Merrow in Brenvale was another god, but apart from that little outburst, she listened without comment.

I was in the middle of describing the massive warrior statues that had barred our way onto Athena's island when a knock on the door interrupted me.

"That's probably Lucas come back," she said. Raising her voice, she called out, "Come in; it's not locked."

But it wasn't Lucas. I leapt up as Apollo walked in, followed by a familiar figure. My heart hammered as I drank him in, from the top of his dark head to his feet, pausing along the way to gaze into his blue, blue eyes and admire his broad chest and strong arms. He wore slim-fitting dark trousers and a white collared shirt. He looked as though he'd just come from casual day at the office.

"Hello, Jake," I said, managing not to sound as desperate to throw myself into his arms as I was. My body remembered exactly what that felt like. Not to mention how it felt to have him moving above me, how his skin smelled when I buried my face in his chest, how—

He nodded at me. "Lady Artemis."

Gods above. I felt like I'd been doused in cold water. He was beautiful, but I'd forgotten how annoying he could be. I took a deep, calming breath and forced myself to keep smiling. "Call me Lexi." He opened his mouth to make some stupid objection, and I snapped, "That's an order."

He closed his mouth again, and I felt a certain satisfaction to see the muscle in his jaw jump as he clenched it. Good to know that I could still annoy him, too.

"I've filled Jake in," Apollo said, giving me a reproving look. Oh, he didn't like me ordering his precious Ruby Adept around? Maybe he should tell him not to be such a giant pain in the arse, then. "Are you ready to go?"

"Go?" Syl repeated, looking from one to the other of us in surprise. "You only just got here."

"Well, those statues I was telling you about wouldn't let us through, and we need to get past them to see Athena. We only came back to get Jake so he could help us. We figured with his metalshaping powers he'd be able to control them."

"As I explained to Lord Apollo, that may not be the case," Jake said. "My metalshaping is fading all the time, and if they have a very strong enchantment on them ..."

"Well, there's only one way to find out, isn't there?" I said briskly. "Syl, please don't panic if we don't come back straight away. We'll be gone at least a day, maybe two."

"Oh, don't worry about me," she said, giving me a meaningful look. "I've got some other things to organise."

"I hope you're not still thinking about bodyguards."

"And why shouldn't I be? You had all of us in a panic when you disappeared without warning—and trust me, you don't ever want to see a wolf pack in a panic. You can't pull a stunt like that and expect there to be no consequences."

"You're sounding like a mother again, Syl. You could give Holly a few tips for when Mireille is a teenager."

"Don't try to wriggle out of it by making everything a joke either. You're not fit to be let out without a keeper. At least Jake will be with you this time."

Apollo blinked in surprise. "What, the sun god's not good enough protection for you?"

She gave him a stern look. "No offence, Apollo, but you gods have already shown that you're vulnerable to whatever tricks the shadow shapers are playing. Jake doesn't have that vulnerability."

"I will protect the Lady Ar—Lexi—with my life," Jake assured her.

"I know," Syl said drily, and he shifted uncomfortably and looked away. Stupid bloody man. Everyone could tell he still loved me. Why wouldn't he just go with the flow? We could all die tomorrow, and I was sure he wouldn't be lying around bleeding out and wishing that he'd treated me with a little more deference. It was ironic, really: I'd been alive for millennia, yet I had a better grasp on the whole *live for the moment* thing than he, a human with a fleeting lifespan, did.

Still, there was no point getting upset about it now. We had a job to do, and I had other things to worry about. But once we had Zeus back, I was going to carpe the hell out of a certain fireshaper's diem.

⁂

Poseidon gave us all rooms so we could sleep while the iceberg made the long journey back to Athena's island. I'll admit, it did cross my mind to pay Jake's a visit in the middle of the night, but I wasn't going to beg, and I certainly wasn't going to order, so I figured I'd be better off getting some sleep. I contented myself with the hope that he would sleep badly, knowing that I was only just down the hall. He could toss and turn all night, as far as I was concerned, wishing he was in my bed instead of his own. It would only help my cause.

When we all assembled on the small, level patch on the iceberg's surface that I now thought of as the deck, he did look pretty tired. Excellent. For a fleeting moment, I wished that I was wearing something more alluring than jeans and a T-shirt, but the main item on today's agenda wasn't seduction, and my practical clothes were much more suitable for trekking through jungle and scaling that damn mountain.

It loomed over the island, clouds wreathing its tip. At the moment, there was no sign of the warrior statues on the beach below it. Even the tips of their helmets were gone. Hidden underneath the sand again, presumably, waiting until the next intruder threatened the island.

The humidity stuck tendrils of hair to my neck and forehead and caused my T-shirt to cling uncomfortably to my back. It would probably be even hotter once we got into that jungle. At least out here we had the sea breeze.

"How far up that mountain is her house?" I asked. Maybe I should have worn shorts. Every inch of me would be soaked in sweat if I had to climb all the way up there.

"It's actually at the base," Poseidon said. He seemed in a much better mood today. Maybe Manannan had had a quiet word with him, or maybe he'd realised that Apollo was right, and he was already stuck in the middle of this mess, so he might as well be helpful. "There's a place where a stream comes down from the hills and forms a lake. It's very pretty, full of water lilies. Her house is out in the middle of the lake."

"Let's go, then," Manannan said. "Are you ready, Jake?"

"Yes, sir."

I rolled my eyes at that "sir". Jake didn't seem to know how to deal with Manannan. He wasn't from the pantheon that Jake worshipped, so apparently, he didn't rate a "my lord", but he was still a god. Jake's devoutness couldn't seem to cope with calling any god by their name unless he was ordered to, so he'd compromised with "sir".

Manannan stepped down onto the surface of the sea and gestured for us to follow him. Jake and Apollo followed without hesitating, and the water bore them up. I closed my eyes for just a second as my foot left the comforting solidity of the iceberg—deep inside, I really expected to fall into the water, despite seeing the three men supported. It was the oddest feeling—the surface gave under my foot, but I didn't sink. It felt like walking on a trampoline, kind of bouncy and uncertain.

Gingerly, I followed the other three towards the shore. As we grew closer and the water paled to that vibrant green shade, it became even more peculiar. I could see the fish swimming beneath my feet. They flocked towards Manannan, as if the sea god's footsteps were a magnet— even some big ones. A couple of reef sharks as big as me joined their brighter cousins, flitting beneath our feet, and it gave me a particularly nasty feeling to see them draw nearer. Reflexively, I reached for their minds, ready to turn them away. But I needn't have worried. Manannan shooed them all away with a laugh, as if they were flies, and they scattered obediently.

Soon, we stood on the wet sand, with waves breaking around our ankles. The sun beat down on my head, and I wished I'd thought to wear sunglasses, as the glare from the white beach was fierce.

"Where are the warriors?" Jake asked.

"You'll see," Manannan said. "Watch this."

He strode up the beach, stopping when the tips of the conical helmets poked up from the sand.

Jake shaded his eyes with his hand and gazed along the beach. "That's a lot of warriors."

"You think you can handle them?" Manannan asked. "It would really spoil my day to get pulverised by some antisocial goddess's welcoming committee."

Jake rolled his shoulders as if limbering up for a fight. "Maybe not *all* of them." He glanced at Apollo. "Will it be enough to freeze the ones directly in front of us? Do you think the others will follow us once we break through the line?"

Apollo shrugged. The sun glinting off his blond curls was almost as bright as the glare off the white sand. Today, he wore a shirt as white as Jake's, which, I realised, was the first time I'd seen him in anything but black. Must be a concession to the heat. "Knowing Athena, they're just as likely to chase us all the way to the bloody house. Best to be ready for anything."

I rolled up my jeans as far as I could, sweltering in the heat. Apollo looked as cool as if he were still on the iceberg. Goddammit. I'd forgotten again. I could regulate my own body temperature. No sooner had I thought it than the bite of the sun receded to nothing more than a pleasant warmth. That felt *so* much better. I could get used to this god stuff.

Apollo and I were to wait on the beach until Manannan and Jake saw Athena and gave us the go-ahead to approach our prickly sister. Manannan started toward the tree line, moving slowly to give Jake time to prepare. He didn't seem to be doing anything, though, unless he was praying. The sun beat down on his dark head as he waited, arms hanging loosely at his sides, his gaze fixed on the metal cones. Little waves foamed around my shoes as I stood next to Apollo, holding my breath.

Even though I was expecting it, I still gasped when the sand erupted and the mighty statues heaved themselves into the light. They were so *fast*. One minute, only the tips of their helmets were showing; the next, the armoured giants were looming above our heads.

"Any time, now, Jake," Manannan called over his shoulder, his steps slowing even further.

I would have been nervous, too, if I were him. Even from back by the water's edge, those statues were intimidating, and he was a lot closer than I was. He took one more step. They grounded their spear butts in the sand. An air of readiness hung about them, and an implacable aura of menace.

"Jake?" Manannan said.

"I'm not sure if this will work," Jake said, speaking through gritted teeth. He held his hands out toward the warriors and flames, almost invisible in the bright sunlight, leapt from his fingertips to the nearest half dozen. With excruciating slowness, the flames spread to others further down the beach. Nothing about the statues changed, but whatever Jake was doing, it was costing him an effort. "This isn't the kind of metalshaping I'm used to."

"Just try not to damage them," Apollo said, from the relative safety of the waterline. "Athena won't be feeling too cooperative if we destroy her pets."

"Can't you help him?" I asked in an undertone. Jake's arms were shaking already, and he'd only just begun. "I know metalshaping isn't your forte, but you could do *something*, couldn't you?"

"I don't want to interfere with whatever he's doing," he replied. "Our shapings could work against each other. Best to just leave him to it."

"I hope he knows what he's doing." I eyed Jake's trembling arms with deep misgiving. He'd been totally wiped out by animating the giant statue of Apollo that time in the Plaza of the Sun, though, admittedly, he'd also been shot, which hadn't helped. But this would not be a good place to collapse, if he didn't manage to contain all the statues. Anyone lying on the sand would soon be trampled by those monsters.

Uneasily, I sent my senses out, hunting for anything in the jungle that could give us an edge. I found plenty of birds, some small monkeys, and a handful of leopards. Lots of smaller things, too—lizards, snakes, rats, and so on. Nothing big enough to take on one of the giant warriors.

I wasn't sure what I'd expected—a dragon, perhaps? I was certainly a lot more open to unusual possibilities than I used to be, but, alas, Athena had no mythical surprises lurking in her jungle. Or, at least, if she did, they weren't animal enough for me to locate and use them with my powers.

"I'm moving again," Manannan announced, taking an exaggerated step forward.

The statues directly in front of him, six in all, didn't react, standing stock still while Jake's flames played around their heads and shoulders. Unfortunately, the same couldn't be said for the rest of their companions. On either side of the still six, warriors raised their spears in threatening poses.

"Damn," Apollo muttered. "I'd hoped for better than that."

True, six out of fifty-odd wasn't a great result. "It can still work. That gap is plenty big enough for them to get through."

"As long as the others don't get involved."

And that didn't look very likely, since the others all had spears raised, responding to the threat posed by Manannan's advance, even though he wasn't threatening them specifically. Damn. It all hinged, now, on what happened once Jake and Manannan gained the safety of the jungle—would it actually constitute safety, or would the attack continue all the way to Athena's house?

"I've just thought of something," I said, speaking quietly so as not to break Jake's concentration. "What if there are more safeguards further in?"

We'd been so focused on getting past the warriors that we hadn't considered that there might be more dangers to face once this one was defeated. There could be traps or other kinds of magic that a sea god and a fireshaper with a side of metalshaping couldn't handle.

"Shit," Apollo said. "I hate standing here uselessly like this."

"Well, there's still the *blast them all to slag* option if we get desperate."

"Only as a very last resort."

"Only then," I agreed, then raised my voice. "Jake, you'd better get moving or Manannan will leave you behind."

He didn't reply, but Jake began to move up the beach towards the trees. He looked distinctly wobbly on his feet, and my heart lurched into my mouth. I was sure that he was going to faceplant into the sand any minute now.

Manannan had upped his pace now that the statues in front of him appeared to be frozen, and he was almost at the trees. The motionless warriors loomed over him. But as he took his next step, he must have crossed some magical point of no return.

All hell broke loose on the beach, and that was saying something, since I'd actually been to Hell. The warriors in front of him quivered but otherwise stayed still. Sadly, they were the only ones. The rest of them hurled their spears and came charging up the beach, their massive feet scoring great gouges in the sand. A few that Jake's flames had touched moved a little slower than their companions, but that was scant consolation.

Jake roared and threw up his arms. The incoming spears rained down in a perfect circle around a stunned sea god.

Unfortunately, that took the last of Jake's strength. He crumpled into a heap on the sand.

"Shit! Jake!" I sprang forward, but the sand made me feel as if I was running in slow motion. The warriors, with their greater strides, were closing rapidly. With a giant shriek of metal, they drew their swords in unison. You haven't known fear until you've had nearly fifty giant metal warriors descending on you, all focused on smiting you into your component parts. Their silence was unnerving. My heart pounded as I forced my legs to move faster.

Apollo sprinted past me and scooped Jake into his arms, scattering sand everywhere.

"Run, Arti!"

I ran.

10

We fled into the jungle. I had wet sand in my shoes and a stitch in my side, but I'd never moved faster in my life, leaping over roots that would have entangled my feet and ducking and weaving around plants and tree branches at top speed. Apollo, with Jake slung over his shoulder in a fireman's lift, was just ahead of me, and Manannan was somewhere in front of him, judging by the sounds of something big crashing through the jungle. We were making more noise than a herd of elephants, but none of us cared. Our number one priority was escaping the murderous monstrosities on the beach.

Apollo pulled up so abruptly that I almost ran straight into his back. "Stop," he gasped. "Listen."

I stopped, but all I could hear was the thundering of my own heart. "What?"

"They're not following us."

I turned to look back, but I couldn't see the beach anymore, only the trail of snapped branches and crushed ferns we'd left behind us. He was right; once I got my breathing under control and listened, there was no sound behind us. It was as if the life had been sucked straight from the warriors the minute we'd passed under the shadow of the trees.

I shooed away a cloud of buzzing insects. That lasted all of three seconds, of course, so I used my powers to gently suggest to the tiny bloodsuckers that they might prefer the view on the other side of the island.

"I can't believe it was that easy," Manannan said, wiping sweat from his face as he rejoined us. He'd probably been too focused on staying alive to worry about regulating his body temperature.

"That wasn't easy," I said, a little shortly. My shoes and socks were soaked with seawater, my heart was still pounding, and I was worried about my favourite fireshaper. "Not for Jake, anyway."

"No, of course not." He noticed my wet feet and dried them with a wave of his hand. "How is he?"

Apollo bent down and lowered him to the ground.

Blue eyes blinked blearily up at us. "Everyone all right?"

I crouched down beside him. His face had a grey tinge I didn't like. "More to the point, are *you* all right?"

"I'll be fine," he said, his eyes searching my face as if he needed to see for himself that I really was unharmed. Stupid, stupid man. "Just a little tired."

"You did well," Apollo said.

Jake's eyelids sagged closed. "Thanks."

He'd forgotten to add "my lord" on the end of that. He really was exhausted. I glanced up at Apollo. "Can you give him some energy?"

Apollo cocked an eyebrow at me. "How do you mean?"

"When Jake and I were in the underworld and I was injured, Jake sort of *breathed* energy into me, and I felt better." I looked to Jake for confirmation, or a more technical description of what he'd actually done, but he appeared to have fallen asleep. It had felt a lot like kissing, but I couldn't quite find the words to suggest to my brother that he ought to play tonsil hockey with his Ruby Adept.

He gave me a blank look. "Don't you think that would be better coming from you?"

"But … I'm not a fireshaper."

"But you're a goddess." He shook his head impatiently. "I can't believe you don't remember this. This is, like, Godhood 101."

"Well, I'm sorry to disappoint you. I'd love to remember it. Don't you think I'm trying?"

"I'm not sure, actually. Are you?"

I turned my back on him, furious. What the hell was he suggesting? Of course I was trying. If trying was all that was required, I'd be firing on all cylinders by now. I was sick to death of not *knowing things* that everyone else took for granted. This no man's land I was inhabiting was a truly shitty place to live.

Jake's eyes were still closed. I bent over him—what was I supposed to do now? There was no way I was asking Apollo. He'd just accuse me of *not trying* again. I'd have to figure it out on my own.

When I'd been lying on the couch in Hephaistos's little cottage in the underworld, wounded and cold, Jake had pressed his lips to mine and flooded me with warmth. So ... lips to lips. That was a good place to start. I leaned closer, until I was breathing in the air he breathed out, and I could smell his familiar smoky aroma. He smelled like a bonfire at night in the forest, or a favourite camping trip. He smelled like warmth and comfort and everything good I wanted in my life.

I hovered closer, our lips almost touching, and drank in that smell of his. We were so close that his features blurred, and I closed my eyes, gently lowering my lips to his. The moment of contact was achingly sweet. I had missed him so much.

He didn't respond—he really was asleep. His lips were parted ever so slightly. Softly, I breathed into his mouth, imagining a ball of light in my core. I pushed some of that light toward him, willing it into him. For a moment, nothing happened, and then his lips moved beneath mine. My very own Sleeping Beauty was awake.

His lips parted further, and his tongue came alive, deepening the kiss. I forgot what I was supposed to be doing and threw myself into kissing him back enthusiastically. His arms snaked around me, crushing me closer to his broad chest, and I twined my free hand into his dark hair, trying to drag him even closer.

"I think he will live," Manannan said drily.

Suddenly, Jake was shoving me away. Fire flickered in his eyes, but an expression of horror warred with the lust, and it looked like the horror was winning. I sat back on my heels as he scrambled into a sitting position. "Lady Artemis! What are you doing?"

"Giving you back some energy." I tried not to feel hurt by that horror, but it wasn't easy. I knew he still wanted me—he couldn't hide his body's reaction. Only his stubborn will was keeping us apart. "Do you feel better?"

A look of surprise chased away the horror. "Yes. Yes, I do." Belatedly, he added, "Thank you."

I sighed. "You know, you keep saving me, and I keep saving you. I think the universe is trying to tell us something."

Apollo and Manannan had moved a little further away, and were discussing something in low voices. It wasn't exactly private, but it was the best we were going to get.

"What?" he asked.

"That we're meant to be together. We're *better* together, Jake." Damn. I'd told myself I wouldn't beg, but having him so close and yet still unobtainable was doing my head in. "You're torturing us both, for what? Some outdated notion of propriety?"

"It's not an outdated notion. It's who I *am*. I can't change my religious beliefs without changing everything about myself." He looked up at me, his blue eyes full of pain and longing. "I'd do anything for you, Lexi. I'd give up my life for you and die happy. But I can't give you this."

What did I say to that? It sounded so … so final. "But I love you."

My voice sounded small and weak, like a child's.

"Please try to accept it," he said. "It will be easier for us both that way."

I got to my feet, shaken. Accepting things I wanted to change wasn't my forte. I blinked a couple of times to clear the moisture from my eyes—I was *not* the kind of girl who cried over men. Now I was annoyed at myself as well as him. Oh, and at Apollo. And a little at Manannan for interrupting that kiss. Basically, I was pissed at everyone and everything.

"Let's get back to business, shall we?" My voice was cool.

I stalked off into the jungle without looking to see if they were following me. I borrowed the eyes of a brightly coloured flock of birds to show me the easiest way through the thick undergrowth. I wasn't spending a minute more on this trip than I had to. It had suddenly become almost unbearable. Thankfully, it wasn't as far as it had appeared from the beach—it was hard to judge distance when you had an almost impenetrable jungle in front of you. Poseidon had been right: the house was nestled in its lake at the foot of the mountain, looking like something off a tourist postcard, or maybe an advertisement for a day spa. Even from a bird's eye view, it looked amazing.

No one spoke as we tramped through the jungle. I kept the clouds of midges and other biting insects away, but I couldn't do anything about the thorns and scratches we were all collecting from pushing our way through the jungle. But the birds guided me well, and in less than an hour, we stumbled upon an actual path that had been cleared through the thick vegetation. After that, the going was much easier.

Still, the sun was high overhead by the time our path landed us on the edge of the still, green lake. It was roughly crescent-shaped, and we had emerged at the southern end, where the tip of the crescent narrowed into a stream that meandered through the jungle, towards the sea behind us. The house was at the northern end of the lake, though right out in the centre, away from the shore. It perched on stilts like a waterbird, and had jetties poking out from three sides. The stilts were tall enough that there was room beneath the house for someone standing in a boat. Stairs climbed up from each jetty to the house level.

Many large windows looked out on the lake and the green jungle surrounding it. They probably let a cool breeze circulate through the interior, too. There was no obvious front door, unless it was around the other side. Presumably, you just boated out to whichever jetty suited your purposes and climbed up to the house. There were a couple of chimneys, including one above the biggest jetty, which I guessed might be part of the kitchen. The size of that jetty would make it easy to unload foodstuffs for the inhabitants. The house was large enough for there to be many of those—it was easily big enough to accommodate several families. But no smoke rose from any of the chimneys today.

It was probably too bloody hot for cooking.

"No welcoming party," Manannan said, eyeing the house with a frown. Indeed, there was no one in sight, though I might have expected at least some signs of life in a house that big. Someone should be outside fishing, or washing clothes, or something.

Apollo also looked troubled. "Can't you feel it?" he asked me.

"Feel what? I can't feel anything."

"Exactly," he said. "We're close enough now that we ought to be able to feel Athena's divinity."

"And she, ours," Manannan added. "What should we do?"

Apollo, seeing my look of confusion, said, "Normally, in approaching another god's territory, we would get close enough for our presence to be noted, then wait to be invited closer."

I frowned. "You didn't do that when we visited Hestia."

"Hestia's different. She welcomes everyone. Athena is … a little pricklier."

And we didn't want to piss her off—though Apollo and I might have already done so by coming so close. Our initial plan to stay on the beach and let Manannan, a third party, make the approach on our behalf had fallen by the wayside when Jake had collapsed. It was probably too late to be concerned about offending her.

"Maybe she's not home," I said. That would explain why we couldn't feel her divinity. Now that Apollo had mentioned it, I realised I *could* feel something from him and Manannan. It was hard to describe the sensation, exactly—it was like another sense, as if I could feel a vibration in the air, or a taste. Whatever it was, it clung around each of them, and presumably around me, too, though I couldn't feel my own. And I wasn't getting any such feeling from the house across the water.

Apollo sighed. "That would be a massive pain in the arse after we've come all this way."

"Well, let's keep going. At least we can ask her servants where she is."

"Maybe she's only gone out for a walk," Manannan said hopefully.

"Maybe." Though why anyone would want to go walking in such a place, I didn't know. I loved the outdoors, but this was too much outdoors even for me. Forcing my way through that jungle had not been my idea of a good time.

So, we left the shade of the trees and walked down toward the pretty green lake. The water was clear enough to make out individual pebbles in the shallows, but further out, it was hard to see any water at all for the profusion of water lilies that spread across the surface. Pink and purple flowers waved on their stems above the water, and fat green leaves the size of dinner plates carpeted the lake beneath them. Dragonflies danced lazily above the wide, green carpet, and the only sound was the occasional plop of water as a fish broke the surface, rustling the blanket of leaves.

We were halfway around the crescent. I wasn't even looking at the house, too busy admiring the pretty picture made by the blanket of waterlilies, when Jake threw himself at me.

As we went rolling down the slope toward the water, a shot rang out, and then someone opened fire with an automatic weapon.

"Jake!" I shouted, trying to wriggle out from under him, but he wouldn't budge, determined to shelter me with his body. "Get off me!"

We needed to get to cover. We were sitting ducks out here, and I wasn't going to let him die being my human shield. I turned my head, which was the only part of my body I could still move, searching for Apollo and Manannan. Who the hell was firing at us?

An astonishing sight met my eyes. A wall of ice stood between us and the house. Jake saw it, too, and he moved enough for me to shove him away and get up into a crouch. Manannan stood calmly behind the wall, as if this was something that happened every day. Where had all that ice come from? I couldn't even *see* the house through it—it must be ridiculously thick. The sounds of automatic fire were still coming from behind it, and I could see chunks of ice flying up into the air as the bullets hit, but they weren't getting through.

The blanket of waterlilies was sagging now, and the slimy stems underneath the beauty were showing, sticking up at odd angles like creepy fingers. The water level in the lake had dropped considerably. I stood slowly, still awestruck by the wall of ice. It extended all the way from the lake's edge into the jungle. Now that I had a moment to look closer, I could even see pieces of water lily stuck inside it, caught up as Manannan—because it must have been the sea god who had done this—drained the lake to form his protective wall.

Jake got up, too, brushing sand from his pants and not meeting my eyes. I found it telling that his first instinct had been to protect me and not the god he worshipped. And speaking of whom—

"Where's Apollo?" I asked. But even as I spoke, a great sheet of flame blasted into the sky on the far side of the ice wall, and the guns fell silent. "Never mind. I figured it out."

So much for not damaging any of Athena's property—or her people. Not that I could really find it in me to care. If they were going to open fire on us without warning, I had no sympathy for them.

"Sorry," Manannan said. "I meant the wall to protect him, too, but he moved too fast for me."

"It doesn't sound as though he needs any protection," I said drily. Everything on the other side of the wall was suspiciously quiet. Had he killed the whole household? My brother had a bit of a problem holding onto his temper. Probably because he was the god of fire—he couldn't help being a hothead. "I just hope he's left someone alive so we can find out where Athena is."

Jake turned a look of surprise on me. "Do you really think those are Athena's people firing on us?"

Oh. Well, now I felt stupid. It did seem an extreme reaction, even for the household of someone so notoriously antisocial as the goddess of wisdom. "Shit. Not the bloody shadow shapers *again*?"

"We need to get through," Jake said to Manannan, and the sea god nodded. In a rush, the ice wall dissolved, and the water went foaming back into the lake. Jake steadied me as the edges of the torrent surged around our knees.

"I didn't know you could work with fresh water, too," I said to Manannan. The water lilies were now looking very much the worse for wear. Half of the leaves had been ripped off, many of them scattered in sodden piles around our feet, and there was barely a single flower left whole.

"You learn something new every day," Manannan said cheerfully, though his worried face rather belied his tone. "It's all water. A little bit of salt doesn't change the fundamentals."

I followed the direction of his gaze and found Athena's house still perched on its stilts above the lake. Thank heavens for that. It did show a few new scorch marks, however, particularly around a couple of windows that faced our way. The shooters must have been positioned there. There was no sign of them now, but I suspected we would find their blackened corpses once we went inside. Apollo was waiting for us at the water's edge and keeping a watchful eye on the house's empty windows.

"Still no sign of Athena?" I asked as we joined him. I certainly couldn't feel her, but I held onto the possibility that the others might have, being in full control of their divine powers.

"No." His mouth was a grim line. "I don't hold out much hope for her."

I swallowed hard. I was slow today—it took me a moment to understand his meaning. When I did, I looked at Jake in horror. Wordlessly, he reached out and took my hand, his expression as grim as my brother's. There could only be two explanations for the shadow shapers being here. Either Athena was the traitor among the gods and they were her servants, or ... or ...

I didn't want to think about the other possibility. I clutched Jake's hand tighter, unable even to feel pleasure in this small triumph over his religious scruples. The other possibility was making me feel sick to my stomach.

There were no boats on the shore; none even on the lake, as far as I could see. I had no idea how Athena's people were meant to cross the green water to the house, unless they swam, but we had the advantage of a master of watershaping in our party.

"Manannan, if you would," Apollo said, and Manannan waved his hand. A pathway of ice formed from the shore at our feet to the nearest jetty. We stepped onto it and followed him out to the house.

The house felt empty. As we came through the doorway into a large kitchen, I knew instinctively that there was no one alive inside it. What had happened to all Athena's people? A house this size must have required quite a staff to run. The kitchen alone had a bank of ovens and enough counter space to occupy several cooks at once. Where was everyone?

Apollo took the lead down a hallway with several doorways opening off it. There were no doors as such, only curtains for privacy, which were drawn back now to allow what little breeze there was to circulate through the house. He stopped in the doorway of a room that smelled strongly of smoke and roasted meat. I closed my eyes and tried not to breathe through my nose as I realised what kind of meat had been roasted in this room. I caught a glimpse of a charred corpse on the floor by the window, and a twisted hunk of metal that must once have been a gun.

I stayed in the hallway while Apollo went in and inspected the corpse. He only shook his head when he came out again—there was obviously no information to be gleaned from the remains his fire had left. We moved down the hall again, finding two more such rooms, with more blackened bodies in them.

"Do you think they were Athena's?" Manannan asked. He was looking a little green around the gills, as if this demonstration of fireshaping power didn't sit well with him. I couldn't blame him.

Apollo shook his head again and kept moving.

The buzzing of flies should have tipped me off, but I was following Apollo without really thinking, too shocked by the attack and its aftermath to put together what I was hearing with the obvious reason. So it was a shock to me when we entered a large dining room.

The table in the middle of it was large enough to seat twenty or more, but no one was enjoying its hospitality now. All of the dining chairs were pushed back against the wall, out of the way, and on the table lay a body, stretched out, her arms and legs tied to the legs of the table with thick rope. A ragged pile of feathers lay beside her. A thick cloud of flies swarmed the body.

Angrily, I sent them away to find somewhere else to lay their eggs. Once the buzzing mass had lifted, the gaping cavity in the woman's chest was revealed. Her heart had been cut out. And the ragged pile of feathers was the corpse of a magnificent owl, its snowy feathers now soaked in blood.

I knew what that meant. My worst fears had come true. The woman's dark hair fanned out around her head, and I guessed that if her eyes had been open, they would have been a cool grey. I looked at my brother, whose own eyes were full of unshed tears. He'd told me once that he thought Athena's avatar was her owl.

"It's Athena, isn't it?"

He nodded, and Jake's hand tightened on mine. The shadow shapers had cut out her heart and stolen her powers.

11

We searched the house, but it was a half-hearted effort. If the lightning bolt had ever been here, it wasn't here now. There were no other bodies. I hoped that meant that Athena's people had either escaped or been let go once Athena had been killed. But, knowing the shadow shapers, their bodies were probably rotting somewhere in the jungle, or even feeding the fish beneath the mangled water lilies.

We reconvened in the dining room. I couldn't bear to look at Athena's body and that of her poor, crumpled owl, so I gazed out the window at the jungle. It was so beautiful outside, so green and lush and vibrant. It broke my heart that, inside, such awful things had happened. It didn't seem right that death should come in the middle of such a paradise.

Jake came to stand beside me at the window. He held a spoon that he was folding and reforming with his metalshaping power, over and over. Perhaps it soothed him to so easily bring back something that had been destroyed. If only it were that simple with people.

"I don't understand how they could sneak up on her like this," Apollo said behind me, his voice full of frustration. "How did they even get past the bloody statues on the beach?"

"Yes," said Manannan. "You would think that being so isolated, she would have been safe here. She should have had plenty of warning that someone was coming. I imagine those statues deploying would have triggered some kind of warning system here. Unless the shadow shapers flew in, I don't see how she could have been surprised."

"Unless it was someone she knew," Jake said. He was no longer holding my hand, but at least he was close. All I wanted to do was put my head on his chest and cry. We'd been so sure of finding the lightning bolt here. I'd thought our quest to recover Zeus was nearly done. Finally, our world would be put right, and the shadow shapers stopped. Now, it seemed that goal was even further out of reach, and another god lost into the bargain.

No one said anything. We'd probably all been thinking the same thing. It seemed certain proof of our theory that there had to be a traitor among the gods. But we were fast running out of suspects. There just weren't that many of us left. I trusted Apollo and Hades, but could I really trust any of the others? What if it was Poseidon? He'd been the only one who knew where Athena lived. I found it almost impossible to believe, but I didn't dare trust my own instincts anymore. Whoever it was, they were obviously horribly good at hoodwinking people. I couldn't discount anyone, however unlikely.

"How long ago do you think it happened?" I asked.

"Probably a couple of days," said Manannan.

He ought to know, since he saw a lot of dead people in his role as lord of the dead for the Celtic pantheon. Poseidon had been with us for most of the last forty-eight hours, so that probably put him in the clear—unless he'd killed her before he'd brought us here the first time.

"So she was dead all along, when we were trying to get in to see her?" Apollo asked, shaking his head. "If only we'd come sooner."

"Perhaps the shadow shapers were here when you were first trying to approach," Jake said. "And that's why they left a few behind, in case you returned."

I nodded. "That makes sense."

Apollo shook his head. "Something doesn't add up. Guns couldn't have killed any of us. Well, except Jake. But I doubt my Ruby Adept was their target."

I turned away from the window and forced myself to look at Athena's body. My sister's body. Her hair was as dark as mine, her long limbs sunbrowned and strong. She had a warrior's build, with muscled arms and legs. Her left hand, which was closest to me, had callouses on it. They would be from gripping her sword; she was left-handed. An image swam up from the depths of my mind, of her swinging her sword in a practice match, a fierce grin on her face. Her hair was braided down her back, much like Syl's, and sweat ran down her face as she hacked and slashed against the man who faced her. He was good, but barely holding his own against the goddess.

I'd accused her of holding back, and she'd laughed. "How else would I ever get a match against anyone, Arti? *You* won't take me on."

I gasped, returning to the stifling heat and the smell of smoke and death.

Apollo stiffened. "What's wrong?"

"Nothing. I was just … nothing." I'd remembered something, but it was too personal and precious to share. I had so few real memories. Tentatively, I reached for more, but the moment was gone, and the inside of my head as blank as ever. I began worrying at the knot that held my dead sister's arm in place. "We should untie her. We can't leave her like this."

Apollo moved to the other side of the table. Together, we removed the ropes and straightened her body as best we could, laying her hands over the gaping hole in the centre of her chest. I smoothed her dark hair back from her face, and Apollo laid the body of her owl next to her head, snuggled in against her neck. Another sudden flash of memory showed me that same owl perched on her shoulder in life, both of them staring at me with haughty expressions.

"What now?" I asked, looking up at Apollo.

He was staring down at Athena, his eyes bright with unshed tears. "Now, we go."

"Shouldn't we bury her?"

"Leave it to me."

We trooped outside into the full heat of the tropical sun and, once again, Manannan created an ice path for us to cross the lake. When we were back on the shore, Apollo raised his arms and bolts of fire shot forth from his hands, arcing over the water and igniting the roof of the building. He bathed the whole place in fire, working in grim silence, and we stood there for a long time, despite the heat, watching it burn. It seemed a fitting funeral pyre for a goddess.

At last, Apollo lowered his arms, and I slipped my arm around his waist. He laid his across my shoulders and rested his cheek on my hair with a sigh. For the first time, he really felt like my brother, as we shared this grief.

"Our family is shrinking," he said.

"She will be the last," I said. "I promise you."

He dropped a kiss on my hair. "Don't make promises you can't keep, Arti. The shadow shapers are even stronger now. They have Athena's wisdom. They grow stronger all the time, as we diminish. And we are no closer to finding the missing lightning bolt. I begin to despair of ever seeing our father again."

There were tears on his cheeks, and the flames reflected in his eyes as he watched the house burn.

"We can't give up hope now."

"How can we not, when our situation seems so hopeless? Hermes was right to go into hiding when he did. Trying to fight back hasn't helped any of us."

"Athena wasn't fighting back," Manannan pointed out. "She was tucked away here, trying to keep her head down, and they still found her. Seems to me you can't afford to stop fighting now."

"But what can I *do*, Manannan?" He threw a frustrated blast of fire at the house, though the structure was collapsing on its own now, burning pieces falling into the lake. "The shadow shapers have the third lightning bolt. And if you're going to suggest a frontal assault to get it back, you must have rocks in your head. These people are *dangerous*."

"You can't be sure they have it," he said. "You're assuming that Athena had it, but she may not have. You need to find Hermes and ask him. Ask Hera, and anyone else you initially discounted. Don't give up until you're sure, Apollo. There may still be a chance."

"Perhaps even reuniting the piece that Poseidon has with Hestia's would generate enough power to recall Zeus," Jake said. "It's worth a try, my lord."

"Maybe." Part of the house subsided into the lake with a roar of flame and a mighty hiss of steam. Sparks shot up into the air, though none touched the surrounding jungle. Whether that was because the air was so still and heavy or because Apollo wouldn't let them, I wasn't sure. He stared at the house with a face like flint.

I had little hope that Jake's idea would work. There was something about the magic of threes: Zeus's lightning bolt had three parts; Poseidon's trident had three prongs; and my favourite hellhound, Cerberus, had three heads. Each of these three brothers, the three major gods of our pantheon, had an avatar that had three parts. I was pretty sure that all three of those parts had to be functioning to access their full power. United, the parts of the avatar combined to make a whole that was more than their sum.

But, still, it was an idea, and something to be doing. Anything to fight off despair. Because that was getting harder and harder. The odds against us had never been so high. We stayed until the last of the house had crumbled into the water, leaving nothing but the blackened piers that had held it up, protruding from the lake like broken fingers.

Then we turned our backs on Athena's final resting place and began the long trek back to the beach.

❦

Poseidon was waiting for us on the deck of the iceberg, as eager as a dog waiting for its owner to come home. As soon as we were within hailing distance, he shouted, "Well?"

I glanced at Apollo's stony face, and then at Jake and Manannan, and walked faster across the bouncy surface Manannan had created for us. By the time we stepped up onto the iceberg, the sea god was in a fever of impatience.

"I can see by your faces that the news isn't good," he said. "Didn't she have the lightning bolt?"

"She may have," I said. "But if she did, she doesn't any more. She's dead, Poseidon."

His face paled until it almost matched his snowy beard. "Dead?"

"The shadow shapers got there before us," Apollo said. "Let's get away from here while we still can. We'll tell you more inside."

Poseidon needed no second invitation. He had no more interest in meeting the shadow shapers than we did. We were underway immediately, with Manannan's yacht tagging behind like a duckling following its mother. The five of us gathered in a beautiful dining room, complete with massive crystal chandelier hanging over a table covered with a feast of dishes hot and cold.

Unfortunately, I had little appetite. All I could think of was the dining room I'd just been in, and what had been laid out on the table there. My hair smelled of smoke, which didn't help, either. I put some fresh fruit on my plate and nibbled on a couple of grapes, leaving the rest untouched. It looked like the others were similarly affected. Even Poseidon, who hadn't seen what we had, was so shocked at the news of his niece's death that he only picked at a plate of roast meat and vegetables.

Manannan told most of the story, with occasional help from Jake. Jake was sitting beside me, and I was aware that his gaze often rested on my face, but he'd been careful to put some distance between us once we left the site of Athena's former home. Gone was the man who had thrown himself between me and a hail of bullets, the man who'd held my hand. The Ruby Adept was back, in careful control of his emotions.

Not as careful as he might have liked, though. He was still fiddling with the spoon he'd taken from Athena's house, and by now, it bore very little resemblance to the elegant piece of cutlery it had started as.

Apollo said very little, sunk in gloom. For a sun god, his disposition wasn't particularly sunny. If it wasn't for the shining golden hair, he could have given Hades a run for his money as a Lord of the Dead.

When Manannan finished the tale, Poseidon sat staring into his wine for a long time, twirling the delicate stem of his wine glass between his fingers. Losing a god was a terrible shock, since they were never expected to die. This last year had shaken up our pantheon in ways that would take a long time to recover from. We might all end up as gloomy as my twin.

Jake's spoon now looked like a child's first efforts to craft a spoon out of clay, and his face was white.

"Are you all right?" I whispered, leaning closer while the others applied themselves to the task of getting as drunk as possible. Even Manannan looked as though he'd seen a ghost, though his pantheon wasn't affected.

Jake crushed the misshapen spoon into a solid lump and let out a shaky breath. "I can't metalshape."

"What?" My glance flew to his fist, still clenched around the lump of former spoon. I thought he'd been soothing himself by fiddling with it, but instead he'd been testing his power. "Not at all?"

"Barely." He had a tight hold on his emotions, but I could sense the panic beneath the surface.

"You're just tired from all that effort with the statues."

"Maybe."

I could tell he didn't believe that. He'd been saying ever since I'd met him that metalshaping was getting harder—was this the end? If Jake, who'd brought statues to life and crafted an exquisite copy of Apollo's avatar with his power, could no longer even mould a simple spoon shape properly ...

We were in big trouble.

I closed a comforting hand around his clenched one, and he didn't pull away. Time was ticking away even faster now, and the buzzer was about to sound. We didn't have time to sit around mourning; we had to come up with a plan.

I turned to Poseidon, who was still staring morosely into his goblet. "Jake suggested that we should try bringing your piece of the lightning bolt together with Hestia's—"

"No." Poseidon didn't even look up.

"There could be enough power even with only two pieces, to bring Zeus back."

"I said no."

Selling second-hand books had never been this hard. I felt a pang of nostalgia for those less complicated days, when all I had to worry about was whether Erik Anders would find me.

"But why? Sitting here hiding it does nothing. It could work—but you won't know if you won't let us try."

He slammed his free hand on the table, making the wine in everyone's glasses jump. "Are you the traitor, to keep nagging me so? Maybe it would suit your plans to get your hands on the lightning bolt, hmm?"

There was a shocked intake of breath around the room, and Apollo surged to his feet. "That's my sister you're accusing."

"And she's my niece, you golden nincompoop. That doesn't prove she's innocent, does it?"

I took a deep breath to calm my rage. "No, but I would

have thought that rescuing both Apollo and Hades from the shadow shapers might have."

He looked away and shrugged. I'd never met a person before who had so much trouble admitting that other people might be right.

"And I'm not *nagging* you for my own amusement, I assure you. I'm trying to work out what to *do*. We can't just sit here and let the world burn."

"Well, it won't work, anyway, not without all three pieces, and I'm not sending this one back out into danger for anything less than a guarantee of success." He glowered at me, his thick eyebrows drawing together in a menacing fashion. "You forget, my brother sent this to me for a reason. He trusted me to protect it. And protect it is what I will do."

"So, if we find the other piece, you'll let us take this one?"

"If you find the other piece, I'll bring you this one myself. But if you don't, this one isn't leaving my protection."

"Fine." I rose from my chair. "I'll be in my room. Let me know when we get back to Berkley's Bay."

12

It was early in the morning when Poseidon dropped us back at Berkley's Bay, and the streetlights were still on. Apollo and Jake headed for the tiny temple, and I turned my steps towards home.

Though … it wouldn't be home much longer. Given our lack of success in locating the damn lightning bolt, I couldn't ignore Syl's advice any longer. It was time to say goodbye to Berkley's Bay, and so I walked slowly, drinking in the familiar sights with new eyes, trying to commit each one to memory.

There was the mayor's house—not that I would miss that old windbag at all, but I had fond memories of stealing his altarpiece. I probably should have mentioned that to Manannan. The statue had been of him, after all. There was the pub on its corner, where I'd spent so many happy evenings arguing with Hades in his guise as Alberto, or trying to drink Syl under the table. I still hadn't succeeded with that one. Despite her small size, she had the advantage of a shifter metabolism to keep her from getting shit-faced. And here was Tegan's hair salon. The big weretiger was one of my favourite people here in Berkley's Bay. I didn't see as much of her as I'd like already—when would I see her again once I'd left?

And there was the bookshop. I paused, resting my hand against the glass, as if the shop were an animal I was patting. So many happy hours had been spent in there, reading books, arranging shelves, talking books with customers. Syl used to lie right there in the window display, where she could bask in the sun. I'd learned to leave that little patch empty for her, since if I put a book in her spot she'd just bat it out of the way with an imperious paw.

And this was where I'd met Jake, the night Joe's son, Cody, had gone missing. So many strange events had been set in motion that night. I'd seen a god killed, I'd been to the underworld, I'd lost Jake and found him again … and lost him once more. Ridiculous bloody man. How could so much of my happiness be tied up in one person like this? The old Artemis probably would have sneered at me—Apollo had said she rarely even let her lovers sleep over. And here I was, pining for a pair of laughing blue eyes and the feel of his strong arms around me.

Strangest of all, of course, of all the strange things that

had happened in the last few weeks, was that I'd discovered my own divinity, and lost the past I'd thought I had. Unfortunately, nothing had arrived to fill the void yet. *Any time now, brain. A working memory would be kind of handy right now.*

I sighed and opened the discreet door next to the bookshop that led up to our apartment. Of course, then I might truly be a goddess, and I wasn't sure I was ready for that. I climbed the stairs slowly. Joe and Holly's door was right across the landing from ours. I'd miss them, too, and beautiful baby Mireille. They'd been good friends to Syl and me, and the best neighbours anyone could ever hope for. Did goddesses have friends like these?

I opened the door of our apartment quietly, not wanting to disturb Syl—and probably Lucas. He stayed over most nights. Despite all Syl's protests that he was just a fling, I wasn't convinced. I'd seen the way they looked at each other when they thought I wasn't paying attention. I was pretty sure she felt the same way about him as I did about Jake. It didn't always take months and months to fall in love with someone. When you met the right person, love could blossom in a flash.

The lounge room was piled with cardboard boxes, everything we owned packed and ready to go. Not that our "everything" was very much. We hadn't been here long enough to accumulate great heaps of stuff. We had kitchenware, some linen, our clothes, and that was about it. Plus a few books, of course, but even those were a minimum. I tended to read stock from the shop and take it back again when I'd finished.

Something moved in the hallway leading to the bedrooms, and I jumped. Lucas loomed out of the dark, wearing a pair of boxer shorts and nothing else.

"You're back," he said, with undisguised relief. "I thought I heard a noise. What happened? Did you get the lightning bolt?"

"Unfortunately not." I looked around the dark apartment and sighed. Outside, the first glimmerings of light were appearing in the east. My last sunrise in Berkley's Bay. I had always loved that ocean view. "Looks like we'll be moving out today."

"Damn." He came closer and rubbed my shoulder awkwardly. "Are you all right?"

"A little discouraged," I admitted. "That's not even the worst news. Athena's dead."

"Shit. I'll wake Syl."

"No, don't disturb—"

I might have saved my breath; he was already gone. In a moment, Syl stumbled out, wearing one of Lucas's T-shirts. She was so short it came almost to her knees. "Athena's dead? What the hell happened?"

We sat there in the dark while I brought them up to date.

As I spoke, the sun climbed out of the eastern sea in a blaze of orange fire, and the world around us lightened. Before I'd finished the story, Lucas went to the kitchen and started frying bacon and eggs. It was only when I smelled them that I realised how hungry I was. How long had it been since I'd eaten a proper meal? I couldn't even remember.

"What a mess," Syl said when I'd finished. "What are we going to do now?"

"Apollo's going to talk to Hestia and see if she knows where Hera and Hermes are. We can contact him through Winston if we need him—he's going to be lying low. And I—well, I'm pretty much useless without a working memory, so I'm going back to Albany. Maybe I can jog something loose there."

"Albany. That's down south, right?"

"I think so." I wasn't actually sure. "It's up pretty high, lots of forest. You'll like it, I hope. Lots of good hunting."

She gave me a quizzical look. "Lots of good hunting? Like, rodents and birds?"

Where had those words come from? I'd spoken without thinking, but no—I hadn't had a cat's point of view in mind. Rather, I'd been thinking of wild boar and deer, like the one whose head was mounted on the wall of Artemis's lounge room. Of foxes. Fast-moving beasts that would give a good chase to something a little larger than a cat. Something like a goddess of the hunt, for instance.

"Never mind," I said, flustered. Bits of the old me seemed to be leaking back into my subconscious, but there was still nothing there when I reached for it. Maybe that was the secret: to stop trying so hard. "How are we going to shift all these boxes?"

Neither of us had a car. Lucas had his motorbike, but that was hardly an ideal vehicle for moving house. If Winston hadn't landed Joe's truck in the repair shop, we could have used that.

Or, if I had access to Artemis's memories and, presumably, her bank accounts, I could have bought my own damn truck. Even a fleet of trucks. I pushed away a flash of annoyance and bent my mind to the problem at hand. Could we borrow Tegan's little car, perhaps? If all else failed, we could lump them all over to Winston's temple on foot, but I'd hoped to be a little less conspicuous about the fact that I was leaving town.

"Don't worry about that. Lucas can borrow his dad's van."

"But doesn't Ray need it for work?"

She snorted. "As if that matters. Your wish, apparently, is the pack's command. They'd happily carry your shit all the way to Albany on their backs if you asked."

"Seriously?"

"Seriously. They're all on standby in case you need something."

"Wow." I didn't know what else to say.

My stomach rumbled, and Syl laughed. "But first things first. We're not going anywhere until after breakfast."

I got up and followed my nose over to the kitchen, where Lucas was serving generous helpings of bacon onto three plates that were already heaped with eggs and toast. "Good plan. Bacon always comes first."

❧

An hour later, Winston had finished ferrying us and all the boxes to the little temple in the woods. It was as pretty as I remembered it, with the early morning sun slanting through the trees outside. The glass was so clean it was as if it wasn't there, and the open door added to the illusion by letting in the mingled smells of pine and eucalypt, fresh and clean.

"I guess we won't see you for a while," I said to Winston. I'd miss him; he'd quickly become a friend. "We could be in hiding for quite a while, until we figure out where the third piece of the lightning bolt is."

"True friends are always in our hearts," he said, giving me a funny little half-bow, as if he knew he'd get in trouble if he tried anything more formal. "Even when they are not in our lives."

We said goodbye, and he jumped back to Berkley's Bay. I felt a momentary longing for the salt breezes of home before I grabbed the nearest box and headed for the door. "It's not far to the cottage. This way."

Lucas and Syl both sniffed appreciatively as we came outside. Their shifter noses could probably detect more detailed aromas of animals and plant life that I couldn't pick out. I breathed in deeply and caught a hint of something sweet and floral—a few late freesias bowed their heads in the shade under a big, red-barked gum to the side of the path.

I set off toward the cottage, Lucas and Syl close behind. Lucas paused at the point where the path to the cottage branched off from the main one. He frowned as he looked along the path that led to the gym and sniffed the air suspiciously.

"What's down that way? It smells … industrial."

"Just the gym. You're probably smelling the car park, or the air conditioning units. It's a big building, ugly as sin. Looks like a warehouse." His eyebrows rose, and I hurried on. "But the cottage isn't like that at all. You'll like it. Come on."

We struck out down the path to the cottage, and it soon came into view, nestled among the trees with the morning sun sparkling on the front windows.

"It's cute," Syl said as we climbed the stairs to the wide veranda. "Very secluded. You wouldn't know it was here."

"That's good," Lucas said, eyeing the bush all around. "Though I'll need to scout around and get a feel for the land. I don't like that the gym's so close. Anyone could wander over here."

"I don't think anyone knows it's here, apart from Ophelia and a couple of Artemis's close friends. No one from the gym would have a reason to go wandering off into the bush."

He didn't look entirely convinced. I opened the front door and his eyebrows drew together into an alarming frown. "That wasn't locked? What kind of security is that?"

"Uh … I think it was." I glanced down at the door handle, unsure. Had it been unlocked, or had it opened to an unconscious use of my powers? Ophelia had offered Apollo a key last time, so she'd certainly expected it to be locked. "I might have magicked it open."

He rolled his eyes and shouldered his way past me, clearly determined to sweep the place for threats before I got inside. I sighed and followed him in. If he didn't cool it with the over-protectiveness, sharing a house could quickly become problematic.

I was carrying the box that contained most of my clothes—which just proved how limited my wardrobe was. It wasn't a very big box. I took it into the front bedroom and dumped it on the bed. There was plenty of hanging space still left in Artemis's wardrobe. When I opened the door to check, a faint scent of lemons wafted out from the clothes already hanging there.

Lucas and Syl's footsteps tramped past, going to collect more boxes from the little temple, but my gaze was caught by the photo at the bedside, of Artemis with Ophelia and the other laughing woman. I still had no bloody idea who she was.

I picked up the photo and studied Artemis's face. It wasn't so different from the one I wore now: a slightly different shaped nose, eyes bigger and darker, lips slightly fuller. Her cheekbones were to die for, high and sharp as knives. My own face looked like the budget version. I checked it out in the mirror, remembering that odd moment last time I had been here, when, for a second, I had taken on the appearance of the goddess.

Nope, it was still just me, tanned a warmer brown than the moon goddess. My own eyes, my own lips, and, sadly, nothing at all striking about my cheekbones. Could I change that? I'd only done it accidentally before.

What had Apollo said? His instructions had been particularly unhelpful, as I recalled. Something about if you wanted to, it just happened, like moving your arm without having to think about the mechanics. *Thanks, bro.*

I frowned at my reflection. Did I want to? The prospect was no longer as horrifying as it had been at first. I guess I'd had some time to get used to the idea of being a goddess, though most of the time, I still felt like an imposter. But I'd opened the front door with my power. I'd saved

Cerberus and Hades and all of us with my power, back when we'd been trapped in that shadow shaper house in Brenvale. And, so far, I still hadn't stopped caring for my friends or become a stranger or a bitch. Well, that last one might depend on who you asked. But I hadn't stopped being *me*.

I was still scared of what might happen if I ever recovered my missing memories, but that didn't seem likely to happen any time soon. Fiddling with my appearance surely wouldn't affect anything on the inside, at least. My hand strayed to the silver chain around my neck, and I pulled the little bow-and-arrow charm out of my shirt, clenching it in my fist.

"Okay, let's give this a go."

I shut my eyes. Apollo had said there wouldn't be any sliding of features, and I certainly hadn't noticed anything weird when he'd demonstrated on Winston's doorstep that time, but it made me feel oddly self-conscious to watch my own face so intently. I took a deep breath. Should I say something? *Abracadabra? Face swap?* My cheeks began to warm, but that was embarrassment, not any kind of change. I opened one eye and peeked, just to be sure, but I was still me.

I could hear Lucas and Syl's voices as they carried boxes in, moving up and down the hallway. Any minute now, they would start wondering why I wasn't helping. If I was going to do this, I'd better get it over with. Syl would laugh her head off if she came in and found me standing in front of the mirror with my eyes shut.

I really want to change. I really want to change. I opened my eyes. Nothing, dammit. I sighed and relaxed my death grip on the little bow and arrow. It had left an imprint dug into my palm.

I looked down at the photo again. Artemis looked so happy, and a fierce longing flooded me. I wanted that happiness, that ease she had, secure in her life with her friends.

The little charm warmed briefly in my grasp. I looked up, hardly daring to hope, actually holding my breath.

The goddess's face looked out at me from the mirror.

I gasped with shock, and instantly, my own face returned.

Lucas stuck his head in the door, perhaps alarmed by my gasp, but merely looked around with interest when he saw there was nothing wrong.

"Nice room," he said. "Ours is a little bigger—are you sure you don't want to swap?"

"Of course not. There's two of you—you should have the bigger room." Besides, this was Artemis's choice. Despite the fact that I couldn't access her memories and had no way of knowing why she'd chosen this room over the larger one, I preferred it, too. I liked the view out the big front windows onto the green of the bush, and the soft green paint on the walls. It felt like a very restful room. I could tell I would sleep well here.

"Cool. Well, Syl's started unpacking the kitchen boxes, so if you ever want to be able to find anything again ..."

"Yeah." I put the photo back in its place on the bedside chest. "I'll come and help."

I checked my face in the mirror before I left the room, though, just to be sure I was wearing the right one. That was so weird. It hadn't felt any different. I stroked my cheek as I followed Lucas's broad back down the short hallway into the kitchen. Those cheekbones were *awesome*.

"Pots and pans here?" Syl asked, busy filling up a deep drawer beside the hotplate with our collection of cookware as I walked in.

"Sure." I figured she'd put them where she wanted them regardless of what I said, despite the fact that I'd always done the cooking. She'd spent most of our time in Berkley's Bay living in cat form, anyway. Lately, it seemed to be Lucas who was wielding the cooking implements, which was fine by me, even though it meant we had a lot more meat in our diet than before. But hey, everything tasted better when someone else cooked it.

The kitchen, though not large, was very modern, a fact I hadn't really taken in last time I'd been here. Everything gleamed in stainless steel, including the fridge, which had one of those ice dispensers built into the door. We'd really come up in the world with this move. Our apartment in Berkley's Bay had been cheap, but nearly as old as the gods. To light the oven, you had to turn on the gas, throw a match into its depths, and hope you didn't get blown across the kitchen. I could see we wouldn't have that problem here. The oven was wide, and the door didn't even creak when I opened it. Plus, the inside was just as shiny as the outside.

Syl had already made quite a dint in the number of boxes stacked in the middle of the floor. I opened another and started liberating our assortment of mugs from their wrappings, stacking them into one of the upper cupboards. There were several mugs already in there. Just as well they were big cupboards. I opened a couple more doors, hunting for plates and bowls, and soon found them. Again, there was still room for our meagre collection.

I'd just filled our kettle and set it boiling when Lucas raised his head, sniffing the air. "Are you expecting someone?"

I opened my mouth to say no, when the front door slammed open, rebounding off the wall behind it. A large figure loomed in the doorway, and Lucas automatically took a step forward, placing himself between us and whoever had come calling so noisily.

"Who the hell are you?" he growled.

"That's just what I was about to ask," the figure growled back.

13

I recognised that voice, and breathed out in relief. "It's okay, Lucas."

"She's a wolf," he said, still holding himself in readiness to attack, his voice full of warning.

"I know." Gently, I pushed him aside. "Come in, Ophelia."

Syl glanced uncertainly at me as the big werewolf stalked down the hall and into the kitchen. Ophelia was certainly an imposing figure. I'd thought so when Apollo took me to meet her, and she'd been smiling then. Now her face was like flint, her posture as hostile as Lucas's.

Her eyebrows shot up as she took in the boxes full of our belongings and the open cupboards we were stacking them into. Then her gaze came to rest on my face, black and piercing. There was no welcoming smile this time. "I don't care if you're Apollo's friend, you have no right to be in this house. Get out."

Lucas stiffened, and she spared him a considering glance. Probably calculating her chance of taking him in a fight. She'd clearly already dismissed Syl and me as any kind of threat.

"And take all this shit with you," she added. "How *dare* you think you can just move in here? Just because you saw it was empty, I suppose, and thought to take advantage of it."

Her dark eyes began to glow yellow, a sign that her wolf was close to the surface. The hands she held at her sides were clenched into fists; no sign of claws yet, but they wouldn't be far behind.

"It's not what you think," I said. "Why don't we all sit down and have a cup of tea while I explain it to you?"

Now I wished that I had let Apollo tell her who I was. Then we wouldn't have had this problem. But I'd hoped to have a chance to settle in before I had to face this conversation. I'd envisaged sitting her down in her office at the gym at a time of my choosing to explain the whole mess, not suddenly being faced with a hostile werewolf about to turn on me. But hey, at least if she did, I could speak to her mind to mind. That ought to convince her.

Not that we wanted it to get that far, of course. I held out my hands in a placatory gesture as the kettle built up steam and began to whistle behind me, the water bubbling merrily inside.

I backed away toward the cupboard where I'd just put the mugs. "What kind would you like? Black or herbal? We have peppermint, and I think camomile, too."

"You can shove your peppermint tea right up your arse!" she roared. "Get out!"

"Ophelia. We have Artemis's permission to be here."

She took a deep breath, controlling herself with an effort. "You're lying."

But her voice was calmer, with a wistful note that said she really wanted to believe me. I knew I had her attention and at least a few minutes to state my case.

I gestured at the dining table. "Take a seat."

She hadn't said what kind of tea she preferred, so I opted for camomile. It was meant to be calming, right? She needed all the help she could get in that department. She sat, but her whole body still quivered with a righteous fury that was ready to boil over if my explanations didn't meet with her approval.

Syl helped me make the tea, her movements small and careful, as if she was trying to make herself as inoffensive as possible. Lucas refused to sit, hovering between us and the dining table, getting underfoot, while glaring daggers at the other werewolf.

I carried Ophelia's tea over and set it on the table in front of her. As I bent over, my bow-and-arrow charm swung out of the neck of my top.

Ophelia gasped and surged to her feet, shoving the chair back with a screech. "Where did you get that?"

Shit. Looked like I was going to have to talk even faster now. She obviously recognised it and knew its significance.

"It's mine." I stared into her eyes, though I had to look up to do it as she loomed over me.

"It belongs to Artemis," she ground out.

"Yes." I closed my hand around the bow and arrow and let the power within it surge. Bright golden light filled the kitchen, so bright I squinted against it and Syl threw up a hand to shade her eyes. Ophelia didn't twitch a muscle, though she swallowed hard as the full-size bow and quiver appeared in my hands.

Her eyes sought mine, confusion and a desperate pleading warring in their depths. She drew in a deep breath, sniffing the air as she had done the first time we'd met. Once again, my scent seemed to confuse her. "But you're not … you're not her."

"A couple of weeks ago, I would have agreed with you. It's a long and bizarre story, I'm afraid, but the short version is that Artemis took human form in order to go on a truly epic hunt, where she needed to disguise her divinity from the prey. In the process, she lost her memory and became … well, me. So, we're both right, in a way. I'm not the same Artemis you knew. But I am her."

Doubt hardened into suspicion in her eyes. "You expect me

to believe that you're the goddess, but you've lost your memory? So if I ask you to prove who you are by telling me something that only she and I would know, you can't. How very convenient."

Lucas stirred behind me, but I didn't dare take my eyes from Ophelia's face to check on him. He'd better stay out of this and leave her to me. Her gaze didn't flicker from mine either. It was as if we were the only two people in the room.

Time to try my new party trick. I focused on my need, my longing, just as I had earlier in the bedroom. I knew I'd succeeded when all three of them gasped.

"I didn't know you could do that," Syl breathed.

Ophelia chewed at her lower lip, doubt still warring with hope in her expression. She'd make a terrible poker player. "Okay, so you look like her. I'm not denying you've got some kind of power. But ..." She sniffed again. "You don't smell right."

Typical werewolf. She trusted the evidence of her nose more than that of her eyes. What else could I do to convince her? Get a signed deposition from Apollo and Hades? I was pretty sure they hadn't heard of birth certificates back in ancient times. That probably wouldn't *smell right* either.

"A person's scent is made up of a dozen different things," Lucas said stiffly. "The kind of foods they usually eat, the detergent they wash their clothes in, their brand of soap and shampoo, their deodorant—"

"I know all that," Ophelia snapped.

"It's all right, Lucas," I said. "Let's all just sit down."

I sank into a chair and, after a moment, so did Ophelia. At least she seemed ready to listen now. Lucas and Syl joined us at the table, though Lucas didn't touch his mug, as if he wanted to keep his hands free. Or maybe he just preferred coffee. I sighed and scrubbed at my face.

Then I looked at my hand. Still mine, with my usual tan. And I'd been looking up at Ophelia, when Artemis was about the same height as her, if that photo in her bedroom could be believed. So I needed to go further. Artemis was more than a set of facial features. She was a body, a certain skin colour, a particular smell that was unique to her. That hint of lemon that still clung to her clothes in the wardrobe.

I quailed at the thought, but then I reminded myself of what Apollo had said. It was easy. You thought of what you wanted, and it just happened. Maybe I hadn't wanted enough. And maybe if I stopped fighting the idea of godhood, my memories would come back and I might even remember something useful, something to help us all in our struggle.

I met Ophelia's lost, hopeful gaze again, and my heart went out to her. She wanted her friend back. Syl had freaked the other day when I'd only been missing for twenty-four hours. I couldn't imagine how much more Ophelia must have suffered. Artemis had been gone so long, without a word in all that time. Ophelia didn't even know whether her friend was dead or alive. Maybe I couldn't give her Artemis's memory of her and their real relationship, but at least I could get the outward trappings right. She deserved that much, at least.

Impulsively, I reached out and covered her big hand with my own. She started but didn't draw away. My other hand closed on my bow, drawing both power and comfort from the familiar weapon. Maybe my brain had forgotten everything, but my body remembered the bow. I stared into her dark eyes and focused on doing this for her, for setting at least one thing in my crazy world right.

I felt nothing more than a slight, tingling warmth in my chest, but now I could look Ophelia directly in the eye. When I glanced down at our hands, there was an even greater contrast between her ebony one and my pale one on top of it. She drew in a deep breath, and I looked up to find her dark eyes glistening with unshed tears.

"It really is you," she breathed, and then she was up again, and dragging me to my feet with her. She crushed me in a fierce bear hug, and I felt her tears wet on my cheek.

We may have been the same height now, but there was an astonishing power in those werewolf muscles. I tried to wriggle, but she'd left me no room.

"Ophelia," I gasped. "You're crushing me. I can't breathe!"

Reluctantly, she released me, but only to hold me at arm's length while she examined every inch of me. I was kind of interested in doing that myself, though I figured now wasn't the time to excuse myself and go check out my reflection. I could see my arms had more muscle definition, and I could tell I was taller, but the rest would have to wait. For now, the joy on the werewolf's face commanded my attention.

"I can't believe it," she said, a delighted grin transforming her expression. "I thought you were dead! Man, I should kill you myself for running off like that without a word to anyone."

"Yeah, sorry about that. I guess she thought it was for the best."

"She?"

"Me. I mean, Artemis." Some of the joy faded from the werewolf's face as I struggled to find the right words. "It gets confusing. Sometimes it's easier to think of her as a separate person, since I don't actually remember being her."

Ophelia frowned and sat down again, folding her hands on the table in front of her in an expectant attitude. "Okay, I think I'm ready for that long and bizarre story now."

❦

I was getting so much practice at telling this stupid story, now, that the telling itself didn't take more than half an hour, but Ophelia's reactions and questions took a lot longer. Plus, she then wanted to fill Artemis in on everything that had happened since the goddess had disappeared, which included giving me potted histories of everyone she thought I should remember.

The day sped past in unpacking and talking, and by the time evening rolled around, my head was whirling, full of new names and facts that I was sure I'd never remember. The sheer amount of information exhausted me. I had to call a halt and kick her out, though she didn't leave without extracting a promise that I would meet her at the gym bright and early for our regular sparring session. It sounded like way too much work for first thing in the morning, but I didn't want to disappoint her, so I agreed and fell into bed with relief.

It was still dark when my alarm went off next morning, and I was seriously regretting my charitable impulses, but I hauled myself up and dragged out a daggy old pair of shorts and a T-shirt. I didn't actually own any exercise gear, per se. Exercise wasn't something that I'd ever had to seek out in my old life in Berkley's Bay—it just seemed to form a natural part of my day. With a beach like that at your doorstep, practically beckoning you to take long walks, and everything in the small town within walking distance, I had always seemed to be moving. Even in the bookshop, I was rarely still, stacking and rearranging shelves, finding books for customers or just pacing around while I chatted.

Artemis had exercise clothes: slim black tights and little midriff tops in soft, breathable fabric. They were neatly folded in the drawer I'd just opened. I chewed my lip as I stared at them—I'd slipped back into my own appearance some time in the night, and I felt weird about appropriating the goddess's wardrobe. My own clothes felt more natural. And yet … hadn't I decided I wasn't going to fight it anymore? I *was* the goddess.

I put back the shorts and T-shirt and pulled on the tights and crop top instead.

With my bow and arrows back in their miniaturised form around my neck, I struck out on the narrow path to the gym. The forest all around was the grey of very early morning, when it was no longer night but not quite day yet, either. I let my senses spread out around me, checking with all the little life forms around me. Some were waking up to start their day, like the kookaburras perched in a gum tree above, their raucous laughter splitting the early silence; others were just bedding down after a night of hunting or feeding. A possum blinked sleepily in a hole in a tree trunk off to my right, and a mother fox returned to her cubs, ready to sleep away the daylight hours with a full stomach. All around me were birds, rats, mice, snakes, rabbits, and insects of many different kinds. The bush teemed with life, most of it well-hidden.

The use of my familiar power settled me. So much was

changing, but the little sparks of animal life were old companions, and reaching out to them felt as natural as breathing. Out of habit, I checked the interior of the gym as I rounded the blank side of the building, but found nothing bigger than a cockroach inside. It was almost a shame my power didn't extend to sensing humans; it would have been so useful.

There were already more than a dozen cars in the car park, despite the early hour. The automatic doors slid open as I approached, and a rush of cool air replete with the scent of sweat greeted me as I stepped inside. The fresh air outside had smelled immeasurably better, but I'd probably be grateful for the air conditioning once I'd worked up a sweat of my own.

"Morning!" the girl at the desk piped cheerfully.

I nodded but kept going, heading for Ophelia's office. I opened the door, but there was no one inside. While I hesitated in the corridor, a woman, freshly showered, her wet hair smelling of apple shampoo, stepped out of the change rooms.

"Are you looking for Ophelia?" she asked. "She'll be warming up in the training hall. Along the hallway and down the stairs."

"Thanks." I took the stairs she'd indicated, my steps slowing as I neared the bottom.

What was I doing here? I didn't want to spar with

Ophelia. She'd expect a goddess's reflexes and get only mine. I'd walk out of here a mass of bruises. And I should be saving my energies for hunting down the shyer members of my own family. We had to find that damned lightning bolt. I had no time to waste in a gym, of all places.

By the time I reached the bottom step, I'd almost talked myself into hightailing it out of there. The only thing stopping me was the certainty that Ophelia would come looking for me if I didn't show up.

I sighed. Might as well get it over with.

I pushed open the door into the training hall. Ophelia was lounging against a wall, crunching on an apple, watching two other women circle each other warily. She looked up and smiled when I came in, but the other two didn't take their eyes off each other. The taller one feinted toward the other, but her opponent merely slid sideways, not taking the bait.

Ophelia straightened and tossed her apple toward a nearby bin as I approached. "I'm going to get dizzy if you two don't stop going round in circles and start actually fighting soon."

The shorter woman grinned, tossing her long ponytail over her shoulder, but again, neither of them stopped watching her opponent. A couple more feints, and then the taller one leapt into action, throwing punches and kicks that her long-haired opponent barely managed to block.

They were both moving so fast I could barely keep track of the blows and the clever twists and turns. Ponytail tried to sweep the other's feet, but she jumped right over the incoming leg, and Ponytail had to scramble out of the way.

I glanced at Ophelia; she was watching it all with keen interest, a little smile playing around her mouth. I hoped she didn't expect me to perform at this standard, or I was toast.

I leaned back against the wall, giving the sparring duo plenty of room. An all-too-familiar song came over the loudspeakers and I rolled my eyes as the guy started his whine about how sexy Lexi was. Seriously? Again? Someone here needed a major readjustment in their musical tastes.

Before I could sigh more than once, the song cut off right in the middle of the chorus, and a new one I hadn't heard before cut in. It seemed to have started partway through, as there was no introduction, just a woman's voice singing, *Look up, look at meeeee*. Weird, but anything was preferable to walking around all day with sexy bloody Lexi stuck in my head. Just as I was relaxing, the music changed again, and sexy bloody Lexi was back—until it wasn't. Again, the woman shrieked, *Look up, look at meeeee*.

I glanced at Ophelia. "What's wrong with your sound system? Why does it keep playing pieces of different songs like that?" The music kept switching between the sexy Lexi song and the other one, repeating the same two phrases over and over again, one from each song.

She frowned, glancing up at the speaker. "I don't know. It's not supposed to. I'll have to get Jamie to look at it. The clients will go crazy if they hear nothing but 'Lexi, look up' repeated all day."

But no sooner had she spoken than the music got over its strange hiccup, and a new song came on, something with an upbeat tempo and no odd stopping and starting.

"Must have been a temporary glitch," she said, returning her attention to the sparring match in front of us.

But mine was caught by what she'd said. Jammed together like that, those two alternating songs had been repeating "Lexi, look up". But until she'd said it, I'd been too focused on my loathing for that stupid Lexi song to realise it.

Could it have been a message for me? Zeus had found stranger ways to communicate with me before.

Lexi, look up. But at what? What did he want me to see? The ceiling? Nothing exciting up there, just regular fluorescent lights and some exposed pipes. The speaker? The girl power sign on the far wall? It was a poisonous bright green, but otherwise unremarkable. At least it wasn't pink. Although, with its jagged lettering, that exclamation mark looked almost like a—

Zeus's balls! I lurched upright, heart pounding. The short woman with the ponytail took down her taller opponent at last, crouching over her with her knee in the other's back, then stepped back as her opponent conceded with a laugh.

Ophelia shot me a concerned glance. "Are you all right? You look like you've seen a ghost."

Not a ghost. A goddamned lightning bolt, hidden right there in plain sight.

It was so brazen—surely it couldn't be? But why else would Zeus have nudged me to look up? It had to be. Artemis had some balls to just bung it on a wall where anyone could see it like that. Yet here it was, safe.

The two sparring partners bowed to each other and then to Ophelia. I barely noticed as they collected towels and headed out the door, too intent on that jagged exclamation mark. I couldn't feel the zing of its power. But then, I hadn't felt the power of the one Poseidon had, either, until he'd withdrawn it from the wall of ice. Maybe I needed to be closer. It was a big room.

I strode across the floor toward the sign.

"Hey, where do you think you're going?" Ophelia protested, assuming I was following the other two out the door. "It's our turn now."

"Have you got a ladder?" I asked. "A big one—tall enough to reach the sign?"

If this was truly what I thought, our troubles were over. Poseidon would stop huddling over his like a mother hen, and we could take them both to Hestia, to be reunited with the one she had. If her theory was correct, together, they would have enough power to coax Zeus out of the wires and back into the land of the living.

A tingle of power swept over my skin as I passed the midpoint of the room, and I clenched my fists in triumph. Yes! I had found the missing lightning bolt. We could get Zeus back and, together, we would wipe out the damned shadow shapers. I could hardly contain my excitement.

"Are you drunk? Why do you want to climb up there? If you can't see it well enough from here, I reckon you need your eyes checked." Ophelia sniffed beside my face, making a show of checking for the smell of alcohol.

In response, I threw my arms around her and laughed. "Just get me the ladder, okay? Pretty please? I promise it will be worth it."

She gave me the side-eye, but trudged out of the room, and soon returned with an extendable ladder over one strapping shoulder. She set it against the wall and held it while I shimmied up, still beaming with delight. Man, if every day at the gym was this good, I'd get up at sparrow fart every day with no complaints. This close, the lightning bolt was practically singing to me.

I touched it and a surge of power blew me backwards off the ladder. My body slammed into the floor and the world went dark.

14

A full moon hung in the sky, huge and silver, its light painting the forest around me with magic. Werewolves howled, raising their snouts to the brilliant orb, then hunkered down on their bellies in obeisance as I walked among them. My steps were sure in the dark, as sure as theirs, my connection to the creatures of the night allowing me to see as well as they—even to see through their eyes, riding inside their heads, if I so chose. I was queen of the night, mistress of the hunt, and all animals bowed to my power, but werewolves most of all.

They were my creations, my beloved children, my endless delight. Together, we flowed through the forest, their golden eyes on me, watching for my commands. My hands brushed their heads as I passed, their fur the only soft thing about them. They were claw and fang; they were mighty hearts and legs that could run forever; they were raw cunning and merciless death.

They were the perfect hunting companions.

Another place, another time: Apollo sat across from me in a tiny rustic tavern. Through the open door, a vista of wide, blue sky and a town full of white buildings cascading down a steep hill to the glorious azure ocean. It was hot, and the light was bright and unforgiving outside, but here in the blessed shade of the tavern, we hunched over our drinks while my brother poured out a tale of woe. I stared into the depths of my wine, my blood boiling with the need for revenge …

I stared into my wine in another pub, a modern building in a big city. Outside, the roar of traffic, of horns and sirens, clamoured—but inside, slow jazz was playing, and Brianna and Claire were attempting to outdrink each other while Ophelia roared encouragement, pounding her big fists on the table.

"Artemis! Join us! Tonight, we celebrate."

I looked up, grinning at the enthusiasm in her dark eyes. "What are we celebrating again?"

"Brianna finally dumped that loser she was going out with," Claire announced, while Brianna looked up at the sound of her name, her eyes bleary but full of a new purpose that had been missing a while. My heart filled with a fierce love for my friends.

Friends. Lovers. A cheap hotel room, the walls paper thin, so thin I could feel the vibration as big trucks rumbled by on the highway outside. The room smelled of stale cigarettes, and the sheets were rough against my naked skin, but none of it mattered. Only his tanned arms wrapped around me, his lips roaming my sweaty skin. He smiled down at me, the corners of his eyes crinkling in that way I loved, and I wanted this moment to go on forever.

"Forever is a long time," Persephone said, eyes downcast.

I sat with my friend beneath a flowering magnolia in a beautiful garden, each rich, rosy bloom the size of my two hands cupped together. The fake sun of the underworld shone down on Persephone's bright head, caressing the curves of her lovely face and pooling in her hands which tore restlessly at a flower. Petals rained down into her lap as she systematically shredded the bloom, her fingers the only things moving in all this unnatural beauty.

The underworld always put me slightly on edge. The palace and its surrounds were adorned with trees and bushes and flowerbeds bursting with blooms, so artfully arranged that they almost perfectly mimicked the real thing—but only almost. They weren't real. They weren't *alive*. No bees buzzed from flower to flower, no breeze disturbed the branches above our heads, or set the grasses to rustling. When I reached out with my power, not a single animal mind greeted me: no mice, beetles, dragonflies, crickets; no lizards, snakes, birds; none of the larger animals, like foxes, rabbits, moles, cats—nothing. Only when the hellhound

Cerberus was in residence could I feel anything even approximating an animal mind in Persephone's home.

It was the land of the dead, and it truly was dead.

Persephone was never meant for a place like this. If sunshine could solidify and become a person, that person would be Persephone. She was meant for grassy meadows beneath the arch of the sky, for running barefoot with flowers in her hair. Today, even her dress was sombre, a blue so dark it was almost black, buttoned right up to her neck.

"Will you leave him?" I asked.

She glanced at me uncertainly, a brief dart of summer-blue eyes, then back to shredding the flower. "I know you care deeply for him."

"I know you do, too."

She sighed. "Yes, I do. But forever is too long to be with the same person. And it's way too long to spend half your life in a place like this."

I'd envied her once, when she and Hades had first fallen in love. She had found love with a fellow god. They could be together forever and not have to bear the pain of losing the people they loved, as the rest of us who gave our hearts to mere mortals did. They'd been together for centuries, the one great constant I could point to and say, *See? It's possible for gods to truly love.*

"He'll be heartbroken."

She lifted her chin. "Yes. And so will I. But we'll both be happier, in the end."

In the end, my one true love is the moon. Anticipating moonrise is like the nervous excitement before a big date, or the moment just before you kiss someone for the very first time, full of spark and promise. And then the moon rises, and my power explodes, shooting through my body like champagne fizzing through my veins. It doesn't matter where I am—whether I can see the moon or not, inside a building or out under the stars—I feel that same thrill as she clears the horizon. Only in the underworld do I lose that connection with the ultimate source of my power.

"Power is everything," Zeus said, his bushy eyebrows drawing together in a fearsome frown. "It's the only game worth playing."

"Maybe I don't want to play anymore."

"You can't spend your whole life cavorting in the forest with your werewolf toys."

"Better than spending it running around, seducing every woman I see."

There was more shouting after that, but I was used to my father shouting at me. It happened nearly every time I saw him. The only one of his children Zeus was ever happy with was Athena, who could do no wrong in his eyes.

Athena shouted sometimes, too. Mostly when I "borrowed" her owl. I don't know, but if I'd been the goddess of wisdom, I might have made a smarter choice of avatar than something another goddess had full control over, even if that other goddess was my sister.

Sisters. Friends. A thousand faces rushed past my inner eye: women I'd known and loved over the centuries, some even dearer to me than my own sister. Men, too. Friends, lovers, even enemies. I lay there, peripherally aware that my body was stretched out on the padded rubber matting of the training hall, stunned by the flow of images. Of memories.

They say your life flashes before your eyes when you're about to die—was this it? But it went on so long, image after image, a parade of people and places stretching right back through time, encompassing the rise and fall of cities, of whole civilisations, even.

Through it all, I remained.

I, Artemis, as constant as the moon.

At last, it stopped, and I opened my eyes. Ophelia, my drinking buddy and companion of many hunts, had just let go of the ladder, her mouth open in a shout. She hadn't had time to do more; the whole thing had taken less than a second. My whole life, my *self*, returned to me in the blink of an eye.

I sat up and held out my hand. She grasped it in hers and hauled me to my feet.

"Don't panic, O." I grinned as her mouth fell open at the familiar nickname. "I'm back."

15

Ophelia came with me back to the cottage, too excited to let me out of her sight now that I was back for real, though I still wore Lexi's face. I'd grown used to it over these last months. It felt comfortable. And the gods knew I'd worn plenty of different faces in my long life.

As we walked the short distance through the trees, my mind brushed against those of the animals hidden in the greenery—such a familiar feeling, and yet so different now that I had my memories back. Richer, somehow. I was aware of them in a way I'd never been before. I felt more alive, more *awake*. The memories of a thousand hunts filled my mind.

At least now I knew that I did play fair—I'd never used this connection to hunt them. For hunting, I relied on my physical skills alone. I was aware as never before of the connections between all living things, and why hunting was sometimes necessary. There was a balance to life that must be preserved. As the apex predator in the system, the goddess of the hunt, that was my role.

I was grateful that Ophelia didn't speak. I was still coming to terms with the door that had opened in my mind, and all the information that had been hidden on its other side. It was a lot to take in, and I moved in something of a daze, Ophelia at my side, just as we had done so many times before. She had made sure to pick the opposite side from the lightning bolt I carried, though.

She'd tried to talk me out of climbing that ladder again, after what had happened the first time, but there was no way I was leaving it on that wall now that I'd found it.

"I'll be fine," I had said. "That little zap was just what I needed to clear the cobwebs away. I'll be ready for it this time."

But there'd been no need; the lightning bolt was as quiet as a sleeping baby, as if Zeus had known that I needed something—a sudden jolt of power—to shake my recalcitrant memories free, and now the bolt's work was done. It only took a moment to detach it from its place on the wall. I carried it down the ladder cradled against my heart as if it were the most precious thing in the world— and, right then, it probably was. I held in my hands the key to the ultimate defeat of the shadow shapers.

It had lost its poisonous green colour now it had been

separated from the sign, and glowed with a soft white radiance. Like moonlight. It hummed quietly against my skin, a pleasant tingle of power. It was about the same size as the one Poseidon had, so I figured it was the other side piece of Zeus's three-pronged lightning bolt.

We followed the sound of Lucas's voice down the short hallway to the kitchen. For once, he wasn't cooking, but lounging at the table, his chin propped on one fist. He sat up straighter as we entered and nodded stiffly to Ophelia. She nodded back, and I grinned at their careful werewolf acknowledgements.

"How's your morning been?" I asked, laying the lightning bolt down on the table.

Lucas's eyes widened as he stared at it.

Syl had her back to me. She was standing in front of the open fridge, inspecting its contents. "It would be better if we had anything decent to drink here."

"It's a bit early in the day for beer, isn't it?" I asked, wrapping my arms around her from behind and giving her an almighty squeeze.

"I meant milk, doofus," she said, squirming. "Get off! What are you doing?" Like most cats, Syl only accepted displays of affection under her own terms.

"Giving you a hug. Doofus."

"What for?"

"Nothing. I just love you." I was lying. It wasn't nothing—

it was sheer relief at finding that I still cared for her just as much now as I had before I got my memories back. I hadn't suddenly turned into a cold, hard goddess. I was still essentially me. A hardier, superpowered version of me, but me all the same.

She succeeded in wriggling out of my arms, and her eyes widened as she caught sight of what was lying on the table. "What the—? That's not …"

"It most certainly is." I knew I was nodding and grinning like a lunatic, but I couldn't stop. It *was* pretty funny when you thought about it: all this time, we'd been searching for the damn third piece of Zeus's lightning bolt, and it turned out it had been right here the whole time. No need to scour the world or take on any giant bloody metal warriors after all. All that effort wasted.

My sudden urge to giggle died once I followed that line of thought to its logical end. No need for Athena to die, if only I'd realised what it was the first time I'd seen the stupid girl power sign with its zigzag of an exclamation mark. I'd been staring right at it while we chatted in Ophelia's office. Right at it, only I never truly saw it. And I might have gone on not seeing it forever, while the shadow shapers picked us off one by one, if Zeus hadn't managed to find a way to get me a message. Again. Zeus had had to give me so much help, he must have despaired of my mental capacity.

But I *had* been operating under a handicap, robbed of

all my memories. That surely had to be a good excuse. And now I was back.

The shadow shapers were in for a reckoning like they'd never imagined.

Syl put her hands on her hips. "Where in the name of all that's holy did you get that? I thought you said you were going to the gym to work out with Ophelia? Where the hell have you *been*?"

I grinned. "To the gym to work out with Ophelia. Only I got distracted when I got there." Quickly, I explained the events of the morning.

She shook her head. "That's one hell of a cheeky hiding place. That was a pretty ballsy move."

My grin widened. "That's exactly what I thought when I realised what it was."

We shared a smile, perfectly in tune. It was weird, but in a wonderful way, to have Syl and Ophelia together now. My friends. I had a history with Ophelia as long as my arm, and I remembered every last bar fight, every hunt, every night spent chatting with her and the crew until the wee hours. I'd known Syl for a much shorter time, but we'd been through so much together that she was every bit as dear to me as my old hunting companion.

Even Lucas felt more like an old friend than a guy I'd only met a couple of weeks ago. He cleared his throat, giving the lightning bolt a look as if he expected it to leap off the table and grab him around the throat. "So, what now?"

I pulled out my phone. "Now I call Winston."

Thank goodness I could use him to contact Apollo now. It was the most reliable system I'd ever had for locating my brother. On one memorable occasion, I'd spent seven months looking for him before I'd finally run him to earth in a tiny settlement on the edge of the desert.

When Winston answered, I told him to send Apollo to me immediately. I didn't tell him why—I might not share my brother's complete paranoia about phones, but I wasn't about to trust such crucial information to an open line. He must have known something was up by the tone of my voice. At any rate, it was only twenty minutes or so until I felt Apollo's divine presence approaching the door to our little cottage.

He flung the front door open and hurried inside. "What's wrong, Arti? Is everyone all right?"

Syl grinned at me in a meaningful way. For a moment, I blanked, then recalled how we'd teased him about coming in without knocking, as if he owned a place. It used to drive me mad when I'd thought myself fully human. Yet now I hadn't even noticed, because it seemed such a natural thing to do. I'd done it all the time, myself. All the gods did. Who would deny us entrance?

Admittedly, Ophelia had had a few words to say on the

subject, and I'd stopped doing it to her. Even gods could be taught.

"Better than all right," I said, trying to put thoughts of humans and gods behind me. So maybe I had changed a little—that was only to be expected. It would be more of a surprise if I hadn't. Syl would keep me grounded, just as Ophelia had. Now that I had them both, I'd be the most downtrodden god in existence. That thought was oddly cheering. "I've got something you might like to see."

Surprisingly, my brother had brought two companions with him. Winston, I'd expected, and I gave the elderly priest a welcoming smile. The Ruby Adept had also accompanied Apollo, which I hadn't expected, after his little speech in the jungle.

They must have been together when Winston had tracked down my brother, but surely it would have been less painful for Jake to stay away? Perhaps he'd seen it as his duty to come. I'd never met a man so dedicated to placing his duty above all other considerations.

Jake was every bit as beautiful as I remembered. I loved him and wanted him just as much, and yet … a new note of melancholy was mixed in with my usual whirl of desire, longing, and frustration. Now I remembered what it meant to be a goddess, to walk through eternity essentially alone. I'd had a thousand lovers over the centuries. I'd even been married once. Never again. This was the reason Artemis slept alone most nights—not because she was a cold bitch, but because she knew the pain of becoming too attached to the short-lived mortals.

Staring at his beloved face, I could already see how it would change, how jowls would form on that strong jawline, how the bags would droop under his beautiful blue eyes, and the jet-black hair lighten and recede. He would weaken and stoop, and in barely more than the blink of an eyelid, I would be putting him into a hole in the ground, just like the others.

All this flitted through my mind in a moment, and I had no more than that for such miserable reflections, because Apollo saw the bolt on the dining table and shouted with delight. "You really found it! You are a *legend*."

Then he swept me into his arms and danced us both around the kitchen in a giddy whirl of relief that left us both breathless and had everyone else joining in the laughter. It felt so good to have something worth celebrating at last.

"Have you told Poseidon yet?" he asked, his eyes alight with the same excitement that boiled inside me. I shook my head and he frowned. "Why not? Call him on your shell phone thing."

"My *shell phone thing*?"

He flapped his hands in an impatient gesture. "Whatever you call it. You know what I mean. Hurry up!"

Grumbling that my first thought had been to tell *him*

and he was an ungrateful bastard, I went into the lounge room, the rest of them trailing me, and dug the shell out of its hiding place in the deer's neck. Everyone jumped— including me—when Poseidon's voice boomed in the air around us after I'd called his name. After the way we'd parted, I hadn't even been sure he'd answer.

"Artemis? What do you want? I wasn't expecting to hear from you so soon." He didn't sound exactly delighted to hear my voice, but at least he wasn't openly hostile.

"I wasn't expecting it either, but something's come up."

"Something good," Apollo put in.

"Apollo's there, too? What's going on?"

"We've found the missing piece of the lightning bolt," I said, unable to hold it in a moment longer.

"You haven't."

"I bloody well have."

"Well, that's … that's astonishing. So quickly?" There was a hint of suspicion in his voice.

Apollo and I shared a look. Poseidon had better not accuse me of lying to get my hands on his stupid piece of the lightning bolt.

"She's a marvel," Apollo said, with gushing enthusiasm. "I'm staring at it right now. This is the end of all our troubles—we can finally release Zeus."

Apollo's support would make it a lot harder for Poseidon to imagine I had any nefarious purposes, unless he was prepared to assume that we were both traitors. It was smart of my brother also to remind him that this meant the ordeal with the shadow shapers was nearly over.

"Where was it?" Poseidon asked, after a nerve-wracking pause.

"You won't believe it—I had it all the time."

I told him about Zeus's hint, and how I'd gotten my memory back. This was the first Apollo had heard of it, too, and there were many exclamations and questions to field. But eventually, I got the conversation back on track.

"So, will you bring your lightning bolt to Hestia's house?"

"Not on your life," my uncle replied promptly.

My heart practically stopped beating for a moment. What the hell? All this effort, and he still refused to let go of the damned bolt?

But then he added, "That's too far inland for me. But you can take it. I'll bring it to Berkley's Bay for you."

The breath whooshed out of me in a great gust of relief. "Good. When can you be there?"

"Tonight."

Tonight. We could get Zeus back tonight.

About bloody time.

16

It was only mid-morning when we arrived back in Berkley's Bay, though so much had happened already it felt as though it ought to be much later. Winston and Jake stayed at the temple, while Lucas took Ophelia to meet the local werewolf pack, since she'd insisted on coming back to Berkley's Bay with us. Now that we'd been reunited, she wasn't prepared to be left behind again. Syl went with them, leaving me alone with my brother for the first time since I could actually remember our relationship. We spent a carefree day, mostly at the pub, drinking and reminiscing about the old days.

And when you were thousands of years old, there were a shit-ton of old days to reminisce about. We could have been sitting there still, but eventually, the call of the moon alerted me to the fact that it was time to make our way down to the wharf to meet Poseidon. I'd felt it in the sky all afternoon, but its power surged after dark.

It was a warm night, with the promise of the coming summer in the air, unusually still for the coast. A breeze nearly always sprang up after dark here. We sat on the end of the jetty with our legs dangling over the water like a couple of kids, and I remembered all over again what good company my brother was. He slipped a companionable arm around me and gave me a little squeeze as I lay my head on his shoulder.

"It's good to have you back, Arti," he said. "Really back, I mean."

"It's good to *be* back. Life won't be so confusing anymore, a fact for which I am most heartily thankful. I was getting bloody sick of being in the dark all the time."

The gentle sigh of the waves lent the scene such a peaceful air I could have stayed there all night. The moon was waxing; it hung in the sky like a giant, glowing pearl, if slightly misshapen, its light silvering the tips of the waves. Its power filled me with warmth and contentment.

"Do you regret becoming human?"

I leaned back so I could see his face in the moonlight, and smiled. "Not a bit. If I hadn't, I might have lost my favourite brother."

"There is that," he agreed. "I don't know if I ever thanked you properly for that. It was a great sacrifice, and I can never thank you enough."

I wouldn't have met Syl either, or the other friends I'd made in Berkley's Bay. Or Jake—and that was unthinkable.

"It wasn't so bad. There were compensations." Not bad at all, actually—apart from all the people trying to kill me. But I guess they would have still been trying to kill me if I'd stayed a goddess, and I might not have been able to inflict the same damage on them. So it had definitely been worth it.

"I don't understand why you didn't tell me you had the lightning bolt as soon as it arrived. Perhaps a lot of drama could have been saved."

He spoke lightly, but I knew him too well. He was hurt that I had kept this secret from him.

"The timing was all wrong. Remember, I was away visiting Poseidon when Zeus disappeared. I was there when his piece of the lightning bolt arrived, but I didn't discover until I returned home that there was another waiting for me there. And unfortunately, I didn't go directly home. By the time I found it, you had gone missing, too."

"Then why didn't you at least tell Hades, when you went to him to ask him to make you human?"

"Because by then I had decided there must be a traitor in our ranks." I held up a hand as he began to protest. "No, of course I didn't think it was Hades, but I realised that he was as vulnerable as everyone else. And he already knew where one lightning bolt was. If I told him I had the other, and he was caught ... Well, I didn't want the shadow shapers to have that kind of information."

"Hmm. Why do you think Zeus sent it to you, anyway?"

"I wondered that myself. We both know I'm far from his favourite child." I shrugged. "I suppose because I'm the huntress. Perhaps he hoped it would encourage me to go hunting for answers."

We fell into a companionable silence after that. It was very relaxing, sitting there, listening to the soft shush of the waves and watching the moonlight glitter on the surface of the sea. Way, way out on the horizon—so far out, in fact, that I could probably only see it because of my superior night vision—was a bulk container vessel. Closer in, still in the arms of the bay, a light marked the progress of one of the local fishing boats heading out for the night. I watched the light's steady journey, enjoying the salt scent of the air.

Another shape began to grow on the horizon, an odd, triangular shape, like a mountain sticking up out of the sea. Almost as soon as I noticed it, it faded from sight. I nudged Apollo. "Looks like Poseidon's on his way."

"Where?" Without the benefit of enhanced night vision, he squinted uselessly into the darkness.

"He just activated the mist. He's a long way out to sea still."

It was another ten minutes or more before tendrils of mist began to creep inland, reaching their hesitant fingers toward us. They were cool and damp, and little beads of moisture collected in my hair, sparkling like tiny diamonds in the moonlight. Gradually, the mist built up, forming soft walls around the wharf, blocking our view of the sky but glowing with the moon's muffled light.

Apollo stood up, and I took his proffered hand and let him haul me up, too. For long moments, nothing happened, and then the iceberg loomed out of the mist, suddenly almost close enough to touch. As it bumped gently against the wharf, the hidden door slid open, and Poseidon himself appeared with the lightning bolt in his hand.

"Where's the other one?"

"Right here." Apollo opened his coat to display it. "Relax."

He stepped onto the jetty, his face full of misgiving. Anyone less relaxed it would be hard to imagine. He offered me the bolt, but I could tell he was reluctant to let it out of his sight. "Be careful. Between you, you're carrying two-thirds of Zeus's power. Don't screw this up."

"We won't." I was fully aware that Zeus would be toast if the shadow shapers managed to waylay us before we made it to Hestia's house, but I was confident that the risk was low. We only had to go to Winston's little temple, transfer to the one near Hestia, then walk to Hestia's, and no one knew we were coming, so there was no possibility that we would run into an ambush.

The shadow shapers' inactivity, strange as it was since they knew they could find at least some of us in Berkley's

Bay, worked in our favour now. Whether they were regrouping or planning something horrendous didn't matter; the fact that they had left us unmolested so far meant we were in no danger now, and in a couple more hours, we would be in such a position of power that their schemes would make no difference.

Poseidon lingered on the jetty, looking as if he regretted giving me the lightning bolt already. I tightened my grip on it.

"Are you sure you don't want to come with us?" Apollo asked, sensing Poseidon's disquiet.

He shook his head. "Being that far inland would give me the willies. I'd be no use to you in a fight. My power is here."

"Let's hope it doesn't come to a fight," Apollo said.

"I'm sure it won't," I cut in. We needed to get out of here before Poseidon lost his nerve completely and tried to take the lightning bolt back. "Let's go," I said to my brother.

"Next time we see you, this will all be over," Apollo said.

Poseidon nodded, but he didn't look convinced. We walked away, our boots clomping hollowly on the wooden planking. I looked back before the mist hid him from view, and he was still standing there, looking grim.

"He doesn't have a lot of faith in us, does he?" I said when we regained the shore.

"The loss of Zeus has changed him. He's really rattled by this whole thing."

"Shame he wouldn't come with us, then. It would do him the world of good to see Zeus again."

"You know how he is—a lion at sea, but a mouse on land. He hates leaving the ocean."

"Manannan didn't seem to have any trouble."

"And that's probably why Poseidon wouldn't take us to Athena's island until he offered to go ashore for us. All that stuff about him having to stay back to protect the lightning bolt was just an excuse. He's the biggest coward around without his precious ocean to back him up."

We passed a handful of people as we walked along the foreshore. Apollo had his lightning bolt hidden under his coat again, but I carried mine in my hand, and got some strange looks. Still, we arrived at Winston's temple without seeing a sign of any shadow shapers, so that was all that mattered.

A surprise awaited us inside—the tiny lounge room was crammed full of werewolves. Not only Lucas and Ophelia, who I'd expected, but Holly and Joe, too, with baby Mireille, and Joe and Lucas's parents, Norma and Ray, who were the alphas of the local pack.

Syl, of course, was there, too, perched on Lucas's lap in lieu of any better place to sit. "There you are," she said. "Did it all go smoothly?"

"Fine," I said. "But what are you all doing here?"

Jake and Winston came in from the next room, and then the room really was chockers. Apollo moved away from the door so I could shut it, and he had to tread carefully to avoid everyone's feet. Once the door was shut, the wolves all stood up at once, and the effect was claustrophobic, with so many large bodies looming at once. They gazed at me with expectant faces.

"The whole pack wanted to come," Norma said, as if that explained everything, "but we thought we'd keep it to just the immediate family."

"Come where? To wish us luck?"

She snorted. "No. We're coming with you, to Hestia's place."

"Except me," Holly said in an apologetic way, as if I'd be disappointed at the news. "I'm staying here with Mireille."

"But ..." I looked around at their eager faces, bemused. What did I need a pack of werewolves for? Why had Lucas and Ophelia even told the pack where we were going? I guess I should have known that they would; packs were very tight, and shared information all the time. And here I'd thought they were just going to pay a courtesy visit on the alphas, to introduce Ophelia as a visitor to their territory.

"There's no need for any of you to come," Apollo said, as surprised as I was by this development.

"You need a bodyguard," Syl said to me. "I told you I was going to work on that."

"And we want to help," Norma added. "Werewolves have always followed the Moon. We would be proud to aid you now."

"But I don't need a bodyguard now. We're in the home stretch. In a couple of hours, this nightmare will finally be over."

"But what if Zeus's power draws the shadow shapers?" Norma countered. "Syl told us they can sense divinity, the same as the gods."

Syl gestured at the lightning bolts we carried. "And the power in those babies has got to be broadcasting for miles: *look at me! I'm a god! Come get some yummy power! It's an all-you-can-eat buffet.*"

"You'd be surprised, actually. I had to get right up close before I could sense the one in the gym."

She looked a little disappointed at this news, but undeterred. "Well, it doesn't matter. There's still a traitor somewhere among the gods, so you need someone to watch your back."

Apollo was starting to look affronted, so I cut in. "Guys, this is really touching, but you're a bunch of werewolves."

"And a cat," Syl said, stubborn to the last.

"And two fireshapers," Winston added, with unusual daring for him.

Jake said nothing, but his folded arms and glowering expression said it for him: he didn't think anyone could protect me the way he could.

"And a cat, and two fireshapers. We're two gods, in full possession of our powers. There have been plenty of times lately when I really could have done with a team to back me up, but this isn't one of them."

"What if there's an ambush?" Lucas said.

"Nobody knows we're coming, not even Hestia. We'll be fine. Go buy some champagne and have it chilled for when we get back. We've got this."

There were plenty of disgruntled faces in the room as the werewolves looked at each other, but to my surprise, no one argued any further.

I should have realised that was a dead giveaway.

17

The night seemed even darker when Apollo and I stepped out of the tiny, rundown temple that was the closest access point to Hestia's house. The absence of streetlights or other buildings meant the only light came from the dim red glow of the sacred fire behind us, and once the door was shut, even that was gone.

Apollo began to glow himself, until he was bright enough to cast light several paces away.

"Dude, you're ruining my night vision," I grumbled as we picked our way across the uneven field toward the road.

"Would you rather I broke my ankle stepping in a rabbit hole in the dark?"

"Don't be such a drama queen. And what if someone sees you?"

"Who's going to see me here, in the arse-end of the universe? The only people who use this road belong to

Hestia." The road was dirt and scarred with deep ruts, but it was smoother going than across country, so he let his light die down to a less eyeball-searing level.

"I hope her people aren't as hostile as last time we came." Her guards had all been fireshapers, and aggressive enough that they'd been on the point of taking on Apollo himself—surely a career-limiting move if ever there was one—when Hestia had intervened. "You'll make such a good target in the dark it'll be like shooting fish in a barrel."

"What is your problem? Last-minute jitters? This will be a piece of cake. Just relax."

As it turned out, I needn't have been concerned. There was no sign of Hestia's men as we turned into the long driveway to her house, though I used the local creatures to keep an eye out for them. Nor were there any lurking closer to the house. I would have worried that something had happened to Hestia except that lights burned in the windows of the house, and smoke curled up from one of the chimneys. There was definitely someone home, and everything seemed peaceful enough.

Apollo would have opened the front door and walked straight in, but I stopped him with a hand on his arm. My time as a human had taught me some manners that weren't in the average god's tool box.

"Let's knock. We don't want to start a diplomatic incident."

He gave me an impatient look, perhaps recalling the lecture I'd given him once on the subject of knocking, but he waited while I rapped sharply on the door.

When it opened, not one, but two surly fireshapers stood there, looking particularly unwelcoming. Golden light spilled invitingly out into the dark, but they did their best to block it with their broad shoulders and muscled bodies.

"Yes?" said one.

"Artemis and Apollo are here to see Hestia," Apollo said.

"My lady has retired for the night. Come back tomorrow."

The cheeky bastard—*come back tomorrow*, as if we were door-to-door salesmen instead of gods. I had even assumed my true Artemis form for the occasion. I thrust the lightning bolt I was carrying into the man's face. "I think she'll agree this is worth getting out of bed for."

His eyes widened in recognition and he stepped back, holding the door open for us with obvious reluctance. "You'd better come in, then."

He led us through to the lovely, airy room at the back where we'd sat with Hestia on our last visit, admiring the vegetable garden outside, while his companion followed behind, as if he wasn't quite sure whether we could be trusted not to steal the goddess's knickknacks if he didn't watch us every moment. It was dark outside now, of course, but I could make out the bulk of the barn off to the side, and the little shed where the third and final piece of Zeus's lightning bolt was housed.

Our gracious host gestured at the armchairs grouped in front of the windows. "Have a seat while I tell Lady Hestia you are here."

Somewhat to my surprise, they both disappeared, leaving us alone. I'd thought for sure one of them would have stood guard over us.

"How does someone as nice as Hestia have such a grouchy bunch of servants?" I asked when the door had closed behind them. I had centuries of memories of the goddess of the hearth to draw on now, and in all of them, she was unfailingly warm and welcoming.

"They're probably just over-protective, because they know she's underpowered compared to the rest of us."

Good point. Apollo could take her in a fight with one hand tied behind his back. So could most of the Olympians. Me, not so much, but it was kind of him to include me in the "overpowered" camp. My power over animals gave me all sorts of versatility, but it was still no match for the powers of a fireshaper. Just because he was the strongest one around, he tended to view Hestia's powers as inferior, whereas she'd probably wipe the floor with *me* unless I got in a shot with my bow first.

He took one of the armchairs, and I sat in the one beside him, which was angled to give me a view of the dark yard outside as well as most of the room. I'd picked up some paranoid habits along with the manners in my time as a human. At least soon I would be able to shake them. Not much longer now before the threat of the shadow shapers would be removed, and the gods could sleep easy at night. Zeus would waste no time seeking revenge on whoever had forced him to abandon this reality for the safety of the wires. I had high hopes that he would remember who it was, since he hadn't actually been taken captive by the shadow shapers. At last, the rat in our ranks would be revealed, and I doubted that any of the gods would be in a merciful mood.

Five minutes ticked past, then ten. Apollo shifted restlessly in his chair. "What's keeping her? They said she was asleep, not dead."

"Probably making herself beautiful for her favourite nephew." I was a little surprised myself. Gods happily kept mortals waiting, but we were usually prompt with our own kind.

But the door opened, and Hestia swept in, wrapped in a silk gown and trailing a cloud of perfume. "So sorry to keep you waiting. I was in the bath. Needed a good soak to get all the dirt off—I spent hours in the garden today. I think I'll have to burn my clothes. You've never seen so much dirt!" She laughed and gave us both a hug. Her greying hair was up in a loose bun, damp tendrils clinging to her neck.

"We have good news," Apollo said.

"So Damian said. I can't believe it! You actually found the missing one. But Artemis! I haven't seen you in so long. Where have you been?"

I grinned. I was wearing Artemis's form, not Lexi's, so she didn't realise just how recently she'd seen me. But I was too impatient to get this done to launch into the familiar story now, so all I said was, "It's a long story. I'll tell you all about it over a cup of tea some day—"

"Tea!" she cut in. "Why has no one offered you a drink? Where are my manners?"

She bustled over to the sink and filled the kettle, setting it to boil. Typical Hestia. I exchanged a glance with Apollo, half-amused and half-exasperated. Neither of us were the slightest bit interested in tea, or cake, or any of the other things she would no doubt try to feed us while we were here. We would far rather get on with the job of restoring Zeus.

"Maybe we could leave the tea until after we've re-joined the lightning bolts," I suggested.

"Or even wait for the celebratory champagne," Apollo said. "When Zeus is with us again."

"Nonsense," Hestia said, as I'd known she would. "There's always time for a cup of tea. You've just walked all that way in the dark. You need something to refresh you."

I rolled my eyes but gave up. Hestia was convinced that the rest of us would fade away unless she plied us with food and drink at every opportunity. It would be quicker just to drink the damn tea than to continue the argument. "Do you need a hand?"

"Not at all. You sit down and relax."

I shrugged and sat back down. A furtive movement outside caught my eye: a black cat scampering around the side of the barn. It was probably hunting mice, earning its keep around the property.

A crash in the kitchen diverted my attention. Hestia had just knocked a tea cup onto the floor and smashed it.

"No, no, don't get up," she said, as the door flew open and Damian rushed in. Did he think we were beating up his mistress? She smiled at him. "Damian will clean up for me, won't you?"

"Of course."

I watched Hestia as she got out another cup and continued with her preparations. She fumbled the second cup, too, making me wonder if she'd been drinking before our arrival, though I hadn't smelled any alcohol on her breath. She was usually so deft. Perhaps she was tired from all that work in the garden, and it was making her clumsy.

When everything was ready, she had Damian carry the tray over and place it on a small coffee table in the centre of the nest of armchairs where we sat. Then the surly fireshaper bowed himself out of the room and Hestia poured for all of us.

"You didn't bring your bow, Arti?" She handed me a delicate cup covered in roses, the dark brown tea within steaming. "Don't you feel naked without it?" She shuddered. "I can't stand to be too far from my distaff, especially these days, with shadow shapers lurking around every corner."

"It's perfectly safe," I said, putting the cup down. I didn't take milk, and it was still a little too hot to drink. My bow was in its charm form, tucked safely between my breasts, out of sight. No need to tell her that, though. Apollo was the only god who knew I liked to carry it that way, and I saw no reason to change that. I was a little surprised that she had so freely revealed that her own avatar was her distaff. "Not that it will matter so much, once we get these babies back together."

I gestured at the two lightning bolts lying on the coffee table between us.

"They seem very quiet," Hestia said, offering a plate of biscuits around. "Not like that brute I've got in my shed."

"Perhaps that's because they're smaller," Apollo said, biting into a biscuit and chewing with obvious enjoyment. Hestia was an excellent cook. "The one you have, being larger, probably has a lot more power than these two."

"True." She took a biscuit herself, and for a moment, satisfied munching was the only sound in the room.

I glanced outside again, wishing we could move on to

the part where we went out to that shed and brought Zeus back. The little black cat was still out there, no longer hunting, but sitting against the barn wall, almost invisible in the darkness. It was washing its face, one paw stroking delicately at its whiskers, and something about the movement roused my suspicions. I sent my awareness out to the little spark of light that was the cat's mind, but just before I made contact, she spoke to me.

Hey, Syl's voice said in my head, *I think we have a problem.*

I thought that was you! What are you doing here? I should have been suspicious when she didn't argue about being left behind. Winston must have brought her through to the temple after we'd gone through. But why? *And what sort of problem?*

There have been a whole lot of people running backwards and forwards from the house to the barn, round the side you can't see, while you've been sitting there with your cup of tea. It's like someone stuck a stick in an ant's nest. There must be fifty of them in the barn now.

Doing what? There were no rules about gathering in barns, but my paranoia began to twitch all the same.

Nothing yet. They're just standing there in the dark, as if they're waiting for something.

Well, that set all my alarm bells ringing, but it didn't make a lot of sense. If Hestia had been in the bath when we'd arrived, where had all these people been? Surely not just hanging around the house without her? It was a big house, and she had a few staff, but nowhere near fifty. But if she had fifty guests, why had she gone to have a bath? And why were those guests now hiding in the barn?

Syl got up and sauntered around the side of the barn, out of my sight.

Where are you going?

I can hear movement. Just checking—yep, a few more have arrived. Where are all these people coming from?

My question exactly. *If she has a temple somewhere in the house ...*

They could be teleporting in, like Winston does, if she's given someone that power. I don't like the look of this. I'm going for reinforcements.

You didn't come alone? No, of course you didn't. That was a stupid question. Apollo said something to Hestia, but I didn't take it in, too intent on my conversation with Syl. I picked up my tea cup and blew on the tea, trying to look as though I were doing something so the other two wouldn't suspect my mind wasn't on their conversation.

You're kidding, right? As if the werewolves would have let me come without them. As if Jake would. That guy's got it bad. He was beside himself when Apollo told him to go back to town.

My heart leapt. Jake was here? *This is a real conspiracy

you guys have got going here. What happened to letting us handle things?

If we had, you wouldn't know there was half a bloody army hiding out in the barn, would you?

I had to admit that was a pretty compelling argument. *Where are the others?*

Back a ways in the woods. Not far. I'm nearly there.

Tell them not to do anything until I give the signal. Let me suss out what's really going on first.

What *was* going on? I put my cup back on the saucer without drinking. When I looked up, I found Hestia's eyes on me, watching me almost avidly.

"Still too hot?" she asked sympathetically. "Want me to add some cold water?"

"No, I'll leave it until later. It will be cooler then."

"No, you must have some—I insist. We can't have you going out in the cool night air without something to warm your insides." She smiled expectantly until I picked up the cup again.

Why did she care so much whether I drank the stupid tea or not? Was it poisoned? That didn't make any sense— why on earth would Hestia, of all people, want to poison me? Besides, Apollo had drunk half of his tea, and he wasn't writhing around clutching his throat or anything. I was being ridiculous.

Yet her intent gaze made me determined that not a drop

of tea would pass my lips. Something was very wrong here—but could I figure it out fast enough? To give myself time to think I picked up the cup and saucer and carried them to the window. With my back to her, I mimed drinking from the cup, then stood, as if pondering the darkness outside, but really watching her in the reflection. Her lips curved in a small, satisfied smile now that I'd apparently drunk some of the bloody tea. I mimed another sip, and her gaze returned to Apollo as she asked him about our trip to see Poseidon.

What the hell was going on? Her own cup of tea sat untouched on the table in front of her. I wouldn't even have noticed if Syl hadn't alerted me to what was happening out in the barn. Was she trying to take Zeus's lightning bolts for herself? That was crazy. Particularly when it had been Zeus himself who'd sent the message "Hestia lightning" that had brought Apollo and me to her door in the first place.

Except … I blinked in pure astonishment as another thought occurred to me. We'd come here knowing nothing, our only clue that enigmatic "Hestia lightning". Zeus's communications were necessarily brief and often difficult to figure out. It was Hestia herself who'd told us that it meant we were to find the other two parts of the lightning bolt and bring them here so Zeus could be freed.

What if Zeus had actually meant us to *take* the lightning

bolt from Hestia? What if Hestia having possession of one was a danger to Zeus?

And now we'd brought her all three.

If only I could communicate mind-to-mind with Apollo. I needed advice here, and quickly. I couldn't stand here much longer, pretending to drink tea which may or may not be poisoned. But I was having so much trouble getting my head around this. Was it all in my head? How could Hestia be the enemy here? She was the most self-effacing goddess around. Half the time even *we* forgot she was a member of our pantheon; she was always kind, always welcoming. Never a threat. If she'd wanted to attack us, she could have done it last time we were here.

Except all those people in the barn weren't gathered for a barn dance. Just standing around, waiting for something to happen, according to Syl. *That* wasn't fishy at all. I clung to that knowledge. I wasn't being paranoid, and I wasn't imagining things. Something was going on.

"Everything all right, Arti?" Hestia asked. "You seem a little pensive."

I turned and flashed a bright smile. "I'm fine, thanks. Just a little tired."

Apollo covered a yawn with his hand. "Me, too."

Why had Hestia's smile widened at that? Her bright, expectant gaze darted between us, and a chill ran down my spine. What was she waiting for? Did she want us to ... fall asleep?

What the hell was in this tea? My mind replayed everything that had happened since our arrival: she'd been so slow to come out to meet us. Was that because she was organising whatever was going on out in the barn? Who were all these people that had arrived so quickly and in such secrecy? Then she'd started making tea. She'd broken the cup, and fumbled another—she'd made Damian carry the heavy tray to the table.

No, I couldn't link that to anything—but wait. I'd almost forgotten: she'd asked me where my avatar was— and how had she known that my bow was my avatar, anyway? It was practically the first thing out of her mouth. Why should she care? Unless …

Unless her barn was full of shadow shapers.

I closed my eyes to prevent her from seeing the shock in them. *Hestia* was our traitor? I couldn't believe it, yet that was where all the evidence was pointing. It would also perhaps explain why the two lightning bolts we'd brought were lying docile on the table, whereas the one she had outside spat and hissed at anyone who came near. It reflected its owner's anger at Hestia, was perhaps even trying to defend itself from her.

She took my closed eyes as a sign of something else. I opened them to find her rising from her chair with a hungry look on her face. Apollo's head was nodding as if he were too tired to hold it up anymore.

"Are you feeling quite well, Arti dear?" she cooed.

"Just … a little sleepy." Out the corner of my eye, I saw Apollo slump in his seat, eyes rolling back in his head. Holy shit. What did I do now? She was a fireshaper and my bow was still around my neck in miniature form. By the time I could put an arrow through her heart, she'd have roasted me.

And she expected me to collapse any minute. At least doing so would hide the fact that I was still holding a full cup of tea. It would also buy me a little time to figure out my next move.

I let the tea cup slip from my fingers to shatter on the floor, then followed it down in a graceful swoon.

18

Quick footsteps crossed the floor to where I lay, then Hestia knelt and laid cool fingers on my neck, checking my pulse. The door into the main part of the house opened as she stood again.

"Damian, get these two collared," she said, "then bring them out to the barn. Oh, and take Apollo's ring."

"Do we have her bow?" he asked, undisguised eagerness in his voice. He moved across the room as he spoke, presumably to retrieve Apollo's ring.

"No, but it will probably be in that hovel she's been living in in Berkley's Bay. We'll send someone to fetch it tomorrow. Her power is little enough compared to that of the sun god and the sky father."

"Those really are the other two lightning bolts, then? We can draw Zeus out?"

"Finally. And then we can take the rest of them down. Has everyone arrived?"

"We're still waiting on the Brenvale contingent. Most of them weren't home, and it's taking some time to track them down."

"No matter. We have some work to do still to prepare the sacrifices. Let's get onto it."

"Yes, my lady."

Two sets of footsteps left the room, and I risked opening my eyes to check. Apollo was still slumped in his chair, but he was the only one here besides myself. The two lightning bolts were gone from the table—Hestia must have taken them. And Damian would be back at any moment with collars for the two of us, to prevent us using our powers.

How long would my brother sleep? Perhaps for hours. I had to assume that whatever she had given him would keep him out long enough for them to collar him, chain him, and get everything ready for the sacrifice. So he would be no help. I sat up, keeping low behind the furniture in case Damian reappeared, while I retrieved my bow and quiver. With my bow in my hand, I felt much better.

It pained me to see my poor, trusting brother collapsed in his chair, mouth open, head tipped back at an awkward angle. He was going to have one hell of a sore neck when he woke. There must be something in that drink she'd given him that had wiped his short-term memories as well as putting him to sleep. "I'd trust Hestia with my life," he'd said once, and now that unwavering trust had delivered him into her power again.

All he remembered of his first capture was going to bed in his own room and waking up in Mrs Emery's prison cell. In between, I was willing to bet Hestia had turned up at his home one night with some sob story, and he'd taken her in without question. She must have laughed at how easy it was to exploit his trust in her by slipping something into his drink.

She'd probably done the same thing to Hephaistos. He'd trusted her, too, and had been captured. But she'd had him even more wrapped around her little finger than Apollo—she'd managed to convince him to make the very collars that proved the gods' undoing before she'd killed him. Probably with some story about how frightened she was. Poor little underpowered Hestia.

And now she was ready to collar Apollo again. But this time, the outcome would be very different. This time he wasn't defenceless. As footsteps approached, I drew an arrow and nocked it. I was still crouched behind the group of armchairs, mainly out of sight from the door. Whoever walked through was going to find it much more difficult to collar the sun god than previously.

When Damian entered the room, I felt a powerful surge of disappointment that it wasn't Hestia. I was building up a thirst for vengeance that would only be quenched by spilling her blood. Damian's would have to do for the moment. Once he shut the door behind him, I let the arrow fly, catching him in the throat. He fell, and the two collars he'd been carrying rolled across the hardwood floor, coming to rest by Apollo's feet.

I picked them up. No point leaving these for the shadow shapers' use. But where to put them? In the kitchen, I pulled open drawers at random and shoved them inside a large pot. With the lid back on, they weren't visible, and I doubted anyone would be making soup or boiling chicken carcases in the next hour or so, anyway. If I'd had a backpack, I would have taken them with me, but I needed a hiding place in a hurry, so this would have to do.

I left Damian where he'd fallen: the pool of bright arterial blood spreading underneath his neck told me he wouldn't be getting up again. I retrieved my arrow, though. That was worth a lot more than some shadow shaper traitor.

Syl? What's happening? I cast my mind out even as I sent the question, and found the bright sparks of the werewolves rushing toward the back of the barn. But Syl didn't answer. Perhaps she was in human form right now. She might even be opening the barn door for the werewolves, because, as I watched, their sparks moved inside. Quickly, I jumped into the head of the lead wolf.

Unsurprisingly, it was Ray, the alpha of the pack. Now the darkness the shadow shapers had been hiding in worked against them—wolves could see perfectly well in the dark.

They fell on the massed shadow shapers, biting and snarling, and chaos erupted in the barn. I watched through his eyes for a moment, to make sure that the wolves would be all right, before leaving his head without speaking to him. He didn't need the distraction right now.

The shadow shapers were so panicked by the sudden appearance of a pack of ferocious beasts in their midst that most of them forgot any power that they might have had and made a concerted rush for the main barn doors. They were desperate to escape the rending teeth and the terrible sounds in the dark all around them, so desperate that they hindered each other as they pushed and shoved blindly. That was the trouble with stealing other people's magic—when the shit hit the fan, drawing on your power wasn't instinctual, developed over long years of living with that power. A couple of them set Zephyrus's stolen winds roaring around the interior of the barn, but that didn't bother the wolves one bit. All it achieved was to slam the barn door shut just when some hapless shadower had managed to heave it open.

Back in my own head, I strode to the back door. *Syl!* I called again, and this time she answered me.

Lexi! Where are you?

Just heading outside. Apollo's unconscious—can you send someone in to guard him?

I'll send Winston in.

Winston's still here? I'd expected Winston's role to have

extended no further than ferrying the disobedient shifters here. Now I was worried about the old man. *He's a bit old for battle.*

He's still a fireshaper, she pointed out. *Probably strong enough to wipe the floor with any second-rate shadow shapers. Besides, guard duty will keep him out of the way.*

Not that we had so many options that I could afford to be choosy. And she was right; guard duty would be safer than the mêlée in the barn. He was also completely devoted to my brother. The only more dedicated guard Apollo could ask for would be Jake, and I had a feeling I'd need his help taking Hestia down.

Speaking of whom, where had she gone? I let myself out into the cool night, where screams and snarls from the barn rent the air. She had the two other lightning bolts, so the logical place to find her was at the garden shed housing the third.

I'd barely moved from the house when I heard running feet and a panicked voice calling for her off to my left. Someone had finally managed to escape the slaughter in the barn. I melted behind a bush as another door opened at the back of the house, down the other end from where I stood, and a small group stepped out, Hestia in their midst. The glow surrounding her could only mean she carried the lightning bolts, though I couldn't see them through the press of people surrounding her. I drew an arrow from my quiver.

"My lady! We're under attack!" the escapee blurted. Even in the dark, I could see the man's chest heaving with the effort to draw in breath. One hand clutched his shoulder, which was bleeding heavily. "The barn is full of werewolves."

"So?" she asked, eyeing him with disdain. "You are shapers now. Blow them away. Metalshape something. Really, Justin, you have all of Athena's knowledge, and you're afraid of a few overgrown dogs? Hurry up. I'm taking Zeus now, and I'm not waiting for anybody."

She swept past him, leaving him standing there uncertainly. He glanced back at the barn with obvious reluctance. Clearly, he didn't relish the thought of going back into the slaughterhouse, and yet his mistress had all but ordered him to do just that. He swayed a little on his feet, and then the decision was taken from him as he collapsed. Probably from blood loss.

Her callousness shocked me, though it really shouldn't have. She was prepared to kill her own family—what could the lives of a few insignificant humans matter to her? Even if they were her most favoured followers, called here to share in Zeus's and Apollo's power. She seemed supremely unfazed by the sounds of slaughter from the barn, though the group surrounding her were obviously ill at ease. Perhaps she had decided that if the people in the barn couldn't defeat a few werewolves, they weren't worthy of sharing in Zeus's power after all.

I tracked Hestia with the arrow nocked at my bow, ready to fly straight to her heart. But she didn't oblige me with a clear shot. The handful of people who walked with her shielded her. I could pick them off one by one, but she would blast me with fire before I could get to her.

I cast my mind out into the night, searching for an edge. A herd of deer slept uneasily in a clearing, but they were too far away to be of use. A pair of owls hunted over the treetops, and I brought them winging my way. Aerial distractions were always useful. But the forest was remarkably clear of other life. No foxes, wild boar, or feral cats anywhere within range. I probably had the werewolves to thank for that. Any creature catching the scent of werewolf on the wind would have hightailed it out of the area.

Keeping low and moving as soundlessly as only a goddess of the hunt could, I began to circle my way closer to the shed that housed the lightning bolt, which was Hestia's target. She was striding towards it with obvious eagerness. There were plenty of low bushes between us, at least until I got to the edge of the vegetable garden.

The shadow shapers with her looked around nervously, perhaps worried that more werewolves might appear out of the night. Hestia herself was so focused on her target that she looked neither right nor left, indifferent to the sounds of people dying inside the barn as she passed. It was a far cry from the nurturing goddess I'd always known. They were her people in there. How could she act as if their fate made no difference to her? Her hunger for Zeus's power must be all-consuming.

She reached the shed and threw back the door. It was like opening the door on the sun, so bright was the light inside. I blinked, my night vision destroyed in the very moment when a clear shot presented itself. Dammit.

The two owls I'd called circled in, and I launched them at the little knot of people shielding Hestia so effectively. They fell back, scattering, shrieking and batting ineffectively at the buffeting wings and darting beaks. Instantly, I drew back the arrow, my arms steady, gaze unwavering. The bowstring thrummed as I released it, sending the arrow on its way, straight to Hestia's traitorous heart.

She should have fallen down dead. I was so close I could have targeted a single freckle on her weathered face, and the golden arrows of the huntress never failed to find a target.

They didn't this time, either, but one of the shadow shapers under aerial attack lurched violently to the right at the exact moment to intercept the arrow's flight. Instead of finding the goddess's heart, it skewered her disciple through the shoulder. The shadow shaper sent up a shriek loud enough to wake the dead and fell to the ground, where she writhed, still screaming.

Hestia's black gaze turned to the bushes where the arrow

had come from, and I threw myself to the side in desperation, knowing what was coming next. She raised her arms and fire burst forth. Apollo's sun-boosted powers were more impressive, but Hestia's fire was still strong enough to kill me. I covered my head, sinking my face into the dirt. Maybe it would roll over me. Yeah, and maybe pigs would fly.

When death failed to overtake me, I cautiously raised my head again. Another wall of flame had met Hestia's, holding it at bay. The vegetable garden, once so lovingly tended, had become a battle ground, and the beans blackened on the vine, shrivelling in the intense heat. The lettuces and carrots were nothing but a smoking ruin. Cautiously, I got to my feet, squinting into the ruddy glow of the flames.

Jake stood by the back door, a look of cold determination on his handsome face. I'd never been so glad to see him in my life. Until the shadow shapers had come along, with their nasty avatar-destroying ritual, gods had been pretty much invulnerable to anything mortals could throw at us, but it had always been possible for us to kill each other. Without him, Hestia's fire would have wiped me out.

"You again," Hestia spat at him. I moved out of the shadows and her eyes widened. "Sneaky. You didn't drink the tea." She tried to see past Jake, into the house, but the windows only reflected the flames back at her. I guessed she was looking for Apollo, since her expression relaxed when it became evident that Jake was the only fireshaper confronting her. "You always were smarter than that big, blond oaf."

She moved a hand to divert a small stream of flame into the air, and my poor owls fell to the ground, mere blackened chunks of meat. Unmolested now, her followers regrouped behind her, straightening their hair and clothes. Most of them had blood running down their faces from where the owls had pecked them.

"But not quite smart enough. What are you going to do now? Set your dogs on me?" She gestured at the barn, and a tongue of fire leapt toward it, landing on the roof. It licked hungrily down the sides of the barn. Horrified, I cast my mind inside, to find most of the wolves were already out. Too bad if any of her people were still in there, wounded. Her callousness took my breath away.

Stay away! I broadcast to the wolves, my mental tone urgent as the last couple scrambled out of the burning building. *There's nothing you can do against fire. Jake and I will handle this.* I couldn't bear it if any of them got hurt. And Holly would kill me if I let any of her family come to harm.

"Shoot me with your shiny arrows?" Her voice was mocking as she tried to send another lick of fire my way. Jake's wall of flame shielded both of us, preventing her from getting through. Beads of sweat gathered on Jake's forehead, and his outstretched arms trembled from the strain of holding her fire off with his own. That wasn't good.

I locked eyes with Hestia; best not to draw her attention to Jake's struggle. "Sounds like a plan."

In a fluid movement that felt as natural as breathing, I drew, nocked, and let fly another arrow, certain of my target this time. She stood right out in the open on the other side of the flames. I couldn't miss.

Yet again the bitch proved me wrong. She batted aside my arrow with a gust of wind that bent the flames, sending them streaming back toward us. Jake countered, finding more strength somewhere to feed into his fiery wall.

I chewed at my bottom lip. Where had she gotten that wind from? That was no part of the goddess of the hearth's powers. Wind had been Zephyrus's strength, but surely I would have noticed if Hestia had been there at his sacrifice?

Idiot. I was still thinking like a human. She could have been disguised as anyone. I certainly wouldn't have felt her divinity back then, or known what it was even if I had.

But Zephyrus would have, and he hadn't said anything. Hadn't cried out for help from the goddess he must have felt in the room. I shook my head. It didn't make sense, but it was a problem for another time. Right now, I had to focus on living through the next few moments.

Jake's fire dipped lower, and Hestia laughed. "I can keep this up forever, little fireshaper. Can you say the same?"

Jake's flames surged upward in response to her taunt, but I could see the effort cost him. The shaking of his arms must be apparent even to Hestia now.

I'm circling around through the trees with the wolves, Syl said into my mind. *We'll come at her from behind.*

There was a wide stretch of cleared land between the back of the shed that housed the lightning bolt and the edge of the trees. The wolves would be completely exposed while they crossed it. If Hestia saw them, or even one of her followers …

I'd just have to make sure their attention was fixed on me. I nocked another arrow and shot one of the shadow shapers, who was trying to circle around the edge of the flames to get at Jake. The others shrank back around Hestia. Good. Fortunately, none of them had guns. I hadn't heard any gunfire in the barn, either, when the wolves had attacked. The shadow shapers' stolen powers had made them cocky.

They didn't look so cocky now, as I shot another arrow. Since I wasn't going for secrecy anymore, and they were all just standing out in the open, I gained nothing by letting them live.

"Use your powers, you fools," Hestia commanded, but one of them broke and ran for the shelter of the trees, and once one of them bolted, the others got itchy feet, too. I let them go, knowing the wolves were waiting in the dark, under the trees. There would be no escape for these god-killers.

Wait for my signal, I said to Syl. There was a scream from the wood, abruptly cut off. Guess I didn't need her to tell the wolves to deal with the shadow shapers I'd just sent their way. They had it under control. A cold smile curved my lips.

"Laugh all you want," Hestia said, a vicious gleam in her eye. "You won't be laughing anymore once your pet fireshaper runs out of juice. You'll be mine, then, Artemis, and your precious werewolves won't be able to save you."

I glanced at Jake. Sweat ran freely down his face now, and the muscles of his neck were taut with strain.

"Look at him shake," she said. "He's only a mortal. A talented one, I grant you, but he's no match for my power. Even now, he's draining his life force to feed that fire."

Shit. That sounded bad. *Come on, Jake, just hold on until the wolves get here.* Hestia's wall of flame didn't extend behind herself. If the wolves were quiet enough, she could be down before she even realised what had happened. *They* might not be able to kill her, but *I* certainly could. All I needed was a second when her attention was distracted to be able to put an arrow through her heart.

I moved sideways along the barrier of flame, keeping an arrow trained on her the whole time. "Your stolen powers, you mean. What exactly do you hope to accomplish by all this, exactly? Are you trying to take Zeus's position as top dog?"

"Top dog," she jeered. "You have no imagination at all. I'm going to be the *only* dog. My so-called family is more trouble than it's worth. You think I want to waste my time adjudicating the squabbles of a bunch of overgrown children? I've done enough of that down the millennia, thank you. Time to clear out the old dead wood and let a new generation of shapers come to power."

"A new generation, who all owe you their fealty for giving them their stolen powers?"

"Now you're catching on. A new generation who all revere one god and one god alone. Since none of you cared to share your powers with me, I'll take them instead."

"And Zeus is next?"

She laughed. "I rather think *you're* next, Arti, dear. You and that stupid, trusting brother of yours. Once I've added your powers to the tally, I should be strong enough to take on Zeus, weak and disoriented as he will be when I finally extract him from his hidey-hole. You don't know how pleased I am that you both decided to deliver the missing bolts in person. If only you'd brought Poseidon with you, too. Still, we mustn't be greedy, must we? All in good time."

Jake's wall of flame dipped alarmingly, and I drew in a shocked breath. He was staggering, his face unnaturally pale even in the red light of the flames. Fireshapers were immensely powerful, but normally, they used their powers in short bursts. This kind of sustained effort, against a goddess no less, was draining him alarmingly.

"Jake, stop," I said.

He ignored me, of course. He hadn't looked at me the whole time he'd been holding Hestia off. The task took all his concentration.

"He probably can't even hear you," Hestia said conversationally as he staggered again. "His body is shutting down, cannibalising itself to feed his fireshaping. Senses will be the first to go, then the vital functions. Shouldn't be long now."

"No!" I sprinted toward her, or tried to, at least, but the wall of flame held me off to one side, angled toward the shed but unable to reach the goddess who stood before its door. I let fly an enraged arrow, but she batted it aside with her wind power. Where were those damned wolves? "Jake, stop!"

His eyes met mine at last, full of a desperate determination. The flames roared too loud to hear him, but his lips moved, and I could read the words he spoke: "Lexi, run!"

In helpless agony, I watched his eyelids flutter closed as he collapsed in on himself. Was he dead? He hit the scorched earth, one arm outflung toward me.

Blinded by tears, I threw myself behind the garden shed as his fire died and Hestia's flames roared free.

19

If he hadn't been dead then, he must surely be dead now, burned to a crisp by Hestia's fire. I squeezed my eyes shut against the pain, drawing deep, gasping breaths of the hot air. My ears were filled with the roar of flame and Hestia's mocking laughter. Hate for her flared in my heart, but what could I do? I didn't even dare peek out from behind the shed to look at Jake's body, because sure as shit the crazy bitch was just waiting for a chance to roast me, too.

And she wouldn't have to wait long. I turned my head, opened aching eyes to gauge the distance between me and the shelter of the forest. Too far to run before the flames caught me—but at the same time, this shed wouldn't shelter me for long. It was made of sheet metal, and already, the sides were buckling and groaning from the heat of the flames.

Part of me just wanted to lie here and let the flames take

me. If Jake was gone, I wasn't sure what the point of continuing was. But the other part of me clamoured for revenge. Hestia had to pay for what she'd done, for all the lives she'd taken, for stealing my love from me when I'd only just found him.

But how? She was facing the shed now, no longer standing with her back to the trees. The wolves wouldn't be able to sneak up on her, and I had nothing against a goddess who could wield both wind and flame. Arrows couldn't find her, and there were no animals that could stand against her fire either …

Except one.

I sat up, heart pounding with renewed purpose, and scrubbed the tears from my face. He'd answered my call once before, when I'd needed him most. I bent all my will to the summons, forcing the call out until I reeled with dizziness.

"Come out, Arti, before I burn you out," Hestia said in a wheedling tone. "I hear that's a very painful way to go."

Would he hear me? Was he close enough to Hades for his master to open the way in time if he did?

"Why should I?" I could barely spare the attention to answer her, but keeping her talking might buy me a little extra time. "You're only going to kill me anyway if I do."

"But a quick slash of the knife would be so much nicer than burning, don't you think?"

"You're a shit negotiator. You could at least offer to spare me if I give up."

She laughed. "Oh, that's so cute! *If* you give up? You think your wolves can save you now? You're a dead woman walking, and your only choice is how you want to go."

"You wouldn't burn me. You wouldn't be able to steal my powers that way."

"Don't flatter yourself, sweetie. Your powers really aren't worth bothering with. I just want you out of the way."

Her voice was coming more from the left now, as if she'd begun circling the shed to get at me. Carefully, I edged to the right. She probably wouldn't come all the way around, for fear of leaving the door unguarded. She didn't want me anywhere near that lightning bolt. Did she still have the other two in her hands, or had she dropped them at the door? If I could get to them, maybe I could use them as leverage.

I took another step, and the ground trembled ever so slightly. If I hadn't been looking out for it, I probably wouldn't even have noticed. My heart leapt with hope.

Shit, Lexi, what do you want us to do? Syl's anxious voice sounded in my head. The situation must look pretty hopeless from her vantage point in the woods. But she didn't know what that tremor beneath my feet signified.

Don't show yourselves, I said urgently. *Tell the wolves to stay well back. She's too dangerous.*

273

But you're—

The earth trembled again, more noticeably this time. *I'll be fine. Trust me.*

I make it a point never to trust anyone who says 'trust me'.

"What was that?" Hestia's voice was sharper. "Have you got an earthshaper hidden back there? It won't do you any good, you know."

"Don't be so sure," I muttered, and then the time for words was over.

The shed heaved to one side as the ground beside it erupted. I staggered back, narrowly escaping falling into the giant hole that appeared. A familiar, beloved figure leapt from it, his great heads swinging around.

BOSSY GIRL NEED? he boomed in my head.

Hestia shrieked and threw flame at him, but it washed over him as harmlessly as water. Fire wasn't a problem for a hellhound.

Get her, I said flatly.

She buffeted him with wind, but it made no difference. He leapt at her and bowled her to the ground, the jaws of his middle head closing on her throat. Her hands scrabbled at him, but she had no chance of moving him. When Cerberus caught you, you stayed caught. She kicked desperately, but he ignored her, patient as a mountain, one enormous paw holding her down.

WHAT DO? he asked. *EAT NOW?*

The left head looked at me hopefully. I opened my mouth to say yes when a voice spoke behind me.

"Is that my *sister* in the jaws of death? What is going on here?" He was wearing his Hades form, the greying older man who looked like everybody's favourite uncle. He was certainly mine. His mild gaze met mine inquiringly.

Hestia kicked harder and shrieked something that was probably meant to be a plea, but the pressure of Cerberus's teeth on her throat made her speech unintelligible.

"That's not your sister," I said, my voice steady, though my blood thrummed with the passion of the hunt, the need to see Hestia's lifeblood spurt from her dying corpse. "That's our traitor, unmasked at last. The leader of the shadow shapers."

"Ah." He strolled closer and stood looking down at her. "What a shame we don't have those shadow shaper collars here, then."

"What a shame she's still breathing, you mean. We don't need collars. Let's kill her."

He quirked an eyebrow at me. "Before we find out the names and locations of every last one of the monsters she's created? I know killing things is your *jam*, as the mortals say, Arti, but let's not be hasty."

"Hasty?" I drew an enraged breath, prepared to argue, but then I caught the steel in his gaze. "Fine."

I marched across the scorched earth to the back door, gaze carefully averted from Jake's body. A world of grief waited there for me in the dark, but I couldn't let it sweep me away yet. There was still work to do, and I had to be strong.

When I returned with the collars from the kitchen, I thrust them both into Hades' hand. His eyes gleamed with satisfaction as he bent to fit one around Hestia's rather chewed-on neck. "Ask and ye shall receive, they say." He stepped back. "All right, Cerberus, you can let go. Our lady of the hearth won't be doing any damage now."

Movement under the trees caught my eye—werewolves, their eyes blazing golden, slinking out of the cover of the woods. Syl walked with them, her hand on the back of one of the largest. I ran my eye over them all, mentally checking them off: Norma and Ray, the alphas, with their sons Joe and Lucas—the big black one with Syl—and Ophelia, almost as well muscled as the alpha, striding tall on Syl's other side. All there. Briefly, I closed my eyes in relief. All there, though Joe was limping.

That meant our only casualty was Jake.

My throat constricted. Jake. Finally, I looked toward where his body lay, but it was only a dark shape on the ground. The killing fury returned, and I clenched my fists. He'd died for me, and Hestia had to pay.

"What do you want us to do?" Syl asked as she reached my side.

The werewolves gathered around me, brushing against me like cats, anxious for my touch. Stroking their soft fur restored a little calm to my battered heart. Cerberus sniffed at them, his tail wagging hesitantly. They might not be hellhounds, but he clearly considered them the next best thing.

The whole scene felt surreal. The stench of blood and smoke was in my nostrils, and heat radiated up from the scorched ground. Hestia lay on it, still prisoned by Cerberus's huge paw, her baleful gaze switching between Hades and me. Hades was unperturbed, but I wanted nothing more than to drive a knife right into her hateful face.

"Winston and Apollo are inside. Kill everyone else," I said.

On this, Hades didn't gainsay me. He was just as keen as I was to destroy every last shadow shaper. The wolves loped away to do my bidding, moving as with one mind.

Syl glanced at me uncertainly. "Where's Jake?"

I jerked my head in the direction of the body. She sucked in a sharp breath and half ran towards him. As she fell to her knees beside him, I turned away, bending to gather the two lightning bolts, which had fallen on the ground.

Not yet. Still more to do.

"What do we do with these?" I asked Hades.

He gave me a troubled look, as if he could tell what a tight grip I had on my emotions. "I think once we bring them together with the main branch, our worries will be over."

We both turned to look at the shed. It had fallen onto its side, shoved away by Cerberus's grand entry, its panels mangled and warped by the heat of the fireshaping battle. The lightning bolt within still stood proudly, rammed into the ground though the shed around it was more than half destroyed. The light of the bottom half, which was all we could see, lit the scene.

"Let's get this out of the way." With one hand, Hades flipped the shed into the air, sending it sailing towards the trees. It tumbled across the ground with a series of metallic crashes. Uncovered, the lightning bolt blazed brighter than ever.

"Lexi, I can't find a pulse," Syl called, her voice tinged with dread.

A pulse? Why was she checking a charred corpse for a pulse? Unless …

A sudden vision of Jake, standing half naked in the holy fire of Apollo during his initiation as Ruby Adept, came to me. Already a powerful fireshaper, he'd been changed by that fire, made even stronger. Had that baptism of fire strengthened him beyond the normal reach of mortals, enough that he could withstand Hestia's flames?

My feet were moving before I was aware of what I was doing, flying across the smoking earth to his side. I dropped to my knees next to Syl, a wild hope fluttering in my heart. There wasn't a mark on him; he looked as though he was only sleeping.

"Jake," I breathed, bending over him.

Syl's fingers were pressed to the pulse point in his throat. She looked at me and shook her head. "I think he's gone."

"No." Fierce determination burned inside me. I would *not* lose him again. I placed the heels of my hands on his chest and began to pump, willing his heart to start beating again. This was what the humans did in a crisis. If only I had a hospital here, and people who knew what they were doing. Despite my long life, I'd only ever seen this done in movies.

Syl tipped his head back and pried his mouth open. I bent to breathe into his mouth, then resumed pumping, keeping a steady rhythm going. Syl watched anxiously.

Light as bright as day flashed over me and I looked up without pausing my rhythm. Hades had brought the three parts of the lightning bolt together. It looked as though they had fused somehow, but I no longer had any interest in the lightning bolt, or the fate of Zeus. Only the fate of a certain beloved mortal.

I covered his lips with my own again, breathing into his mouth. Syl took over the chest compressions, and I bit my lip. He wasn't moving.

"It's not working," I choked. We needed a doctor or, at the very least, a defibrillator to shock his heart back into life.

Wait a minute.

I looked up again, squinting into the glare of the renewed lightning bolt. The damn thing was practically fizzing with electricity. Okay, so it wasn't a defibrillator, but what other choice did I have? It was Jake's only hope.

"Hades! Give me that!" I leapt up, vaulted over Jake's body and practically snatched the lightning bolt from Hades' hand. "Get out of the way, Syl."

Syl scrambled aside, and I slammed the tip of the lightning bolt down onto Jake's chest.

20

"Zeus's balls, girl," Hades shouted. "Are you trying to kill him?"

Blue fire snapped and sizzled. A powerful smell of ozone and burnt flesh filled the air as Jake's body jerked.

"I'm trying to save his damned life."

I held my breath as the moment stretched into eternity. Then Jake shuddered and began to cough. Syl dropped to her knees and rolled him onto his side. Her eyes were shining when she looked up at me.

"Interesting first aid technique," she said. "Not one to try at home."

All the lights in the house suddenly turned on and off, on and off, flickering like something out of a horror movie. The motor of an air-conditioning unit turned over with a thud, and through the back windows of the house, I could see every light on the front of the oven start blinking.

A power line stretched from the roof above the back door out to the burning barn, and it began to hum. Blue fire danced along its length. I glanced at Hades and found him grinning.

"Looks like big brother's on his way," he shouted over a rising wind.

The lightning bolt in my hand hummed in tune with the power line and every hair on my body stood straight up. Power coursed through me until I felt as clear as glass, lit up from the inside. The buzzing of the lightning bolt felt as though I held a hive of hornets in my hand, and I drove it into the ground and backed away.

Wind moaned through the trees behind the house. I helped Syl drag Jake further away from the lightning bolt. He was barely conscious, his head lolling as if it were too heavy for him to hold up.

Cerberus barked. His fur was standing up, too, and little sparks of static skittered across his black body. I tilted my head to the sky and saw clouds gathering above us, swirling like a film of a storm watched on fast forward. The air felt alive, charged with tension.

A drop of rain fell on my upturned face, big and fat, swollen with the promise of storms to come. The wind's voice rose to a scream, and the blue fire leapt from the power line to the roof of the house, dancing along the eaves and flashing at the windows.

"Is he trying to kill us all?" I shouted to Hades, tearing the hair from my mouth so I could speak as the wind whipped it around my head. Syl hunched protectively over Jake, and I dropped down by his side, too, supporting him against me.

"You know Zeus," Hades shouted back, his voice competing with the shrieking of the wind and the zinging of the blue lights as they spread, each a tiny flicker of lightning. "He likes to make an entrance."

It was still night, but the scene was as brightly lit as day time, though with a bluish cast to the light. Hestia had curled herself into a ball on the ground under Cerberus's watchful eye, her arms wrapped around her head, as if she expected to be struck by lightning at any moment.

Blue sparks began leaping from the power line, arcing through the air to land on the tip of the lightning bolt. It quivered like a live thing as each one struck, and they rained faster and faster. A shriek like a finger run over the rim of a crystal glass, only a hundred times louder, rose from the lightning bolt. A column of blue light shot from its tip into the sky, and the rest of the blue sparks screamed back as they coalesced around it, spinning faster and faster. Every light in the house blew in a shower of sparks, and lightning arced up into the sky, so bright I was momentarily blinded.

When I had blinked my vision back again, the wind had died, and a figure stood in the eye of the storm, the blue lights flickering in his hair like a caress. He was massively built, with a grey beard, his shoulders so big he looked as though he could wrestle Cerberus and win. He was also completely naked, which allowed me to see that the hairiness of the beard extended over quite a large expanse of flesh.

With an effort of will, I kept my gaze on that bearded face. Some things a girl just did *not* need to see, and her father in his birthday suit was one of them. Swearing by Zeus's balls occasionally didn't mean I wanted to get personally acquainted with them.

"Hello, Dad."

A soft rain began to fall as he looked around, taking in the scene in the now-reduced light of the lightning bolt in his hand. The blue sparks began to fade, winking out as the wind died.

"Congratulations, Artemis." His sharp gaze fell on me with more favour than he usually showed. I was more accustomed to seeing a frown from him. "I had my doubts at times, but you finally figured it out."

"It was a close thing at the end there," Hades said, cheerfully. "You could have been a little more helpful with your clues, brother. We nearly all got killed."

Zeus scowled at him. Ah, there was that expression I was used to. "I was having a little difficulty of my own, *brother*. It's not easy being scattered to the four corners of the earth.

It turns out that possession of a body is something of a prerequisite for structured thinking."

Structured thinking? That was a laugh. Zeus had never shown much interest in thinking, structured or otherwise. From the smirk on Hades' face, I assumed his thoughts were running along the same lines. Zeus was a doer, not a thinker. He loved to fight, to drink, to feast, and always—always—to chase women. A good three-quarters of our family's troubles had been caused by his inability to keep his pants zipped.

"You're here now," I said. "That's the main thing. Although some clothes would be appreciated."

He looked down at himself in surprise, then a pair of pants and a short-sleeved shirt covered his form. Perhaps he'd spent so long without a body that he'd forgotten they were usually clothed around other people.

"I hope there aren't any ill effects from your little sojourn in the wires?" Hades asked, earning himself another scowl.

"Of course not." Zeus flexed his massive arms, showing truly impressive muscles. "I could still wipe the floor with you."

Hades held up his hands in a placatory gesture. "No need for that. I think we have a far worthier target for any floor-wiping right here."

He indicated Hestia, still curled on the ground. All the

fight had gone out of her once Hades had collared her. Of course, it helped that Cerberus was still standing guard, ready to pounce if she made any move.

"I say we kill her," I said, flatly. "She deserves to die for everything she's done."

Jake sat up, pushing away from me, and Syl helped him to rise. I stood, too, close enough that I could feel the reassuringly alive heat of his body, and he didn't move away. Probably didn't have the energy. From the way he sagged, it looked as though just staying upright was taking most of it.

"She nearly managed to kill *me*," Zeus said, as if that was the greatest of her crimes.

"How did she?" Hades asked. "Your powers are so much greater than hers that I've never understood why you had to flee into the wires to escape her. Why didn't you just kill her?"

"Because by the time I realised she was a threat, I only had a second or two of consciousness left. I could guess what would happen to me if I lost consciousness around her."

"She gave you tea, didn't she?" I asked.

"Bloody tea. I don't even like the stuff, but I took a sip to be polite. I discovered later it was water from the Lethe mixed with a powerful sedative, but at the time—"

"The Lethe?" Hades repeated. "How did she get her hands on that?"

The Lethe was one of the rivers of the underworld, part

of Hades' domain. Drinking water from that river removed people's memories. Hades gave it to the newly dead, to ease their passage into the underworld, so they wouldn't mourn what they'd lost.

Hades guarded access to his domain carefully. There was no way Hestia could have stolen in and helped herself to the waters of the Lethe, and certainly none of us had helped her. Who else had access to the underworld?

"From Persephone," Zeus said, frowning at the interruption.

Hades looked stricken. He and Persephone weren't together anymore, but they still cared for each other. "Surely Persephone's not involved in this?"

"Don't be ridiculous," Zeus said. "Persephone had some in her home, and Hestia stole it from her. Anyway, as I was saying, at the time I didn't know what she'd put in the damn tea, just that I was going under, and I was already wobbly and far from my best self. I only had a moment to act. I tried to send the lightning bolt out of danger, but she caught hold of it and it broke in the struggle. She was left with the main branch, but I managed to send the two smaller pieces away. Everything was going black, and she thought she had me then, but fortunately, I was near a power point. She didn't expect that. When I came to, I was in the wiring, and I didn't have enough power to get out again. So there I stayed, keeping an eye on her and trying to help anyone who opposed her."

The back door of the house crashed open, and Apollo staggered out, followed by Winston, hovering anxiously behind him. Apollo looked at us all and blinked. "What did I miss? Why are you all standing out here in the rain? And why is the barn on fire?"

I rolled my eyes. "What did you miss? Let's see: werewolves and shadow shapers duking it out in the barn, desperate danger, death and resurrection, plus the last-minute arrival of the cavalry." I patted Cerberus's closest head and he slurped happily at my hand with a giant, pink tongue. "Zeus's triumphant return." I glanced at Hades. "Did I miss anything?"

He shook his head solemnly. "That just about covers it."

"I must have been out a while."

"Not that long. We've been kind of busy out here while you were napping."

Apollo's eyes narrowed. "It was not my intention to take a nap. Or my decision." He glared at Hestia, collared on the ground. "I can't believe I was so taken in by her."

I didn't say, *I can't believe it either.* That would have been rubbing his nose in it. Though he was all fury now, I knew the pain of betrayal would sting later, when the crisis was past. He'd had a real soft spot for Hestia.

"We're just discussing what to do with her now. I want to kill her, but Hades says we need the names and locations of all the shadow spawn she created first."

"Especially that Mrs Emery bitch," Apollo said fervently.

"You're looking at her," Zeus said, nodding pointedly at Hestia.

What? That couldn't be right. Mrs Emery had lost her arm at the elbow. Of course I knew gods could change their appearance—hadn't I done it myself? And also that gods could survive all manner of things, even to the extent of regrowing limbs. I'd done that, too, a couple of times over the centuries; it was slow and painful, but it could be done.

But not if another god had caused the injury. We were as vulnerable to our own kind as humans were. If I put an arrow through her heart right now—and that option was well and truly still on the table, as far as I was concerned—she would die. And Cerberus was Hades' avatar, a part of his divine power. When Cerberus had bitten Mrs Emery's arm off, that arm was gone for good, even if Mrs Emery was in fact Hestia wearing a human disguise. "But her arm …"

"You mean this?" Zeus bent and tore Hestia's arm off.

She struggled and screamed, but it wasn't a sound of pain. Zeus punched her in the head almost casually, and she slumped into unconsciousness.

He held out a prosthetic arm for inspection. It must have been a very expensive one, as it looked almost like the real thing, but not so much that I wouldn't have noticed it was fake. "She had a glamour on it, so that no one would see it wasn't real."

Holy shit. The dropped tea cup. She'd pulled it from the cupboard with that hand. Obviously, the prosthetic had good functionality, but not as good as a hand of flesh and blood. And after that, she hadn't trusted herself to carry off the deception. She'd made Damian carry the heavy tray to the table, afraid she'd drop it if she tried.

"But …" Apollo looked stunned. "I would have known if Mrs Emery was Hestia. I would have felt her power. She was a human, I swear."

"The cuff," Hades said. "We wondered what it was for, but none of us cared to try it on."

"I thought it gave her some special control over the collars," I said.

"No," said Zeus. "I've been watching her for months, listening in on her conversations. The cuff was to hide her divine power, to make her disguise as the human Mrs Emery complete. Only her inner circle knew who she really was."

No wonder she'd said, *You again*! when she'd seen Jake. That had struck me as odd since, as far as I knew, Hestia had never met Jake, but in the heat of battle there'd been no time to ponder it. But Mrs Emery had measured her fireshaping powers against Jake's before. Jake was lucky she'd been wearing the cuff to hide her divinity that first time; it must have damped her power, too, otherwise she would have killed him then.

"She was playing the same trick you were, Arti," Hades said.

"Yeah, only her way was much easier." Hestia hadn't had to give up her memories for her disguise.

"How did she persuade Hephaistos to make such a thing?" Apollo asked.

"The collars were worse, and he made those, too," I pointed out.

"It all started when she killed Boreas and stole his power," Zeus said. "As the god of the North Wind, he was no match for a former Olympian, even a weak one like Hestia. Then she used his death to start a rumour that someone was killing gods and stealing their power. After that, it was easy to persuade Hephaistos that she was terrified and needed the cuff so she could hide better. He's always been sweet on her. She could wrap him around her little finger."

"But the collars?" Hades asked. "They were a direct threat to him and all of us. Why would he create such dangerous things?"

"She suggested them as a way to capture whoever was killing the gods. Apparently, the plan was for him to make one for all the gods to carry with them, so they had some protection if they were accosted by the killer. At least, he thought that was the plan. But as soon as he had completed the first half dozen, she used one on him and killed him."

Bitch. We all glared at her, though she was still unconscious, lying limp on the scorched ground, her face spattered with rain and ash from the burning barn. It was the only way someone like her could have overpowered the stronger gods. Poor, trusting Hephaistos. He hadn't had many friends, and he would have done anything for the few he had.

"Death is too good for her," Apollo said.

"I don't know," Hades said, "I'm sure I could rustle up something suitably horrific for her. A nice cell in Tartarus, perhaps?"

Zeus bared his teeth in a fierce grin. "I like this plan. Take her away, and make sure you get all the names out of her."

"It will be my pleasure," Hades said. "Cerberus, bring her."

All three heads bent and took the unconscious goddess up in their mouths. She'd have a few wounds to add to the egg on the side of her head that Zeus had given her, but none of us would shed any tears for her. And there were plenty worse things in store for her than a few bite marks.

Hades leapt into the gaping hole he'd come from, and Cerberus followed him, with Hestia dangling limply from his jaws. Soundlessly, the ground closed behind him.

I became aware that the wolves had returned, and were standing in a loose circle around us, keeping guard, though I assumed that their presence meant they'd killed all the shadow shapers they could find. Their wet fur clung to their powerful bodies, just as my hair was sticking to my head.

"Why *are* we standing out here in the rain?" I asked, but Zeus ignored me. Would it have killed him to make it stop? Typical Zeus—it didn't bother him, and that was all that mattered, as far as he was concerned. My father was hardly the best role model for how to win friends and influence people.

"Well," he said, rubbing his hands together with enthusiasm, "it seems we have an opening for a new goddess of the hearth."

"Among other things," Apollo said, his face gloomy with thoughts of all the people we'd lost. "We're missing a few gods now."

I just about swallowed my tongue as an idea occurred to me. I grabbed Jake's hand and drew him forward. "With Hephaistos dead, metalshaping's getting harder and harder. Without a new metalshaping god, it could die out altogether. Jake would be perfect."

Jake threw me a startled glance, but I wouldn't let go of his hand, and after a moment, he stopped trying to pull it away.

Zeus considered him thoughtfully. "I've seen you before, haven't I, following Artemis around?"

Jake looked as though he'd like to argue with that description, but he was too overawed by Zeus's presence to protest. He stood stiffly in the rain, eyes fixed on a point somewhere around the middle of Zeus's chest.

"He helped me save Apollo," I said, giving his hand a reassuring squeeze. There would be no better way of curing Jake of his extreme reverence for the gods than to join their number and discover what they were really like.

"And get the collars off," Syl added. "He went through hell and back—literally—to get that star-metal so we could make a key to unlock them."

At least Syl didn't seem in awe of my father. He looked at her in a very different way than how he'd looked at Jake, like a man who liked what he saw. Lucas stepped forward to Syl's side and growled. Hurriedly, I diverted Zeus's attention before he got twitchy with that lightning bolt. Fried werewolf was not on the menu tonight.

"That's right. He's a fine metalshaper. And Hephaistos likes him. There's no one better suited for the job."

"Perhaps an *actual* metalshaper might be a more suitable candidate than a fireshaper with a metalshaping secondary," Zeus said mildly. "I'll bear him in mind, but I'll have to look—"

"There's no time for that," I cut in, remembering the spoon Jake had taken from Athena's island. "Metalshaping is all but dead already. While you dick around searching for a 'more suitable' candidate, metalshaping will be lost to the world."

"Father, you may find a better practitioner, but you won't find a braver man, or one more deserving of this honour," Apollo said. "He has proven himself worthy of godhood a dozen times over. His loyalty to us, to our family, is beyond question."

"Is that so?"

Jake wilted under that frowning gaze. "My lord, Lord Apollo does me great honour, but I'm not sure I'm the right person—"

"Shut up, Jake," I hissed, but Zeus was smiling. Belatedly, it occurred to me that his protest had probably made him look more appealing, not less, in Zeus's eyes. Zeus didn't like competition, and Jake had just demonstrated an extreme lack of ambition.

"Well," Zeus said, "since the need is urgent, and my children have earned a favour for all they've done, perhaps we can dispense with a search."

He smiled at Jake, who looked stunned by his sudden promotion. "But …"

"Don't argue, Jake." I threw my arms around his neck. "There's no law against being happy. Stop fighting it."

"Being happy?" He blinked down at me, confused.

"Yes. You know, when two people love each other, and there is no longer anything keeping them apart? They get to be together. Generally, it makes them happy."

A slow smile spread across his face as his brain finally

caught up with what his change in circumstances meant for our relationship. His arms tightened around me. "I love you." He dropped a feather-soft kiss on my lips. "I can't believe I finally get to say that."

"About bloody time." Happiness welled in my heart as I pulled him down for another, deeper kiss. "I love you, too."

Zeus raised an eyebrow at Apollo. "Isn't he one of yours? Does this leave a gap in your organisation?"

"Yes. I'll need a new Ruby Adept." Apollo looked pointedly at Winston, who jumped like a kid caught with his hand in the cookie jar, shocked to find himself the centre of attention.

"Who, me?" He looked around at us, horror on his face. "Oh, no, my lord. I couldn't do it, I'm not strong enough."

Apollo grinned. "Are you arguing with your god, Winston?"

21

The Great Temple of Apollo in Crosston was bursting at the seams, standing room only. Outside, the crowds who lined the streets roared as if they were at a football match.

"Winston must be nearly here," I said to Jake, just as the temple doors were thrown open, letting in a blast of noise and golden sunshine.

Everyone who was anyone was here, gathered to watch the newest Ruby Adept take office and to gawp at the gods. Four of us were here—Zeus, Hades, Apollo and me—and soon to be five. My wolf friends, including Ophelia, formed an honour guard behind my seat, taking their devotion to the moon goddess very seriously. It was strange to remember, now, how afraid I'd been of fully becoming the goddess again, worried I would lose myself or my friends. None of my fears had come to pass.

Syl stood in their line-up, too, practically part of the

pack by now. Our friendship had only grown through the trials we'd faced together—and now those trials were finally over. This was a very different ceremony than the last one: no sneaking around with only a few fireshapers in attendance. No constantly looking over our shoulders, wondering when the shadow shapers might strike again.

The shadow shapers were all dead, hunted down with great gusto by Hades and Cerberus over the past week while the preparations for today's ceremony were made. Their leader was chained in a pit in Tartarus, with only monsters for company. Zeus had snapped her distaff over his knee, destroying a good three-quarters of her power. She might never die, but she would never truly live again, either.

Today felt like a giant party—the crowds waving flags, the bunting stretched across the streets. It was only midday, but more than half the good people of Crosston appeared to be smashed already.

A golden chariot nearly identical to the one that Jake had once brought to life in the Plaza of the Sun pulled up outside. I squeezed Jake's hand and he smiled at me.

"You look nervous. It'll be fine."

"Easy for you to say," he muttered. "You're not the one becoming a god today."

"It only hurts for the first year or so."

He shot me a startled glance. "Really?"

"I'm kidding. Relax."

Outside, Winston waved shyly to the crowd, who roared in appreciation as he got down from the chariot. He wore a white tunic identical to the one that Jake had worn for his investiture, with red embroidery around the neck and hem. His head was bare, but his hair looked thicker than normal. Darker, too.

I turned to Apollo, seated on my other side. "Did you slip Winston a little something extra? He looks younger."

"This is the second investiture I've been to in as many weeks— I'm not doing this again for a good long time. Had to make sure my new Ruby Adept wasn't going to die of old age on me."

"He wasn't *that* old, surely."

"Well, now he's younger." Apollo didn't seem at all repentant, though technically we weren't supposed to fiddle with such things. "I had to boost his power, anyway, to make him fit for the job. Thought I might as well throw in a little rejuvenation."

"Does Zeus know?"

Zeus was seated on a golden throne on the other side of the dais, sufficiently elevated above ours to make him feel superior. He probably could have heard our conversation if he'd cared to listen in, but he was too busy flirting with the pretty young fireshaper standing beside his throne, who was supposedly there to assist him.

Apollo grinned. "As they say in the classics, Zeus can bite me."

I grinned back. No one would care, anyway. We were

all giddy with the relief of having the whole shadow shaper debacle behind us. Anything felt possible now.

I held Jake's hand a little tighter. Anything at all. "Nice shirt, by the way," I said to my brother.

Today, Apollo was wearing a shirt the blue of a summer sky. It accentuated the colour of his eyes and made him look a million dollars.

Amusement danced in those eyes. "I decided to take your sisterly fashion advice."

The little knot of red-robed priests in front of the dais moved forward as Winston entered, alone and barefoot. The high priest, whose octopus hat I was sure was bigger than last time—what was he compensating for?—ordered in his deep voice: "Let the candidate come forward."

As soon as Winston had cleared the doorway, the great doors boomed shut behind him, shutting out the raucous crowd, who would be watching this on the big screens set up outside the temple and in the Plaza of the Sun.

The ceremony proceeded much as the previous one had done, with the candidate being presented to Apollo—and Zeus, this time—then the vows, the symbolic crowning and the long, long prayer praising Apollo. Zeus shifted restlessly as that droned on, but it eventually ended, and we were on to the part where Winston walked straight into the sacred fire. The assembled dignitaries, who included many non-fireshapers, murmured in awe at that.

I leaned closer to Jake. "I nearly had kittens when you did that."

"It wasn't so bad," he whispered back. "Just a gentle warmth. The bad part was when that dick Adani started blowing a gale around the place."

"Fun times," I agreed. "Life is going to be awfully quiet now without the shadow shapers jumping out of the bushes at every turn."

His blue gaze held mine. "We'll just have to find another way to entertain ourselves."

I swallowed, sudden heat flaring deep inside me. The temple melted away, and there were only the two of us in the whole world. "Sounds appealing. Tell me more."

"I swear," Syl said behind me, in a fierce whisper, "if you two start making out again, I'm going to puke down your backs. Can you at least wait until they stop roasting poor Winston?"

I returned my attention to the ceremony, holding in a laugh. I'd laughed more in the last week than I had in a long time. The priests were draping Winston in the red velvet cape again now he was out of the flames, and that part of the ceremony appeared to be over.

"You're up next, Jake," Hades said. He was seated on Jake's other side. "Last chance to change your mind."

"No one's changing their mind about anything," I said, giving Hades a warning glance. I knew he was joking, but I had trouble seeing the humour in it after all we'd been through.

"Relax." Jake's eyes shone with love and purpose as they met mine. "You're not getting rid of me that easily."

Zeus stood, drawing all eyes like a magnet, and cleared his throat. "I'm not much for speeches or ceremony, so I'll make this quick. Jake, come over here."

Jake rose and crossed the dais to stand in front of Zeus. Tall as Jake was, Zeus still towered over him. Zeus hoisted his lightning bolt aloft, and blinding white light filled the temple. The crowd rippled as the front rows tried to step back, but there was no room to move.

"Today, we welcome a new god to our ranks," Zeus shouted over the gasps and murmurs of the gathered throng. "I give you Jacob, Lord of Metalshaping!"

For the second time in his life, Jake was zapped by Zeus's lightning bolt, though in the hands of its master, the effects were quite different than when I'd done it. Jake began to glow, as if filling up with light. His head fell back, and he held his arms out to the sides as power filled him. I squinted into the light, not wanting to miss a moment. Something was growing in Jake's hand, too bright to make out what it was. His hair stood on end, streaming out from his head in a non-existent wind, and blue sparks leapt from the lightning bolt to play in its dark strands.

Finally, Zeus lowered the lightning bolt and the dazzling

light faded, though Jake himself still glowed softly. In his hand, he held a hammer—a solid smith's tool.

"That's his avatar?" Ophelia muttered to Syl. They were standing beside each other in the line-up behind me. They'd become fast friends already, since they shared a similar sense of humour and a love of taking the piss out of me. "A hammer? Seems a bit old-fashioned. No blowtorch?"

"Maybe he should change his name to Jakaistos or something, to match," Syl replied, making me snort in a very ungodlike way. "I don't know, *Lord Jake* just doesn't have that godly ring to it."

"Lord Jake sounds absolutely perfect to me," I said. "He can shape my metal any old time."

Syl made gagging noises, but Ophelia laughed. Cheers rose from the crowd as Jake raised his hammer above his head. Outside, the crowds watching on the big screens added their voices to the noise. The creation of a new god was a truly special moment.

Hades shifted to Jake's empty seat beside me. "Congratulations. If I'm not mistaken, you got your happy ever after."

"I think you may be right." I couldn't wipe the grin from my face. Jake looked stunned by the applause—stunned and delighted. Not to mention good enough to eat. "I'm glad some good came out of it all, at least."

He sighed. "Yes. I'm sorrier than I can say to lose

Athena, in particular. I hope Hestia enjoys the rewards of all her plotting."

"Why do you think she did it? Why turn on us after all these centuries?"

"I think she's been chewing on her resentment like an old bone ever since she gave up her throne for Dionysus."

"But she offered to do that. No one forced her." To the surprise of absolutely no one, Zeus had become enamoured of his son, the god of wine. They were like two peas in a pod, drinking and sleeping their way around the world. What *had* surprised us was his desire to make Dionysus one of the great Olympians. None of us had been much in favour of that idea. Hera, in particular, had argued that taking our numbers from an even twelve to an inauspicious thirteen was asking for trouble, so he'd been stymied until the idea of replacing one of the twelve began to take shape in his mind.

"I think it was more of a case that she realised she was on the bottom of the pecking order, so thought it better to retire gracefully and earn Zeus's gratitude than wait to be kicked out. I watched her for a long time after that, afraid she might turn on us, but she seemed happy with her new status, and as charming as ever." He shook his head. "She was just playing a longer game than I'd ever imagined. I feel sure she sold it to her human accomplices dressed up as some kind of democratic 'let's get rid of the gods and let humans have their day in the sun', but in reality, I'm sure her goal was nothing more noble than to kill us all and reign supreme."

"Such a waste. She was a clever woman; she could have used her intelligence for good."

Hades nodded. "Sending you all out hunting for the pieces of the lightning bolt she was missing was an inspired touch. She never would have gotten them otherwise."

"Much good they did her in the end. I don't understand, though, why she left those shadow shapers behind at Athena's house to attack us. She didn't actually want to capture us at that point, because we were more valuable to her in the hunt for the lightning bolts. Plenty of time to cut out our hearts *after* we'd brought her the lightning bolts."

"I suppose she wanted to create a sense of mounting danger, to make you feel that bringing the lightning bolts to her was urgent. She didn't want to attack you while you were in Berkley's Bay, but once you were on the way, she wanted to hurry you along a little."

Apollo rose and held up his hands for silence. When he told everyone gathered, both in the temple and outside, to go home and party, an even louder cheer went up. Red-robed figures crowded around Winston to congratulate him and slowly, the temple began to empty.

We all rose as Jake came back to us. Apollo and Hades offered handshakes, but I went into his open arms with a glad heart.

"Welcome to the rest of your life," I said.

"It hardly hurts at all," he said.

"What?"

He grinned. "Just kidding."

I was forced to kiss him just to shut him up.

"When you guys finish playing tonsil hockey, maybe we could get out of here and grab a drink," Syl said. "I hope I never have to endure another one of those endless prayers again. No offence, Apollo."

"None taken," he said mildly. "I often nod off partway through myself. Shall we adjourn to the Ruby Palace? I hear the fireshapers put on a mean feast."

"Did someone say feast?" Zeus asked. He had his arm around the pretty fireshaper girl, and looked ready to party.

"I'll show you the way," Hades said, and the three of them left together.

The wolves gathered around us, and I leaned against Jake with a contented sigh. Even baby Mireille was there, wearing the cutest little green jumpsuit, fast asleep in Holly's arms.

"She was so good," I said, and Holly smiled proudly. "Not a peep out of her the whole time."

Apollo laughed. "She was better behaved than Zeus."

"Do you think someone should rescue that poor fireshaper?"

"She'll be fine. Zeus will be too drunk soon to get up to anything."

I shared a look with Jake. We had sumptuous rooms next to each other back at the Ruby Palace. "And speaking of getting up to things …"

Syl groaned. "No more public displays of affection!"

"Actually, I was thinking of something more private. I think I need a little alone time, so I can get to know our new god a whole lot better."

She sighed. "So if I hear you screaming his name, I should just assume you're praying?"

"More *worshipping*."

Jake dragged me into his arms and stopped my mouth with a kiss. "Stop talking, woman. You'll make me blush, and that seems a little ungodly."

"Oops." I trailed a line of apologetic kisses along his firm jawline. "I'm just so excited I get to spend forever with you."

"Forever is a long time," he said, in an unconscious echo of Persephone, so long ago. "Are you sure you want to put up with me that long?"

I wrapped my arms more firmly around his neck, pressing my body against his. Our love would fare better than hers and Hades' had done. "Try and stop me."

He smiled, a world of love in his beautiful blue eyes, and lowered his face to mine.

"Zeus's balls!" Syl cried, exasperated. "Will you guys get a room?"

So we did.

Don't miss the exciting new series, Thirteen Realms, coming soon! For news on its release, plus special deals and other book news, sign up for my newsletter at www.marinafinlayson.com.

Reviews and word of mouth are vital for any author's success. If you enjoyed *Caged Lightning*, please take a moment to leave a short review where you bought it. Just a few words sharing your thoughts on the book would be extremely helpful in spreading the word to other readers (and this author would be immensely grateful!).

ALSO BY MARINA FINLAYSON

MAGIC'S RETURN SERIES

The Fairytale Curse

The Cauldron's Gift

THE PROVING SERIES

Moonborn

Twiceborn

The Twiceborn Queen

Twiceborn Endgame

SHADOWS OF THE IMMORTALS SERIES

Stolen Magic

Murdered Gods

Rivers of Hell

Hidden Goddess

Caged Lightning

ACKNOWLEDGEMENTS

Thank you to all the readers who have followed Lexi's adventures through this series. It's been wonderful to hear from you and to know that you were just as keen as I was to discover the fate of Lexi and her friends. Thanks also to my family for your support, especially Mal, Jen and Connor for beta reading. Love you guys!

ABOUT THE AUTHOR

Marina Finlayson is a reformed wedding organist who now writes fantasy. She is married and shares her Sydney home with three kids, a large collection of dragon statues and one very stupid dog with a death wish.

Her idea of heaven is lying in the bath with a cup of tea and a good book until she goes wrinkly.

Made in the USA
Monee, IL
14 March 2021